Beyond Mali

By
R. L. Scott

LBP

www.thelionsbrood.com

First printing, third edition

ISBN: 978-1-7363861-1-8

PUBLISHED BY LION'S BROOD PUBLISHING, LLC

www.thelionsbrood.com

Printed in the United States of America

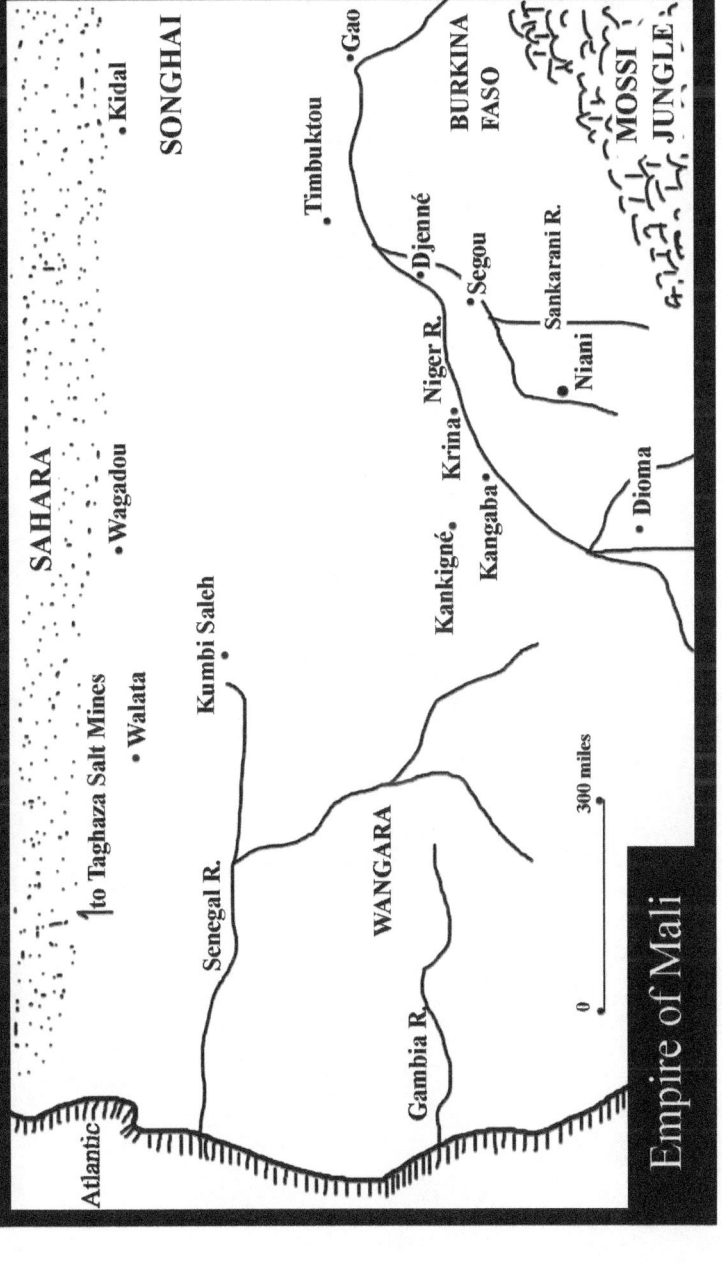

Empire of Mali

African
Lunar Calendar Year
8 days = 1 week (Izu)
368 days = 1 year
13 months= 1 year

Days of the Week (in order)
Ekenta, Orienta, Afonta, Nkwonta, Eke, Orie, Afo, Nkwo

Months of the Year
I) Fijioku, II) Ikenga, III) Igwuji, IV) Mkpocha, V) Ekwuruochie,
VI) Ipieali, VII) Imonmiri, VIII) Amadioha, IX) Kamalu,
X) Eze'elu, XI) Anyanwu, XII) Ofufe, XIII) Agwunsi

Hours of the Day
12 a.m.—Hour of the Owl, 1 a.m.—Hour of the Crocodile,
2 a.m.—Hour of the Hare, 3 a.m.—Hour of the Serpent,
4 a.m.—Hour of the Hyena, 5 a.m.—Hour of the Leopard,
6 a.m.—Hour of the Gazelle, 7 a.m.—Hour of the Goat,
8 a.m.—Hour of the Blackbird, 9 a.m.—Hour of the Boar,
10 a.m.—Hour of the Elephant, 11 a.m.—Hour of the Cheetah,
12 p.m.—Hour of the Buffalo, 1 p.m.—Hour of the Zebra,
2 p.m.—Hour of the Sable, 3 p.m.—Hour of the Dog,
4 p.m.—Hour of the Hippopotamus, 5 p.m.—Hour of the Leopard,
6 p.m.—Hour of the Lion, 7 p.m.—Hour of the Warthog,
8 p.m.—Hour of the Antelope, 9 p.m.—Hour of the Porcupine,
10 p.m.—Hour of the Jackal, 11 p.m.—Hour of the Wolf

PROLOGUE

I will tell you a story of two oceans. One lies towards the lands of Nubia, the other where the sun falls from the sky, the known and the unknown. Within their waters raged the blood of two brothers.

For I am a djeliba; we are vessels of speech, keepers of memories. We are the repositories, who harbor secrets many centuries old. Without us, the names of kings would vanish from oblivion. We are the memory of mankind. By the spoken word, we bring to life the deeds and exploits of kings for younger generations.

History holds no mystery for us. We teach the vulgar just as much as we want to teach them, for it is we who keep the keys to the Twelve Doors of Mali. I teach the kings of their ancestors so that the lives of the ancients might serve them as an example.

For the world is old, but the future springs from the past.

Djeliba Mamadou Kouyaté
(Paraphrased from D.T. Niani,
Sundiata: An Epic of Old Mali)

1.

1294 C.E.

The two young princes led the party of hunters on foot across the tall, dry grass of the vast Wangara plains. With spears in hand and *sassas* on their sides, they cautiously stalked a small herd of buffalo in the clearing not far away. All decorated with ceremonial body paint and cotton cloth draping from their hips, they slowly crouched to within a few meters of the wild beasts. The white paint mixed with their ebony skin to project an auburn hue, camouflaging them against the light brush of the savannah.

The wiry Abubakari fearfully checked his immediate perimeter, while shielding his gaze from the unforgiving sunrays striking his brow. As his father had instructed him, he reached inside his sassa to ensure that his trusted dagger had not fallen from the goatskin hunter's bag. After fingering the weapon and settling the rapid pounding of his heart, Abubakari rested on one knee and caught his breath. He had not forgotten the tales of horror recited to him by Malian *sofas* returning from their rites of passage. Oh, how his father's soldiers were adamant about the maiming and the goring, which were intensified by the howls in the night as the boys slept. At 12 years of age, Abubakari could not see the exaggeration of the soldiers and how they were simply jesting with the young lad.

Abubakari shared his trial of manhood with his younger brother by one year, Kankan Musa. It was customary for many young Mandingo warriors to carry the name of their mother. Thus, Musa was referred to as Kongo Musa, and as he grew older, he became Kankan Musa. Although, only Abubakari still called him Kankan Musa. Most simply called him Musa. He was lean, yet tall for such a young age. As he tenaciously moved closer to his older brother, Musa lowered his hand, and the two boys, including the ten young men behind them, crouched down to hide in the brush, not far from the tranquil herd.

"Be careful, Abu," whispered Musa, "Once the buffalo is attacked, it is even stronger and is *daffeké*."

Abubakari nodded uneasily and wiped his eyes of any obstructions. The rod in his hands shook from the fear that permeated his thin frame. He began to calm himself by mentally reciting the words of his *djeliba*. *A bird is in the air, but its mind is on the ground*. Abubakari respected the spiritual man that was chosen by his father and tasked with recording the history of the future *mansa*, though many of the court historian's words escaped his young mind. His thoughts were focused on earning his hunter's tunic and fulfilling the destiny preordained by his bloodline.

The Africans pounced on their prey, and the buffalo scattered while snorting at the encroaching war party. The young men darted after their fleeing targets with spears in hurling positions above their shoulders. Their tiny war cries succeeded in intimidating the herd. They began launching their javelins. One after another, the spears plunged into the animals' flesh, and many quickly fell.

After having his spear dart through the air and connect, one young warrior was very pleased. *"Wassa wassa ayé!"* he shouted with joy.

One of the beasts refused to go down, even with several

spears lodged in its midsection. It stumbled back forth until one of the young warriors mounted the bull, unsheathed his short blade, and lodged it into the neck of the powerful beast.

Unfortunately, all did not fare so well. One young hunter misread the strength of the buffalo, and before he could flank the howling beast, he found two horns impaled in his abdomen and chest. It was a brutal goring with blood splattering the dry African plain. It wasn't until the boy was nearly ripped in half that he was thrown several meters from the site. He died before he hit the earth.

Abubakari darted in the direction of a still buffalo in the distance, slowing down once the massive buffalo's frame came into his full view. The young prince stood still and gazed at the bull. The bull's large round eye stared back. Abubakari observed his target as it slowly circled to face him. He could no longer hear. He could no longer see clearly. He became oblivious to the chaos surrounding him. Abubakari could only discern the pounding of the hooves, the swinging of the tail, and the sharpness of the horns before him.

In an instant, the bull charged in his direction with horns extended to plunge into the young Abubakari the Second. At less than forty paces, Abubakari launched his spear at the approaching buffalo. The spear whistled towards the animal.

It was perilously off target.

Abubakari reached frantically into his *sassa* and clenched tightly to his dagger. He stood ready, nervously awaiting his inevitable doom. The heavy rumble of the beast's hooves moved closer, snorting louder.

Rumble. Thirty feet.

He held the dagger close to his face.

Rumble. Twenty feet.

Abubakari extended his palm to the buffalo and stooped

into a defensive posture.

Rumble. Ten feet.

Suddenly, before the bull came to within a few feet of trampling the young warrior, a hurled spear flew into its belly and propelled the bull from its original angle. The buffalo slid headfirst past Abubakari's feet and came to a dusty halt.

Abubakari swayed back and forth as sweat poured down his face. He listened to his heart pounding rapidly as dust blew through him. He gazed at the spear protruding from the beast and followed the blood trickling to the earth below. The eye of the buffalo was still wide, and the animal lay on its side. Abubakari stared into the eyes of the animal as the bull gasped for air and screamed in pain. Soon, the breathing slowed and its cries ceased. The nostrils no longer flared, nor did the spiked tail dance back and forth.

Musa ran up and yanked the spear from the carcass with all his might, ripping the flesh as it separated from the bull. He then reached in his sassa and pulled out his knife. Musa nodded and silently offered the blade to Abubakari with a nod. Abubakari shook his head, refusing to take the knife.

Musa sighed and quickly took a knee next to the head of the bull. Abubakari watched his younger brother slit the throat of the beast. Blood spilt out and covered Musa's hands. The satisfaction in the eyes of Musa contrasted those of Abubakari, who was horrified by the sight. Musa then severed the horns from its head and proudly stood with satisfaction.

The hunt was complete, and Musa was now a man in the eyes of the Keita clan, for he had slain the beast and carried from it a symbol of the bull's power. Abubakari could only watch in bitter admiration. He knew that Musa was always the swiftest, the strongest, and had the better dexterity of the two. *My younger brother saved my life.*

"You will need this." Musa handed one of the horns to Abubakari.

Abubakari hesitantly let the bloodstained ivory horn fall into his extended hands. He did not want it, but Abubakari knew that a prince of Mali, chiefly the next mansa, must return with a charm from the beast. So he humbly accepted what his brother had earned. Before he could express his gratitude, Musa dashed away, cheering his accomplishment to the other hunters.

As the golden glow of the sun covered the horizon, Abubakari and Musa rode horseback along the river, watching it pour into the vast western ocean in the distance. Separated from the camp inhabitants young hunters, and the Malian soldiers adorned in dark tunics and the beads of their clan, the pair stopped. Their brief pause allowed Abubakari to gaze at the sun meeting the sea. They watched the silhouettes of the Djallonkés medicine men ritualistically delivering the slain young hunter unto the ancestral plane. The poor lad was covered with henna body decoration before being draped with indigo cloth. Because the boy was the son of a Dogon noble, the witch doctor prepared the corpse for travel, for the young warrior must be buried within Bandiagara Escarpment, befitting his status.

Abubakari dismounted and reached into the warm, murky water of the river with a huge smile.

"Remember when we sailed down the Sankarini with Father, Kankan?" said Abubakari with an ear-to-ear grin.

"Yes, I do, Brother." Musa watched from his steed.

"Look, cowries!" Abubakari's eyes glowed with even more excitement as he plunged his hands into the cold river water. He withdrew two colorful glass-like shells with mollusks inside and carefully wiped the water from their surface.

"They smell," snarled Musa.

"No, they are beautiful," responded Abubakari. "I wish Niani was closer to the water."

"Why do you wish always for the impossible, Abu?" sighed Musa as he rubbed his mount to calm its sudden neighing.

"Ever wonder what is out there?" Abubakari grinned, placed the cowries on the ground, and utilized the river's water to cleanse his face of impurities.

Musa shrugged as he panned the wide ocean. "The sea."

"No, there…beyond the sea." Abubakari did not point. He allowed his stalwart gaze and the flutter of his voice communicate how far he was actually looking. What he saw could not be seen.

Musa espied the horizon and returned a cynical glare to Abubakari. "Nothing is there, Abu." Musa reared the reins of his small steed and hurriedly galloped towards the camp.

Abubakari remained by the embankment. He lifted two cowries above his head and let the water trickle from the shells onto his pate. Abubakari quickly snatched more cowries from the river's edge. Once he was satisfied with a handful, he lifted his head for one final look at the horizon just as the sun disappeared into the deep black waters.

Night had arrived, and the hunting party prepared to camp along the river. The huge carcasses from their game hung in the shadows, away from the fire that the twelve young boys surrounded, digesting the spoils of their hunt. One of the boys plucked away at the five-stringed *ngoni* as some of the young warriors accompanied the sharp whines of the lute with song. In the distance, several lightly clad *sofas* stood guard near the tents with large spears in hand and broadswords in scabbards. *Mansa* Abubakari himself tasked these elite royal guards to protect his sons on their most important journey.

As the light of the flame from the campfire danced off the young warriors' bodies, *Djeliba* Mamadou Kouyaté, who appeared older than his age because of his scruffy beard and decorative silk robe, sat among them. Sitting with his legs crossed, Mamadou used his long wooden staff to raise himself from the earth. With his unworldly gaze, he found Abubakari, who frolicked with the lad beside him. Mamadou raised his staff and the boys became silent as the *djeliba's* gritty voice resonated through everyone present.

"The Initiation of the Bush has been fulfilled by the son of Abubakari. His eldest son by thy same name has honored the Keita clan, as had his great ancestor, Sundiata, the Hungering Lion, liberator of Niani-ba. You are now a Mandingo warrior of Mali. And soon, Abubakari the Second, tales of your achievements shall resonate across the Sahel."

"Wassa wassa ayé!" cheered the other hunters. Those seated beside the young prince pushed and patted Abubakari for his achievements. Abubakari humbly bowed his head to them.

The boy who hit the first buffalo finished chewing his stew and flicked a little on Abubakari. "Once you become *mansa*, Abu, make sure your warriors receive better food."

They laughed boisterously, except for Musa who stared

closely at Abubakari. *If they only knew how he cowered before the horns of the beast. It was I who saved him from the hands of death, though he receives praise from the others.* Musa unsheathed his knife and began quietly hacking the tip off a nearby log.

Mamadou stood abruptly. "Silence! N'ko!" Mamadou was just over twenty years in age, but he commanded respect from the deepness of his tone. Only the chirping of frogs and the crackling of the fire were heard, and every boy's eyes focused on the mystic.

"Holder of the Great Bow of Mali Kings is not an object of banter, for he commands the Twelve Doors of Mali. So many lives…so many decisions to be made."

Abubakari nervously raised his hand. "As my *djeliba*, Mamadou, may I ask you a question?"

"Yes, young lord."

"I am only one. How can I alone choose for so many?"

Mamadou grinned, almost within. "To ask such a question is worthy of a *mansa*. Yet at this moment, your father and sofas of Mali are laying assault on Djenné to expand Mali even beyond the reaches of *Djoulou Kara Naini*."

Abubakari had studied Alexander the Great, among other notable leaders known to Mali. Alexander was one of his favorites, though Sundiata was the greatest in his eyes. He was fascinated by their stories of distant travels, and because he shared the same bloodline as the legendary Sundiata.

"Impossible," mumbled Musa.

"Why is that impossible, young Kankan Musa?"

There was a prolonged eeriness as everyone awaited Musa's reply. Musa was surprised that the djeliba heard him but remained strong from the stares. "It is not the will of

Allah. I do not wish Father to fail, but Mother has said that Allah is a god of acceptance, not of conquest." He continued to shred the log in his hand.

"The will of a foreign god does not control the destiny of the great kingdom of Mali and the wills of Mandingoes. Are you not familiar with the Almoravids? I see that your mother continues her piousness," responded Mamadou to the chuckles of a few.

Musa tossed the log into the fire and sheathed his blade. He had grown accustomed to the ridicule brought upon by the mysteries surrounding his mother. He only offered a resigning exhalation and turned within. Though they were half-brothers, Musa and Abubakari's upbringings were far from similar, after having been raised in their formative years by royal courtiers.

"Mamadou, is it possible that we share one god, even more powerful than our ancestors?" asked Abubakari with great curiosity.

Mamadou leaned over and placed his palm on Abubakari's shoulder. "We have very powerful tribal ancestors, young lord. And though one does not speak Mande, do others not understand them? Do they not exist? The spiritual plane is very wide indeed. Continue with your studies and learn what is to be."

"Tell us more of the Son of the Buffalo and Lion," shouted one of the lads, followed by the cheering support of others.

"We will return to Niani very early, young lord. You will need to be well rested for the journey," sighed Mamadou.

Mamadou served as a surrogate father when the *mansa* was performing his duties as king. It was inevitable since Mamadou was selected by *Mansa* Abubakari to serve as his *djeliba*, just as Mamadou's father served young Abubakari's father. He was to watch over, and often guide, Abubakari the Second, from childhood until Abubakari the Second himself held the title *mansa*, his inherent destiny. Mamadou was there to chronicle the boy's existence and boast of his accomplishments, so that the future *mansa's* legacy would not be forgotten.

The grumbles of the children erupted and Abubakari begged in support. "Just a little, Mamadou. It is a good night to tell of Sundiata."

"Perhaps, a *mithkal*," smiled Mamadou while pinching his thumb to his index finger.

Once the voices of disagreement from the young warriors dissipated, Mamadou continued with the legend that he had began before departing Niani. Mamadou gazed at the dark, starry sky above in search of the place he had finished earlier.

"Once the great Sundiata reached manhood, he knew that his destiny lay in Niani-ba. And although he was banished from there, he would return to face The Untouchable King, the most ruthless man you can imagine."

The boys leaned forward, waiting through the crackling of the fire for more.

"Mamadou, was he afraid?" asked Abubakari.

"Yes, young lord. Soumaoro Kanté was truly a symbol of the evil spirits, a torturer of souls." The campfire flickered in the eyes of the storyteller. "Within his secret chamber in Sosso, Soumaoro kept weapons not from this world. His fetishes held great power. And as a symbol of his wrath, he held within that room the nine heads of slaughtered kings. They were his trophies of a sort." Mamadou faced only Abubakari. "But fear evades a man when faced with destiny."

"How did Sundiata defeat him?" asked Musa, for even

he was intrigued.

"The spur of a white hen placed on an arrow. This was Soumaoro's tana. And just its touch would destroy his magic.

Sundiata's arrow found its mark, and he chased the powerless Soumaoro into the dark caverns of Koulikoro, never to be seen again.

It is said that his evil spirit travels with the snake and dwells in the darkness of owls, waiting to join the living once more."

A strong breeze slowly overpowered the campfire, and the boys shivered from fright. Mamadou stopped there and eventually sent the boys to slumber.

Abubakari could not sleep. His eyes followed the mist of the starry sky, as those around him were sound asleep. A shooting star zipped overhead and faded away. He gazed at the cowries he had constructed into a necklace and placed around his neck. The day's rite of passage continued to haunt the young Mandingo throughout much of night. However, he would never realize that, on that day, he was initiated into a world of self-doubt that would never again reverse itself.

2.

From Timbuktu to the Sahel, the beauty of the dark tributary sliced through the savannah and danced with the hills that surrounded it. A herd of buffalo pounded their way across the fertile plains beside the Niger, kicking up dust as they sprinted in unison. Large, eagle-like secretary birds sailed above the buffalo and skimmed the large mesa below, revealing the city of Niani—a majestic, walled community with spires that towered into the sky.

Surrounding the fortress made of curvature structures were hundreds of huts constructed of handmade, oval-shaped mud brick and bitumen. These small straw-roofed homes were nestled just outside the city's massive gate, which was made of the strongest stone and gypsum. Canals networked to the Niger fed the main reservoir and gave Niani inhabitants their water for the day. The central part of the city provided many basins and bridges for children to swim. The markets bustled with African artisans, Moroccan traders, and provincial farmers presenting their goods to unsuspecting passersby. Musicians who had not received the privilege of performing strictly for royalty played their koras and *ngonis* for the many travelers stirring through the narrow pathways.

It was within Niani's center that the stone castle of kings dwelled, ornamented with gold upon its ceilings and filled with balustradeprotected verandas that overlooked the gardenias. Platforms allowed sentries keep a watchful eye. The Palace of Canco's blue metallic roofs and glazed kiln-fired brick walls shimmered under the afternoon sun. From the palace's minaret, marabouts alerted the faithful Moslem that it was time for prayer.

Feather-adorned spears and halberds hung upon the walls in the battle-practice chamber of the palace. Standing on the marble floor of the pillared room, the seasoned *sofa* officer's rugged face snarled with discontent as he corrected Musa and Abubakari on their poor battle posture. They remained frozen in their stance with staves extended as the scarred officer slapped the boys across the legs and arms with his short staff. They trembled in their tunics but did not budge while the officer circled them.

"Discipline is required in battle as well, young lords." The sweat poured down both of the boys' faces. They were in obvious pain. "In the eyes of the ancestors, you are weak," continued the officer. Remember this. Such thoughts make the Mandingo fierce warriors. A desire to be strong, to remain strong, will keep him alive."

"The *mansa* has returned!" echoed the screams of courtiers and servants from the outer halls of the palace. Abubakari wavered slightly from the sudden news. As their father and younger brother, Sulayman, entered the chamber, the *sofa* officer immediately corrected Abubakari's lack of focus with a swift blow of the staff to the boy's legs. Musa fought every urge within to burst out in laughter.

Mansa Abubakari paused for a moment to admire his two eldest sons in their stances. A smile penetrated his hale and hearty beard. The tall and handsome *mansa* placed his golden helm on the floor and loosened the straps of the golden chest plate covering his tunic. He maintained his muscular physique, since Abubakari the First was still fairly young to hold the title of *mansa*. The scars covering his dark skin and the dullness of his war-torn armor was softened by the innocence of the youth beside him. It was customary for the shy, four-year-old Sulayman to cling to his father's every step. After such a long campaign, *Mansa* Abubakari welcomed the warmth and loyalty that only a child could provide.

"*Mansa*." The *sofa* officer immediately fell to one knee with staff raised and head lowered.

"Proceed with your instruction," said the mansa with certain gladness as several servants hastily placed pillows down for him and Sulayman to sit upon.

"Yes, *Mansa*." The officer rose and continued his lesson. "Breathe." The two boys came out of their stances and relaxed their bodies, all the while breathing heavily. "Combat is a melody of aggression and digression," said the officer sternly. "Let the pounding of the *deba* guide your actions. Now, ready yourselves."

Musa and the young Abubakari slowly pivoted to face one another with their staves extended. A small boy scurried into the room carrying a *deba* drum. He sat and immediately began drumming with his small palms.

The drum reverberated a steady heartbeat, slowly speeding up as the tension built between the two young warriors. Their fierce stares met from a few meters away. If one had entered the chamber through happenstance, he or she would not have known that the same blood ran through both Abubakari and Musa.

"Kankan Musa, attack Abubakari!" grunted the instructor.

Instantly, Musa launched himself at Abubakari, twirling his staff, synchronistic with the rhythmic beat of the *deba*. Their wooden staves clashed as Abubakari repelled each blow while retreating. Once the drum ceased, Musa fell back in a defensive posture. Abubakari regained his stance and focused on the recovery of the precious air that quickly escaped his lungs in the melee.

"Go!" shouted the officer.

It was Abubakari's turn. Once again, the drumming started at a rapid pace. Abubakari aggressively moved at Musa, striking downward in hopes of tripping up his more dexterous brother. Musa danced backward, avoiding each blow that glanced off his staff and to the porcelain below. The *deba* stopped as Musa hopped out of the way of Abubakari's final swing, nearly grazing Musa's knees. They gazed at one another as sweat poured down their dark frames.

In their few years of training, Abubakari had never defeated Musa, but the desire continually crept into his soul with contempt. He was the oldest, but his younger sibling constantly bested Abubakari. He wondered where such dark thoughts hid in his heart, only to bloom into a simmering rage. In the presence of their father, Abubakari had hoped to draw blood from the confident Musa.

"Go!"

The *deba* thumped and Musa attacked once more. The staves connected with the clangor of wood against wood, until the deba stopped beating. Unsure of whether the fighting would continue, Abubakari lowered his defenses. Musa saw his opening and continued without hesitation. Abubakari could barely maintain his balance as he was struck in the side, which immediately brought him to his knees. Abubakari sacrificed his staff for the pain in his side, and the pole rattled to the floor.

The instructor reached down and returned the fallen staff to the wrenching Abubakari. "Where you lost focus, Kankan had not. You must hear the tempo at all times and never give in to the rage. A warrior must remain at peace even in the heart of battle. Well done, Kankan Musa."

Musa nodded and immediately sought to help Abubakari to his feet.

"Let go of me!" cried Abubakari as he angrily pushed Musa away.

"I was trying to help you!" snapped Musa.

"I do not need your help!"

"Silence!" The instructor became nervous once he saw the look of displeasure in the *mansa*. "Children of the Keita do not behave in such a manner!"

"Children of the Keita do not rely on trickery either!" spat Abubakari while regaining his feet.

Musa slammed his staff on the marble floor. "We were

never told to stop! You are a terrible fighter!"

"And you are a two-legged goat!"

"Silence!" intervened the officer.

Before the boys could utter another word, their father also castigated the pair. "*N'ko*!" bellowed *Mansa* Abubakari. The two boys fell silent as Abubakari turned to Sulayman. "I rule lands larger than all of Wagadou, and yet cannot command the discipline of my children. You would not behave so badly, would you, Sulayman?" Sulayman comically shook his head, which amused the ruler.

The instructor quickly fell to his knees and let his head touch the floor. "Forgive me, *Mansa*. I am the one who is to blame for their anger. I have not instructed them properly."

Mansa Abubakari rose. "No. Maybe I have spent too many years in the battlefield. Perhaps it is now my responsibility to instruct my sons. You may leave."

The officer humbly came to his feet and departed. The *mansa* slowly approached Musa and Abubakari, who continued to exchange angry glares. "After bathing, you will both accompany me to my *pempi*." And he departed to the obedient nods given by the sons of the Keita clan.

Later that day, Mansa Abubakari sat with his sons at his feet on a three-tiered pavilion with silk-carpeted steps, upon a knoll just outside the palace's gate. Dressed in his red velvet tunic of Mutanfas, the mansa sat upon his pempi, shaded from the sun's rays by a huge silk-cotton tree looming over the pavilion. The weary warrior scanned the villages and people that dotted the vast landscape. Carefully placed sofa warriors maintained a perimeter to ensure their safety and solitude.

"The Tree of Malabar has outlived us all," the mansa

stated regretfully. "My father ruled from here. His father ruled from here. As far back as the great Sundiata, the destiny of Mali was decided from the protection of this very tree. If only my wraith could remain after I am gone."

"Where are you going, Father?" softly said Abubakari.

Mansa Abubakari affectionately caressed the pate of Abubakari's head. "Nowhere, Abu. Nowhere. I will always be here, under this tree."

"It is going to rain." Musa looked to the sky and watched the clouds slowly move in. As the winds increased, the lands appeared to move rapidly under the troubled heavens.

"Yes. It should be a plentiful harvest for the villagers," said the mansa as he gazed upwards. "All praise belongs to Allah."

"I made this from our hunt." Abubakari held tightly to the cowry necklace as he lifted it into his father's view.

Mansa Abubakari smiled. "It is worthy of a Mandingo." He turned to Musa. "I understand that both of you did well. Such brave warriors are you."

Abubakari lowered his head in shame. He could not explain why he felt compelled to share this with his father, but he was torn between what was and what should be. "I could not say this before, but I failed." Abubakari could feel the storm quickly approaching, and his soul sought shelter. He wanted to play along the Niger and float within its waters before the desire was washed away, before the suffocation began.

"What is this you say of failure?" demanded Mansa Abubakari.

"The buffalo would have killed me if it wasn't for Kankan," murmured Abubakari. "He is much stronger than I. He is worthy of mansa, not me."

Musa had never heard such words uttered by his elder brother. Though Musa possessed a normally quiet demeanor, Abubakari's statement left the young prince still frozen in awe.

Mansa Abubakari, on the contrary, was clearly irritated. "What else should he have done? That was his duty as your brother. And as long as you are brothers, you must stay united, for each of you possess a gift." The mansa's glare shifted between both his sons. "There are those who will try to divide you, but you must not let them. You will be mansa, Abu, and you will one day rule the greatest empire. Do you understand?"

Abubakari reluctantly nodded.

Mansa Abubakari focused on his other son. "Musa, always be there by your brother's side," continued the graying mansa. "He will need you in the darkest moments, as will Sulayman."

"Yes, Father," agreed Musa with a confident tone.

Mansa Abubakari smiled to them both before walking to the edge of the pavilion to watch the warm golden glow of the sun peekthrough the dim sky and glitter off the Niger. "Still, I have not fulfilled my destiny. Djenné, I must have it to complete my legacy. Attack after attack, they repel my sofas." He allowed himself a boisterous laugh. "Your mothers consider me a fool, for a man with an empire at his feet to dither over one village. But they do not understand, that all must yield under Mali, under the Keita. It is the only way we can finally achieve peace."

The mansa paused for just a moment to watch the flash of lightning light up the sullen sky. "If I am unable to conquer Djenné, you must swear to me as my sons that you will complete what Allah would not allow me to complete." The boys nodded, which immediately brought another smile to Mansa Abubakari.

Abubakari the Second saw the single tear trickle down the sharp cheekbone of his beloved father and felt the coldness of a thousand rivers funnel through his thin frame. Abubakari somehow knew that they would never again view the beautiful savannah together from under the Tree of Malabar. His father had the eyes of defeat. Abubakari had always gazed upwards and reveled in the strength of his father, the mansa. Yet on that day, his father was just a man, of this world and more mortal than he had previously perceived.

"What an auspicious time we live in," the mansa whispered to the sky, for he was content with the knowledge that perhaps his sons would succeed where he failed. From that night forward, Mansa Abubakari lived for the afterlife as every Moslem did.

Abubakari's eyes never left the mansa. He had a premonition of his father's bleak future. As fear grappled Abubakari the Second, thunder rattled the horizon and dark clouds overtook the sky. In beautiful synchronicity, the lightning flashes illuminated the faces of the future rulers of Mali and the Keita.

3.

1298 C.E.

The tiny young girl swayed back and forth in her ox-drawn carriage as it slowly made its way up the narrow path. Once it was through the surrounding village and past the gates of Niani, thecarriage approached the Palace of Canco.

She peeked nervously out the shutter to get a glimpse of the massive fortress she would call home. Namandje's swirling, plaited hair was nicely decorated with amber glass beads and secured by shiny black thread, so that her soft, oval face remained undisturbed. Enormous gold crescent earrings hung from her tiny ears, and the blue dye that covered Namandje's lips only accentuated the beautiful, unblemished auburn skin underneath the ivory silk robe that enveloped her.

Namandje was only twelve years of age when her father, a nobleman of the northern Dogon tribe, offered his youngest daughter to the imperial throne of Mali. After two years and several bartering sessions involving cola nuts, twenty cows, jewelry cast from gold, and hundreds of tribal horsemen who promised to support Niani when needed, her destiny was set in motion. She had already been slated as the next Malian queen, and it was time for her to meet the young prince for the very first time. The initial ceremony was only days away.

Namandje looked over her shoulder to espy the procession of carriages following her, flanked by armed sofa escorts on horseback. She viewed the villagers littered along the path with their heads lowered in reverence. "Lift your heads. I am only a girl from a village very much like this one," whispered Namandje to herself. Namandje painfully longed for her home and her family. Even after such a long journey, she occasionally shivered from the thoughts that darted through her nervous mind. The comforting attendants that accompanied Namandje did little to reassure the frightened child. Again, she prayed to her ancestors for guidance and that the young mansa would reject her. With that possibility, she had hope of returning to her village in Burkina Faso. She was indeed naïve to believe that young Abubakari even had a decision in the matter.

"Why must I marry?" young Abubakari argued. His personal chamber befitted the crown prince, for its walls were decorated with precious stones, and gold lined its door. Uncut plinths beneath the room's columns displayed floral ornaments and ivory mosaics.

Abubakari had nicely grown into his years, no longer the scrawny youth. Yet he still remained slender and timid, though his boyish features were slowly transforming into the beginnings of a man. As his two young female attendants, no older than Namandje themselves, rustled around the prince to adjust his hunter's tunic and riding trousers, Abubakari awaited reasoning from his trusted djeliba.

"As future mansa, you must have a queen, young lord," responded Mamadou as he peered out the chamber's window. His eyelids flickered from the bright sunrays shooting through the portal.

The robed storyteller had become a great influence in the rearing of Abubakari, and their relationship had grown closer. With every breath, every thought, and every muscle, Mamadou would dedicate his existence to this strapping young man. Although this was the character of any djeliba towards his mansa, Mamadou became a protective older brother for Abubakari the Second, with only the lad's interest in heart.

"Of course, Mamadou. But I am not yet mansa, am I?" Abubakari contemptuously waved the attendants out of the chamber, irritated by their touching and nipping.

"Your time will come soon enough, young lord." Mamadou faced Abubakari. "It is best that you prepare yourself for its inevitability."

Mamadou's comment warranted pause by Abubakari. "I know of Father's health. I am not a fool. But he will return as strong as ever." Just the thought of his father's illness angered Abubakari to no extent.

Mansa Abubakari had unintentionally revealed his physical decline to his son two years before as they rode their steeds across the palace's recreation grounds. Father and son laughed that day and shared a rare moment of isolation from the rigors of ruling the citizens of Mali.

As Abubakari had raced ahead of his father on the cloudy, moist morning through the green meadow, the neighing of his father's horse forced the youth to rein in his mount and reverse direction. Abubakari watched as his father pitifully attempted to wipe away the bright red blood dripping from his nose and mouth. The mansa quickly dismissed any notions of illness that day and many moons after to his courtiers. However, profuse coughing and blood soon became a daily occurrence, impossible to hide from public view. Eventually, the weakened mansa found comfort only in his bedding, where he spent most of his days in the care of his attendants and wives.

It had been months since Abubakari had seen his father. For his mother, the queen, would not allow anyone an audience with the mansa. *How could she deny me the right to see my father? He is my father!* Young Abubakari had no idea that his father was dying and that his mother was only protecting the boy's psyche as well as his health.

"A bird may fly in the air, but its mind is always on the ground," Mamadou stated sternly, returning his eyes to the world outside the window below. He watched the line of carriages approach the main gate of Canco Palace as one of the sofa escorts commanded the carriages to a halt. Immediately, the sentry atop the northeast tower ordered the opening of the gate. The clangor of levers and pulleys welcomed the Dogon party that proceeded past the walls of the pristine fortress. The banging of drums signified her arrival to the palace occupants. Mamadou caught a quick glimpse of Namandje, who momentarily peered through the sliding portal cover to watch the crowd that gathered around the party.

Abubakari sauntered over to Mamadou to investigate what or who had attracted the djeliba's attention. Just before Namandje shut the portal cover, she gazed upwards, and their eyes met for a brief, uncomfortable moment. Her eyes were burnt into Abubakari's memory, long after he turned away. Except for the two girl attendants that served as his shadows, Abubakari was somewhat afraid of the feminine character; he had little experience with it. He spent most of his days studying philosophy, language, and war science, all of which were taught by handpicked male tutors. His only other encounter with a female had been with his mother, whom he loved dearly.

"She is beautiful, young lord," said Mamadou with a grin. "You should honor the queen for handpicking such a favorable bride."

Abubakari viewed Mamadou with contempt. "It is my life. I shall do as I please!" In disgust, Abubakari slammed his fist on the window ledge and fled the chamber.

Moments later, Abubakari mounted his steed with little effort, just as Namandje and an entourage of newly appointed attendants entered the West Garden. As Abubakari sat upright in his saddle, everyone fell to their knees and lowered their heads in submission, including Namandje, who waited for an attendant to place a velvet mat for her comfort. As an autumn breeze moved through, it carried with it the snow-white flower petals of the baobab tree and the chirps of nearby blackbirds calling for their mates. Abubakari silently panned the prostrate aristocrats and attendants until his eyes found Namandje, who was now clothed in red silk that wrapped snugly around her petite waist and expanded around the curvatures of her breasts and hips. A tightly wrapped hijab of the same hue hid her elaborate coiffure from Abubakari. At that moment, he could only think of his father's health.

"Abu, I expected a more pleasant response, especially after viewing your future bride." A lone woman suddenly appeared from behind the kneeling audience and approached Abubakari.

Mariama wore a purple chador and hijab that blended with her ebony complexion. Her face was free of powder and clear as the open savannah. A voluptuous woman at the very least, her outline was a jewel that tempted all the thieves. She carried a certain purity and sophistication worthy of only a queen.

"Of course, I am pleased, N'na," said Abubakari as his steed danced in a circle and neighed in excitement. "I must regret that I do have one question that must be answered." The horse's heavy hooves pounded the green below. "Can she ride a horse?"

Namandje lifted her head as sounds of astonishment worked their way through the kneeling courtiers. Abubakari the Second centered his horse to within a few feet of Namandje and extended his hand downward. The deep blue that adorned her lips and the yellow amber beads that covered her neck intrigued him.

"You would have the Princess of Mali sit upon that beast?" Mariama was annoyed by her son's imprudent request. As queen of Mali, she understood well that this was not etiquette befitting a lady of the court.

"It is not a beast, N'na. It is a horse." Abubakari continued to offer his hand to the nervous Namandje.

After a brief silence, Namandje slowly rose to her feet and firmly grasped Abubakari's forearm. Abubakari pulled her closer and lifted her into the saddle behind him. Namandje sat with both legs to one side and her arms clenched around the waist of Abubakari. They quickly galloped out of the garden and into the expansive palace grounds where buffaloes and sheep grazed. The warm sun beat down on Namandje's back as she leaned forward to stabilize herself.

The horse dashed through an encapsulated wooded area and carried the two up a small knoll that presented a panoramic view over the palace walls. Abubakari carefully lowered Namandje to the lush, green field and dismounted the steed. While gently stroking the mane of the horse, Abubakari turned his back on Namandje.

"Forget about your marriage to me. The union will not happen," said Abubakari with conviction.

Namandje said nothing. With her head held low, she stood motionless as a slight zephyr cascaded across her dress. She held tight to her elbows to fend off the chills that rippled through her small frame.

"Have you nothing to say?" said Abubakari the Second as he faced a trembling Namandje.

She said nothing.

"I have better interaction with my horse," Abubakari snorted.

How dare you reject me? Though it was what Namandje had earlier desired, she had never believed it would evolve in such a hurtful manner. But since it did, Namandje now understood how impossible it was for it not to happen. She was considered the most beautiful girl in the entire province surrounding the Banifing River. From childhood, she was educated in the ways of the royal court and, in essence, bred to one day marry an emperor. Tears began streaming down her soft cheeks. It was not solely the words of Abubakari that caused turmoil in her heart. She wept for the utter disappointment of her father, which her rejection would surely engender. Namandje became annoyed at Abubakari for deciding their fate without understanding or considering her feelings. She felt the heavy burden set upon her by the many desires of those who scrupulously wanted this marriage to happen, whether for political or financial gain. The tears ceased, allowing Namandje to regain her composure.

"That was all I had to share with you." Abubakari mounted his horse once again and courteously extended his hand to Namandje. "It is decided. You will return to your village."

Namandje angrily tottered in the other direction, nearly stumbling from her hurried pace.

Abubakari laughed at the awkwardness of her departure. "Where are you going? I will deliver you to the garden... Wait!" Abubakari prodded his horse ahead until he rode beside the vexed lass. In fear of trampling Namandje, Abubakari alighted and followed her on foot. "Wait! I command you to wait!" His eyes followed the waves in her red silk garment created by the brisk wind. Still filled with giggles, Abubakari reached Namandje and gently clutched her arm. Abubakari caught his breath. "Wait," whispered Abubakari.

Namandje came to a halt.

"That is better," said Abubakari with relief. "How would

it look if a common villager stormed away from a prince?"

Namandje angrily faced Abubakari. Her watery eyes trembled with fury. She moved to within a breath of the crown prince. Abubakari secretly enjoyed her pleasant scent of perfumed berries and cautiously took a step backwards. Namandje stepped forward, bringing her lips as close as possible to his without touching. She stood on the balls of her feet to make sure her eyes met his. Abubakari ceased smiling as he took another step backwards. Namandje closed the space once more as she reached into her chador and removed a peculiar item.

"Aiee!" Abubakari did not see the large, lonely stone embedded in the knoll under his feet. He stumbled backwards and fell on his rear end just as Namandje knelt beside him. Abubakari raised his forearm in a defensive motion. He had little experience with the other sex, and this discomfort erupted into utter fear. *Is she going to kill me? I have been warned about the craftiness of female assassins!* Abubakari slightly calmed himself upon realizing that his mother, his N'na, would not have procured him an assassin to wed.

Namandje opened her clasped hands to reveal a necklace constructed of cowries, similar to the one Abubakari made as a youth. She slowly placed the necklace over his head and past his gaping mouth. Abubakari's eyes sunk into his chest as the cowries clicked against one another. Namandje's eyes became mere slits upon her oval face, while Abubakari could only manufacture an uncomfortable smirk after viewing the glistening shells around his neck.

"How did you know that…?" said Abubakari to the air where Namandje once knelt. She rose to her feet and hastily abandoned the crown prince in his prone position. The sound of Namandje's small sandals hitting the field slowly dissipated as she moved down the embankment and out of view.

Abubakari stood and brushed the fur of his hunter's tunic to ensure the grassland did not soil it. As he stared at the cowries, memories of the hunt with his brother surfaced. Abubakari had not seen his brother for several years, once Musa was sent to Timbuktu to study. He wanted so badly to share with his brother the grand event that had taken place. She knew. Abubakari's heart, from that moment, yearned for Namandje, and he was determined to have her in his life. Abubakari mounted his horse and rode at full speed to tell his father of the news.

Daylight became darkness, and Abubakari forced his way into his father's private chamber. The guards initially resisted the crown prince as ordered by his mother and their queen, Mariama. With some persistence and his threats of eventually becoming the king of Mali, Abubakari convinced the sofa guards to rethink their duties.

"He is the son of our lord," said one guard.

"And one day, he will become our mansa," added the other. They parted and allowed the young Mandingo prince to enter.

Furs from various lands throughout Africa covered the mansa's plush and expansive chamber. The white glow of torches lining the walls alternated between bright and a flicker. Abubakari had stumbled upon a clandestine meeting between his father, the royal physician, several royal retainers, and Mamadou, son of the mansa's former djeliba. The men prostrated themselves around the king, whose fragile frame lay feebly in his bedding. Abubakari's eyes grew wider as he witnessed his father's sunken eyes and leathery skin. Abubakari's slow entrance had not alerted those present, allowing the prince to meld with the shadows and listen intensively.

"He will need your guidance," the mansa whispered.

The men who surrounded him were brought to tears at the sight of their ruler, who was weaker than they had ever witnessed. Many had not conceived of the mansa dying at such a young age, to fade in this way. A few of his most loyal retainers considered entering the next land with their beloved king, but at the request of the mansa, they had new duties to honor. Nevertheless, the heartfelt pain that permeated the chamber brought the dispirited gathering to cries of sorrow.

"Stay well, my lord."

"May Allah be with you, my lord."

"Why have the ancestors forsaken our lord?"

Mansa Abubakari coughed profusely, spewing blood from his mouth. The physician quickly cleaned his cheek and administered an elixir. As he drank the medicine, the mansa clenched Mamadou's robe to force the liquid down his swollen throat. The storyteller gently lifted the mansa's head until the flask was empty and slowly lowered him onto the pillow once more. The king mumbled incoherently to himself before gazing over their shoulders.

"Abu, is that you?"

"Yes, Father," replied Abubakari.

The sight of the young prince startled the men, with the exception of Mamadou, who felt his young lord's gaze but refused to draw attention to his presence. A son should see his father in his final days. Mamadou had not had such an opportunity. His father had served as djeliba to the mansa before him. While in service of the mansa, during the subjugation of Gao, Mamadou's father succumbed to an illness and died before his return to the palace. There were elaborate burial ceremonies, the sacrificing of the sacred cows, and the passing of the Kouyaté clan leadership to Mamadou. And then it became the responsibility of the young djeliba to chronicle that last years of the ailing mansa as well as the boy who would take his place.

Mamadou took Abubakari's hand and led him to the lion-skin bedding on which his father wheezed. Abubakari knelt at his father's side; the youth's hand trembled in the air above the prone mansa. Abubakari was afraid—afraid to touch the king who had shared very few words with his son during his reign. The only memories Abubakari could muster were those of his father calling for his council or for the master of the stables to prepare his horse for riding. Then there were the many days that he was gone on long campaigns to unite Mali. Everything his father lived for involved a united Mali. At times, Abubakari despised the people of Niani, the kingdom of Mali, and those who resisted the rule of the Keita. In the end, he blamed them all for his father's illness.

Abubakari let his hand rest on his father's chest. The mansa's cheek twitched as his frail hand crept up to caress the hand of his son. Soon a smile pervaded his face and he waved his courtiers out the room.

"As you wish, my lord." Mamadou led the weeping men out the chamber.

Mansa Abubakari slowly opened his watery eyes. They glowed under the torchlight. They were the eyes of a young man that still held dreams within his heart. That was the greatest sadness for all in those last days—how the mansa accepted the next world without fear, but only a smile, as though he knew more than those further away from death. His father's touch was cold to Abubakari.

"You are afraid to greet your father?" whispered the mansa.

"Never." Abubakari resisted the urge to cry. He wanted to remain strong in the presence of his father.

"It is tolerable, Abu. I am such a burden these days." The mansa coughed heavily and quickly covered his mouth with the cloth in his other hand. "I had to be certain that my illness would not become yours before I could see you. Do you understand, Son?" Abubakari nodded. "How is your brother faring?"

"He is well," said Abubakari with a forced grin. He adjusted the wool blanket to warm his father. "In his last letter, he expressed how pleased he was with living in Morocco and serving Mali."

"Is that so?" replied the mansa with a chuckle of satisfaction.

"His mother and yours were vexed by my decision. And Sulayman?"

"He is also well. He has just begun his equestrian training."

"That is good."

Suddenly, Mansa Abubakari rolled over and leaned on his elbows. Huffing for air, he pushed himself up until he came to his knees. Completely astonished, Abubakari watched his father struggle to his feet. The ebony king stood proudly above his heir and gazed downward with warm eyes. His bare chest was skeletal, yet it was his glare that made the mansa appear as the strong Mandingo warrior before Abubakari.

"Let us ride together as father and son," roared Mansa Abubakari.

"The mansa is in the palace's recreation grounds on his

horse," screamed the attendants as they scurried through the halls of the palace and alerted all those who could prevent what could be perceived as childish antics from a sickly man. The attendants feared that if the mansa's condition became known throughout the provinces, his place in immortality would be ruined.

That was what it meant to be mansa. You were one with God because you represented him to the living. You did not die or become ill. Your feet did not touch the ground, nor did you consume repast as the others. You were an immortal to be worshipped by the people. Allah sent you, and after His work was completed, He would return the mansa to His kingdom. There, paradise awaited.

Abubakari held tight to the reins as the powerful horse ripped through the palace grounds, cleared a small creek, and galloped up the face of a small knoll. Mansa Abubakari clung to his son as they shared the same steed. Abubakari was unable to see the joy emanating from the man behind him. Yet he could hear the occasional raspy chuckle over his shoulder. They stopped at the apex of the hill and gazed at the blue silhouette of Niani under the starry sky.

"It is warmer than normal. Is it not the eighth month, the Hour of the Antelope?" Mansa Abubakari rested his hand on the angled shoulders of the young Mandingo prince.

"It is, Father," agreed Abubakari as he smiled with the mansa. Abubakari was pleased that the evening had remained clear for his father. He knew that the opportunities for the mansa to see the kingdom that he enlarged were waning each day.

"Are you pleased with your wife?"

"Yes, Father. She is as beautiful as Mother."

Mansa Abubakari chuckled and coughed intermittently

under his breath. "That is yet to be determined. However, you must know that she was chosen for so much more. She will be the pole to your spearhead."

"Pole?" Abubakari attempted to decipher what his father meant, but eventually shrugged the remark into his subconscious. Instead, he stroked the mane of the horse as it became slightly unsettled. The steed eventually calmed down. "Shall we continue?" Abubakari was eager to let the wind batter his face once more, though he worried about his father's weak state.

"No...not at this moment. Allow me to see Niani-ba." Mansa Abubakari slowly scanned the rich landscape with a symphony of crickets in the backdrop. The wind picked up and offered a gentle breeze on a rather muggy evening. Father and son enjoyed the moment of silence alone, away from the courtiers, family, and menial tasks of governing.

"Father, I am afraid," whispered Abubakari. He carried many fears from his youth, but at that moment, he encountered fear of another kind—uncertainty. Loneliness hovered above in the darkness ready to engulf Abubakari. The trembling young warrior awaited the normal chastising from his father, for the mansa believed that fear lay in the hearts of children, not within the soul of a Keita Mandingo warrior.

"You will not be alone," muttered Mansa Abubakari over his son's shoulder. "Remember your dreams, Abu. Always remember your dreams, but never forget the hearts of the people."

"I shall, Father," said Abubakari. "I shall share my dreams with the people." Abubakari curtailed his sorrow. He recalled the days when they rode until the sun baked their coppery skins and the rippling heat danced above the open savannah. "I will never shame you," continued Abubakari with a flutter in his voice. "Father?"

The mansa's grasp had weakened on the young Abubakari's shoulders, until the sickly man's limbs went limp and his body leaned heavily on the lad's back. Abubakari did not turn around to see what he already knew. Tears streaked down his face, and he allowed himself to cry for his father who would no longer share his wisdom with the Crown Prince of Mali.

Abubakari wrapped his father's arms around him and held tight as he circled the entire recreation grounds before returning to the palace as the new king.

4.

1299 C.E.

As always, the subject of Djenné came before the Niani royal council. It was the first time that Abubakari the Second resided over his father's loyal courtiers, though each of them had their own agendas. In many ways, the courtiers were linked to the provincial lords, often exchanging economic favors.

Within the council chambers, surrounded by stone columns crowned by blackbird capitals, eight men prostrated themselves as Abubakari and his two attendants entered and sat at the head of the gathering. Whenever the council convened, the meeting remained traditional. Everyone, including the mansa, sat on pillows. There were no stools or chairs. It was believed that sitting on the floor put their minds and hearts closer to the land, thereby making wiser decisions for the people of Mali.

"It is very early. Can we not meet later in the day?" Abubakari began, petulant.

"Forgive us, my lord," replied the elderly Azikiwe, the most senior council member. "Your father preferred to begin each day discussing the matters at hand."

"No longer," snapped Abubakari. "In the future, we will gather at the Hour of the Buffalo."

"A wise decision, my lord," answered Azikiwe to the approving nods of the other council members. "Also, we would like to congratulate you on your choice of queen. I understand that the first ceremony between you and Queen Namandje is occurring as we speak."

Abubakari scanned the faces of the men who lined before him. It struck him that they were all at least forty years his senior. Although Abubakari had been trained to handle the leadership role, he masked the uneasiness that simmered in his gut. He did not want to be exposed as a child to the council, regardless of the fact that they were there to do his bidding. Though Abubakari often imagined the beautiful face of his future queen, frivolous thoughts and words had no place in his heart while commanding the people.

"What is the matter at hand?" said Abubakari as he adjusted his velvet red tunic of Mutanfas.

"Djenné, my lord." Azikiwe's cat-like voice did not match the long white beard and dark-green council robe that covered him. "As you are well aware, the late mansa continually attempted to subjugate the rebellious village."

"And we were unsuccessful," Abubakari snapped.

"It is a strong garrison, my lord," another council member interjected. "It is difficult to penetrate their walls."

"Chief Abayomi is a stubborn goat," added another. "But in time, he will surrender to your will, my lord." The other council members voiced their agreement.

"Is that so?" Abubakari looked upon the men with contempt. "I wonder. Why must they surrender to my will? Why will they not freely follow their lord? Or perhaps, ruling Djenné is not my will at all. It is very costly to the farmers, and many Mandingo warriors have perished."

The council members began muttering among themselves. Some even publicly smirked at Abubakari's remarks.

"It is not as simple as that, my lord," chuckled Azikiwe. "There are years of bitterness between the Keita and the people of Djenné. Bitterness that began well before your birth."

"What is so humorous?" hissed Abubakari. "I understand that I am young and inexperienced as mansa, but do not take me lightly! All the knowledge that my father possessed was passed on to me. So, I am aware of my history, Azikiwe!"

Surprised by the roar of their young mansa, the council members quickly lowered their heads in fear. They had not expected Abubakari to respond so strongly. Earlier thoughts of manipulating the young king were quickly washed away.

"Forgive us for our insolence, my lord. We do not wish to be looked upon unfavorably by our lord," Azikiwe cowered.

After a few moments of allowing his presence to sink into their minds, Abubakari continued the discussion. "I believe that they will willingly come under the hand of Mali, for are they not Mandingo?" The confidence in Abubakari's tone concealed his adolescent voice and gave power to his words. "As my father told me, it is preordained. We will send envoys with offers of peace for the Djenné chief. He will wholeheartedly submit when he learns that this is the mansa's will."

The room was silent.

"I welcome your comments," added Abubakari.

Only Azikiwe, as chief council, had the courage to respond. "My lord, we have tried several times to send envoys to Chief Abayomi."

"And?"

"Words offer little consideration, if any. They were all killed in the most grotesque manner. They cannot be reasoned with. Your father knew this and had grown weary of their savagery."

Abubakari was unaware of this. His father had not shared those details. Abubakari rubbed his hands in thought, until he began coughing again—a condition that had suddenly erupted nearly a month before and showed no signs of leaving. He did not feel ill, and his strength had not diminished. But the incessant coughing had not stopped.

One of his attendants quickly poured Abubakari some water from a nearby basin. Abubakari drank the water-filled, wooden bowl down.

"Are you well, my lord?" wondered Azikiwe.

"The summer has brought dry air to Niani. It is nothing." Though the young ruler was concerned, he did not want anyone one to learn of it. Besides, he did not feel feverish. It could only be due to the savannah air. Only Mamadou knew of the persistent coughs, and he persuaded Abubakari to see the royal medicine man. That would come soon enough.

"Ah, it is very common for a young man to feel unwell now and then. But you have a strong constitution, my lord. I am sure you will overcome this dry air," cajoled Azikiwe.

"Very well," said Abubakari as he stood, seeming to ignore the old man's kind word. "I have decided. Let us attempt a peaceful resolution first. I shall send a female envoy this time, someone very dear to me. I will write a letter to Abayomi in ancient Mande as a symbol of our common blood. That should create a more favorable response."

"My lord, there is the matter of village taxes to discuss."

"We will continue this discussion tomorrow at a more suitable hour."

"As you wish, my lord." Azikiwe lowered his head, followed by the other council members, as Abubakari and his attendants departed the chambers.

Once they felt it safe to do, the elders began voicing their discontent for their new mansa.

"He is well-spoken for such a young age, but his ignorance is quite unbearable."

"How foolish it is to ignore the wisdom of the council."

"Djenné will only react in the same manner."

"His laziness is disconcerting, indeed. It is better to meet at the beginning of the day."

Azikiwe raised his hand to silence the bitterness in the room. "We must remember that he is young. Not since Sundiata has someone so young become mansa. In time, he will easily learn his place. Let us respect the wishes of the late mansa and try to guide the lord in the meantime."

Mariama stormed into Abubakari's private chambers, the place where his father once contemplated the future of the Keita.

"N'na," Abubakari said pleasantly from the veranda. He dared not face her as she moved through the room behind him and out to the terrace. Azikiwe had already notified him of his mother's disapproval.

"Why did you send Oni on such a foolhardy errand?"

Mariama said as she stood beside him.

"What do you mean?" Abubakari did not take his eyes off the golden glow of the setting sun. His gaze trailed a flock of blackbirds soaring westward over Niani village. *If only I could follow them beyond the Senegal.*

"You sent my lady-in-waiting into the teeth of Djenné without my permission."

"Who embodies the concept for peace more than a woman?" Abubakari said with a gratifying smile. "It was a wise decision."

"Your father also searched for a peaceful solution. He quickly learned that peace is not something the Djenné people recognize."

"Would you prefer that I wage war immediately, or are you just jealous, Mother, that I did not send you instead?" Abubakari said as he glared at Mariama.

Mariama was silent. She let her look of disappointment counter her son's thoughtless attack. She sighed and turned away from Abubakari.

"Forgive me," whispered Abubakari, "I am already weary, and I have just begun."

Mariama faced Abubakari. "I am your mother. I forgave you before you asked to be forgiven."

"N'na, I am not well." Abubakari inhaled his lower lip to fend off the tears. "I fear that I am to suffer the same fate as Father. Why did he lie to me? He was dying, yet he said nothing! Blast him! How could he abandon me?" Abubakari's grip tightened on the stone balustrade.

Mariama had no idea that her son harbored such feelings. She knew that his words were rooted in guilt, not anger. "Your fate is not that of your father's. You must understand that." Her sympathetic hands caressed his face.

"If that is true, N'na, then why was I named mansa? He put me on this path!"

"Because you are the rightful heir," Mariama said sternly. "And I am certain you will serve Mali admirably."

Those were comforting words for Abubakari. Nevertheless, he always felt that Musa would have made a better choice to rule from Niani. Abubakari missed his half-brother. I am sure that you are having a wondrous time in Timbuktu. Oh, how I envy you, Kankan Musa. Once they had sent Musa away to study, they had very little contact with each other. Royal messengers occasionally arrived with letters from his brother, but eventually, Musa ceased writing Abubakari. Thus, Abubakari held his feelings inside. He was unable to share his dreams or fears with anyone else. There was Sulayman, but he was still a small child and became more of a nuisance than a brother to Abubakari. His stepmother, Lady Kongo, often reminded the young mansa of his coldness to his younger sibling.

Abubakari brought his hands up to cover his mother's hands around his face. He closed his eyes and imagined that he was a child once more, collecting cowries and sailing down the Sankarini with his father and brother.

In Mariama's eyes, Abubakari was still a child. She knew that she would have to impart her strength onto him, even if it weakened her to the point of death. Mariama pulled his head to her chest and held her son, protecting him from her worst fears—at least for that moment.

"Lord Abubakari, please enter."

Guedado was an elderly Fulani medicine man who had served under Abubakari's father. He eventually became Abubakari's personal physician, though the newly crowned mansa never had a reason to be examined in the past.

Guedado pressed one palm on Abubakari's bare chest and the other palm on his back. As he repeatedly breathed deeply at the behest of his physician, Abubakari surveyed the mysterious plant life in the medicine man's chamber. Wild plants and pottery filled with unique aromas crammed the shelves. The bones of various animals also intrigued Abubakari. They reminded him of his Initiation of the Bush and when Kankan Musa severed the horns of the bull.

"Have you coughed up blood?"

"No," answered Abubakari with his brow crunched.

"That is good. You may put your tunic back on." Guedado spoke Mande, but with a deep Fulbe accent, the native dialect of his nomadic people. He had traveled through different lands as a young man, learning his trade from the masters of each village. It had been said that the medicine man had even journeyed to the far reaches of India during his scholarly adventure. Nonetheless, Guedado was quite adroit with medicine, and he knew it.

Abubakari fastened his tunic and rose from the feathery bedding. He waited for the medicine man to return from selecting several flasks from the shelf.

"What is wrong with me?"

"Unsure." Guedado shrugged.

"You do not know?" screeched Abubakari in his juvenile tone. "You are a medicine man, are you not?"

"Yes, I am. But I am not a fortune teller." Guedado placed three flasks in Abubakari's hands. One contained minced leaves of some sort. The second was a hideous root soaking in a yellow-hued liquid. The third contained white powder, most likely ground bone, from what Abubakari could determine.

"What are these?" Abubakari lifted the flasks to his face.

"Mint, ginger, and camel bone to help build your stamina." Guedado stepped over to the nearby basin and cleansed his hands. "Add a pinch of each to your tea before retiring each night."

"So, you do know why I have started coughing?"

The old man scratched his gray, scruffy beard and raised his cottonlike eyebrows, also a dirty gray. "It is hard to say. It may simply be due to anxiety, or you may have inherited your father's heart consumption. I would think nothing of it, if not for your father's illness."

"Heart consumption?" Abubakari did not know what it was, but he knew that it had killed his father, injecting fear into his veins.

"As I said before, it difficult to determine at this moment. Do not be troubled. It may go away in a short period of time."

"You tell me that I may die, and I am suppose to remain calm?"

"Perhaps, I should examine the lord's ears before letting him depart." Guedado began organizing the instruments used for the examination—a conch shell, gold tongs, and a magnifying glass he acquired during his travels. "I never said that you would die."

"But you said that I will be sick like my father." The combatant child surfaced in Abubakari. "That is the same as sentencing me to death."

"Your father's condition came very suddenly, unlike your condition." Guedado chuckled. "You are a cynical young Mandingo."

"How dare you address me with such commonality," pouted Abubakari. "I am your mansa, and—"

"I am an old man," Guedado interrupted. "I do not

distinguish a lord from a beggar. I only see the ill. I treated your father in that manner, and I do not see why I should treat you differently. Have me killed if you desire. I still will not know the root of your illness. Besides, I have lived far too many years. I am tired." He sighed and continued as if his previous words were never spoken. "Ah, and try to not overexert yourself. Get as much rest as possible."

Abubakari stood motionless, unsure how to respond. Since becoming mansa, no one had ever spoken to him with such forthrightness. Abubakari admitted to himself it was becoming an annoyance that every one within his royal circle bowed before him, agreed with every word he said, and laughed loudly when he only chuckled— Mamadou being the exception. This bitter old goat has insulted me, he thought. And then: It is very refreshing. Abubakari smiled, placed the corked flasks inside his tunic, and walked towards the draped exit.

"Lord Abubakari, one more thing."

"Yes, I will return if the condition continues." Abubakari stopped at the exit and faced a moist-eyed Guedado, which stunned the young mansa.

"If it is consumption, I must tell you that a cure may not be possible." Guedado sat on the floor with his legs nimbly crossed. "That is, even in my many travels, I have never uncovered a cure that would have given your father his life."

Abubakari sensed the pain in the medicine man's voice. Yet he was too young to understand that the old man's bitterness came from guilt. Guedado had tried every remedy he knew, but none succeeded. He begged the late mansa to not burden his body with his duties, but

Abubakari the First was incapable of slowing down. He was a hunter-king after all.

"So I am destined to die?"

"We are all destined to die, Lord Abubakari, but we have yet to see any blood. Yours could be a simple cough. I continue to search for the cure, if not only for my own knowledge."

"Where do you search?"

"Djenné. I believe they are well skilled in the art of medicine. Perhaps, behind their muddy walls lies a cure. Your father knew that, but he refused to lay down his arms to find out. Do not follow the same foolish path, Abubakari the Second."

Abubakari's eyes also watered. "What an old fool. You tell me that I will live and die at the same moment." Abubakari fought off the tears with a hearty laugh. "You forget, old man, I am mansa. I am the will of the ancestral gods…I will live forever."

Guedado laughed as Abubakari exited the chamber. "Let us hope so, Lord Abubakari. Let us hope so! Remember, if there is any sign of blood, come and visit me."

"I will, foolish old man." Abubakari exited, leaving a trail of laughter.

In the eleventh month, Abubakari received his first lesson in diplomacy.

Abubakari met with his council once he learnt that the special envoy to Djenné had returned to Canco Palace. The young mansa wondered how negotiations went. He predicted a positive response. The letter that Abubakari carefully crafted was written to reveal his true feeling. Abubakari refused to let the village that whittled away at his father do the same to him. A peaceful resolution had to be achieved.

Day of Afonta, Month of Eze'elu,
Chief Abayomi,
Much blood has been spilt between our two proud
lands. And why? Perhaps, only my father and yourself
can explain. Yet I cannot, for I am now mansa, and our
embittered history has never entered my heart.
Therefore, I come to you on equal ground.
I am lord of the richest lands known to man. Yet I am
young and hesitant in my ways. I look to the support of
my noblest chieftains for support. I request the same
support of you, for it is I who control the Twelve Doors
of Mali. Are we not Mandingo brothers under the gods?
We must open our eyes to the truth that runs from our
limbs to our hearts.
Please, come to the palace and join me in a repast. It
will serve as a worthy symbol of what I desire to be an
alliance, long past its due.
I await your consideration,
Mansa Abubakari the Second

Abubakari had gone to great lengths to personally pick his special envoy. She was Oni, the beautiful daughter of a Keita noble who, at seventeen years of age, served as one of his mother's ladies-in-waiting. As a boy, Abubakari had admired her from a near distance; as children they had often frolicked about the palace, teasing one another until one of them cried to his or her wet nurse. Thoughts of the day he had given her a wolf's tooth from his hunter's tunic raced through his mind. She strung it on thread and wore it around her neck, never removing it. He secretly wished that Mariama could have considered Oni as one worthy of marriage to a prince. That was before Namandje.

In the Month of Anyanwu, the rainy season produced a downpour that lasted many days. Earlier in the year, Abubakari had received news that Kankan Musa would visit to celebrate the mansa's seventeenth birthday, but his younger half-brother never arrived, only a letter explaining his extensive studies at the Timbuktu University and the lack of time as a consequence. The soggy and heavy gray sky that filled the council chamber's portal reminded Abubakari of that time. He sorely needed a lift in his spirits.

"Where is Oni? Of course, she is late as usual." Abubakari turned to each senior official with a grin. "Should I expect less from a woman?" He immediately turned to the two female attendants seated behind him. "Surely, I mean no harm. It is banter in good humor." The two attendants simply bowed with smiles and regained their statuesque posture.

The heavy chortles from the royal council came as Abubakari predicted, except for its eldest member. Azikiwe's white-mane covered head remained buried in his chest.

"Azikiwe, you are one without words. Are you ill?" Abubakari continued chuckling at the detriment of the pensive old man.

"No, my lord. I am well."

Abubakari could sense the turmoil in the way Azikiwe responded, never making eye contact with the young mansa. As the weeks became months, and the months became a year, Abubakari had gained the respect of his venerable staff, but he knew that he had much to learn. His administrative skills had improved dramatically. Abubakari was fair to the chieftains he taxed, and he delegated properly and swiftly when crisis arose—for example, if not for the rapid decision to dispatch sofa warriors to the fires that set the village of Sibi ablaze, nearly all of its inhabitants would have perished.

However, most of the villagers survived, though their homes and small merchant shops were burnt to the ground.

Eventually, Abubakari depended on the recommendations of Azikiwe exclusively. They consulted regularly, almost equaling the close bond shared by Abubakari and Mamadou. "I know you too well, Azikiwe," interrogated the amiable Abubakari. "Tell me what thoughts clutches your mind."

Azikiwe's mouth slowly opened his mouth, and he mumbled incoherently. He could share with his lord what he had predicted several months prior. Azikiwe also feared that the young mansa would take up the same futile cause as Abubakari the First. The experienced statesman wanted the young mansa to improve the already prosperous economy and expand trade routes beyond Arabia. He had learned from several merchants that the People of the North, who dwelled across the Mediterranean, had increased their need for coinage, which required Malian gold. The burden of sharing his knowledge with his mansa demanded that he speak up.

Just as Abubakari leaned closer to hear him, a messenger sped into the chamber and prostrated himself before Abubakari.

"Where is Oni?" Abubakari spied the empty space behind the young boy.

Without lifting his head, the messenger handed Abubakari a letter, wrapped in silk cloth. Abubakari accepted it.

"You may leave," said Azikiwe to the youth, who graciously departed.

Abubakari slowly unwrapped the silk cloth and surmised that the letter was the one he had sent to Chief Abayomi. Upon unfolding the papyrus, Abubakari's lower lip trembled at what he saw. Inside was the wolf's tooth that he had given Oni in their childhood, covered in dry blood. He held the tooth and let the letter fall to the floor, realizing that the Djenné bastards killed the entire envoy party.

Azikiwe cried at the sight of his grief-stricken mansa. "They are unable to forget the transgressions of the past. Forgive us, my lord." He quickly prostrated himself, along with the other advisors.

"We will strike back with ferocity, my lord!" cried one council member.

"How could they slay a woman? Wicked creatures, they are!" screamed another.

Dreadful anxiety rumbled through Abubakari's body. Words were inconceivable for him. He had trusted his feelings, and they had failed him. All he could see was the memory of a joyful little girl, Oni, chasing him through the gardens, until he was able to squeeze his puny limbs into his personal hiding place that she never found.

From that moment forward, Abubakari swore vengeance. Though he wanted to reduce Djenné to ashes, Abubakari listened to the wisdom of Azikiwe after his attendants and the other advisors were dismissed.

"What have I done, Azikiwe?" Abubakari felt like a cornered bobcat, unsure whether to eject his claws and strike or run away as fast as possible.

"Do not fret, my lord," hissed Azikiwe as he stooped before Abubakari. "Refrain from acting hastily."

"Why would they do this knowing that the power of the Keita could destroy them with one wave of my hand?"

"Precisely, my lord," the chief council responded with a satisfying grin. "They are obviously prepared for our retaliation. I am very impressed with how your forward-thinking has improved."

"Yet I cannot let them go unpunished," whispered

Abubakari, obviously still aghast by the tragedy. "Is this what it means to rule? To thrust the Keita into war?"

"Do not fall into Abayomi's trap, my lord. I beseech you!" Azikiwe slid closer to the young mansa. "My lord," he whispered as his cotton-like brows curled at the edges, "A master drummer must have seven eyes. Abayomi is plotting. Let us do nothing for the moment."

"Do nothing! Oni is gone, and I am at fault!" Abubakari cried out. "My naïveté caused her death!" He clutched his forehead and cocooned himself on the floor. Abubakari became tentative in his thoughts, afraid to make any more decisions. The boy in the boy-king surfaced, and tears dripped from his chin. "Father, you have abandoned me when I need you the most!"

Azikiwe mustered the little strength he possessed, grabbed Abubakari by the tunic, and lifted the young mansa to a more presentable posture. "Gather yourself, my lord, and behave like a king!" Azikiwe shook the young Mandingo's limp body in anger. Unsuccessful, the statesman slapped Abubakari across his wet cheek. "You are king! You must behave as one!"

"I do not know what to do! I do not want this anymore!" Abubakari barreled past Azikiwe and stumbled to the edge of the room. "I was not meant to be mansa."

"My lord," delicately said Azikiwe as he stood and ambled over to the cringing mansa, "as with every mansa before you, you must learn to welcome death, for more is surely to come. It is the cost of unity." He placed a hand on Abubakari's shoulder. "You alone must be strong for your father, for the Keita, and for Mali."

Abubakari came out of his stupor and dried his face. "What if I am not strong enough?" His lost stare met the old man's gaze.

Azikiwe placed his other wrinkled hand on Abubakari's other shoulder. "It is said that one must do a thing at its time and peace follows it." Rage filled his face, although his beard covered most of it. "In time, you will…in time. For now, let Abayomi have his way."

Abubakari took a deep breath and, without any hesitation in his voice, said, "I shall never forget this day." He came to his feet and picked the wolf's tooth from the floor.

"The burden falls on you, my lord. You will always remember this day."

5.

1301 C.E.

"Dooni dooni kononi b'a nyaga da," whispered Mamadou, meaning, little by little, the small bird builds its nest. The other wedding attendees did not hear the storyteller's plea to his ancient ancestors. All eyes were focused on how elegant Namandje appeared in her free-flowing, sapphire-colored robe. Nearly five hundred people traveled from all over Mali to witness the coronation of their new queen.

Two years had passed since Abubakari and Namandje's first wedding ceremony. The traditional ceremony involved family only. There, the families of both parties discussed Namandje's dowry, future rituals for the couple's success, and the duties of the queen to her mansa. Since Mariama arranged the engagement, she handled the specifics for

Abubakari's benefit—with the help of her late husband's loyal retainers, of course. On Namandje's behalf, seven senior administrators, including tribal soothsayers, traveled from Dogon territory. After several days of bartering, an agreement was reached and the legal ceremony was set to proceed.

Abubakari and Namandje knelt before the African marabout performing the second ceremony. The cleric praised the gathering of the two and spoke of Allah blessing the union. He chanted ancient Arabic verses from the Qur'an and finished the ritual by having husband and wife swear unyielding servitude to Him, The Benevolent One. The marriage was deemed law after Abubakari and Namandje shared a goblet of blessed water, signifying that they and the land were one.

Before returning to their private chambers to consummate the marriage, Abubakari and Namandje sat alone in their ox-drawn carriage as it rode through the streets of Niani's Merchant District. Escorted by many sofa guards, the procession of carriages and wagons slowly passed each merchant, allowing the people to touch the carriage that held the mansa and offer gifts to the young, royal couple. Thousands lined the narrow roads, hoping to get a peek at their new queen.

At the front of the cavalcade, Mamadou stood atop the first wagon and sang for the onlookers. Tam tam drums accompanied his deep, bellowing verses.

Welcome your new queen
Wife of Mansa Abubakari the Second
Welcome Queen Namandje
Mother to the people of Mali

Princess of Dogon, this is a glorious day
Princess of Dogon, this is a glorious day

The way people banged on the carriages in celebration startled Namandje initially, but she soon grew accustomed to the loud noise and cheers. While merchants placed various items in the wagons as they passed, children ran alongside the royal carriage with flowers in hand.

"You cannot do that," warned Abubakari. He had prevented Namandje from opening the sliding window and taking the flowers from the smiling children. "The villagers must never touch the queen, nor address you in the common. Do not fret. Their gifts will be collected."

"But they are children carrying flowers," pleaded Namandje. "How can I deny their beautiful faces?"

"You simply must," plainly replied Abubakari as he gazed out the other carriage portal.

"I understand." Namandje's defeated tone did not affect her husband the least bit. She peeked out the tiny window and waved to the approaching children.

"It is uncommonly warm today," Abubakari said. He reached in his velvet tunic and withdrew a fan, which he used with vigor.

Namandje smiled and said nothing. She thought otherwise. It was a rather pleasant autumn day to her, though she could feel the humidity of the rainy season looming overhead. Thoughts of the evening worried her more than anything. Namandje had received superior training on ways to please her husband since her pubescent days. However, Namandje's virginity was still hers, and she would have to surrender it by nightfall.

Suddenly, a dirty man in a tattered robe ran towards the

royal carriage. "My queen, have mercy on a lost soul!" Rarely did Niani natives bare witness to such a man living in harsh circumstances.

"What are you doing here, pitiful man?" screamed one.

"You are disgracing the mansa!" spat another.

Others pushed the vagrant away and cursed his very presence. The ruckus he caused alerted the sofa guards, and they began dragging him away.

"Wait!" Namandje could not ignore the beggar's pathetic voice. She turned to Abubakari. "Why are they handling that man so brutally? He has done nothing wrong."

"There are those that even I cannot help," sighed Abubakari. "He is a man without hope. It would better serve him to be dead."

Frustrated, Namandje reached into her elaborate coiffure and extracted a gold pin from her hair. She reached through the forward slit and tapped the sofa guard that sat next to the carriage driver. "Give this to that man." She handed the hairpin to the unsuspecting guard. "There! That man there!" Namandje pointed to the restrained beggar. "And they are to release him."

"As you wish, my queen!"

The sofa guard jumped off the slowly moving carriage. Namandje's eyes followed his path to the man. She heard the guard mumble, "This is a gift from the queen." The guards released the man. Namandje could faintly hear the joy in the man's exuberant reaction.

"Bless you, my queen! Bless you!" He danced before everyone as they cheered him for his newfound fortune.

"It is done, my queen." The carriage guard returned and retook his place next to the driver.

Namandje smiled and gazed out the window as if nothing happened. She could feel Abubakari's frown on her neck but refused to acknowledge his displeasure.

"I wish my mother had informed me of your unending desire to give away our family treasures to street dwellers." Abubakari could not chastise Namandje, since she did not break Malian law, but he did not know how to handle her quiet independence. So instead, he pouted. In fact, Mansa Abubakari sulked the entire way back to Canco Palace.

That night, a feast was held within the Great Hall of the palace. Royal cooks prepared couscous and wosobula na sauce in several huge pots for the influential attendees. There was music and dancing, and all were elated...except for the two who were not permitted to attend.

Within the mansa's dining chamber, Abubakari and Namandje sat alone. It was a simple room, without the elaborate furnishings one would expect of a king's quarters. They sat across from one another on pillows separated by some five feet. There were no tables, chairs, or windows, only the trays that servants hurriedly brought in with their meal. The servants placed the trays down and left them alone in the small candlelit room.

Although they had met three years before, Namandje had not visited the palace since that day. Only their respective families communicated back and forth. Neither had seen the other's face for so long, they shyly avoided eye contact. Abubakari and Namandje kept their heads buried in their chests, leaving the chamber in utter silence.

Abubakari slyly lifted one eye to see what his wife was doing. Namandje had matured faster than his mind could decipher. Her face carried the same innocence, but her petite frame had become shapelier, and her mannerisms had grown even more refined. Abubakari watched as she gently held the bowl filled with seasoned hippopotamus broth to her full lips and slowly sipped without a drop leaving the corners of her mouth.

"I still have the cowries," mumbled Abubakari. "The ones you gave me. I added them to the cowries I possessed."

She remained silent.

Abubakari reached in his tunic and felt his chest. "They are too large to wear anymore. So, I keep them in my chambers. But I do look at them from time to time. Would you like—?"

"No," blurted Namandje with her head buried in her chest.

"Oh," resigned Abubakari. "I guess that would be very awkward for you."

"No, my lord."

"No?"

"No," reiterated Namandje. "It is just that…I know that you really do not want to show them to anyone. Somehow, you feel obligated to show them to me because I gave you cowries three years ago. But there really is no need for you to inconvenience yourself, my lord."

Abubakari blushed. It was as if she read his mind. She understood his feelings even before he grasped them, which was more than he was comfortable with. "That is not it at all. Just recently, I displayed them for my djeliba," smugly rebutted Abubakari. "Ha, you think you know me so well, do you?"

"Should I not understand your feelings as your wife and queen?" Namandje responded softly.

He did not answer.

"The past three years have been very troublesome for me.

I wondered if you had changed since that day. Part of me hoped that you had," she said with a smile. "Yet another part of me hoped that you remained the same." Namandje's head was still tucked into her chest. "We cannot change who we are for anyone, nor can we expect others to change for us. But that is what I want to do." She lifted her head. "I want the people to praise you for being their mansa and believe that it is was I who made you more than a warrior king. They will praise their queen for making you a kind and merciful king."

She will be the pole to your spearhead. Abubakari remembered the words of his father. Once again, she left the stubborn young mansa without words. He was unsure of whether it was the words she used or the serene manner in which she said them, but the wisdom in Namandje shined through to Abubakari. The love that he felt for her in the West Garden returned.

Namandje came to her feet and prostrated before Abubakari. "Please be good to me as your wife," she said with her head and palms on the floor.

The water in Abubakari's eyes glittered from the candlelight. "I will," he said with a quivering voice. "I also ask of you to be good to me as your husband." Abubakari prostrated before Namandje.

"I will," replied the queen.

Mamadou turned another page of the dusty volume while seated in the comforts of his personal chambers. He enjoyed reading the ancient Arabic tomes that were handed down through countless generations of Kouyaté djelibas. Though djelibas recorded Malian history using stories and song acquired from their own memories, they were knowledgeable about the affairs of their nation and the lands beyond. Malian kings relied on the spiritual historians for matters concerning political, personal, and procedural affairs.

Mamadou was a fourth-generation djeliba. He was named after his grandfather, Mamoudou Kouyaté, djeliba to Sundiata and son of Kedian Kouyaté. From the age of five, Mamadou would listen to his father revisit past Keita glory. By the age of manhood, Mamadou could recite the words of his father, his grandfather, and his great grandfather without a single oversight.

"My lord, it has arrived," announced the attendant beyond the velvet drapery covering the entrance.

"Enter," answered Mamadou as he closed the book.

The attendant entered and handed Mamadou something neatly wrapped in cloth. The storyteller nodded and the attendant exited the chamber. Mamadou placed the item on the desk before him and carefully unwrapped the cloth.

"She will be good for my lord." After reviewing the contents of the item, a bloodstained virginity pagne that proved the consummation of the royal marriage, Mamadou re-wrapped the item. He sighed and returned to his reading.

6.

1307 C.E.

"Tuaregs!" Musa's eyes slowly tracked the tribal people of the Sahara, renowned for their ruthless raids of neighboring villages.

From the advantage of his horse, Musa, with the raise of his palm, brought the small cavalcade of miners, camels, ox-drawn wagons, and sofa horsemen to a halt. The party of forty men, most of them enslaved Fulani workers captured in the previous years of subjugation, had traveled several days across the expansive Saharan Desert. They were returning from the Taghaza salt mines, hoping to escape the dunes and reach the Sahel before the approaching storm in the distance fell upon them. Already, heavy winds were battering the line of African travelers.

Musa, just within the prime of manhood, had grown handsome and muscular. His shoulders had broadened and his face displayed a light goatee. After finishing his study at the mandrasa in Timbuktu, he continued to keep his head clean-shaven, contrary to the fashions of that time. A heavy cloth that wrapped his head and cloaked his tunic offered little protection from the sand grains whipping through the air. Only his piercing eyes were exposed to the chilling winds. He knew that their survival depended on speeding up their trek and circumventing the inevitable sandstorm. The Tuaregs would surely jeopardize that cause.

"How many are there, Fela?" said Musa to the officer mounted on the steed next to him. Even squinting did not help his vision in the dust-filled breeze.

The graying sofa officer scanned the barbarian horde of horsemen that rapidly neared. He removed the lower half of the cloth that covered his mouth to speak clearly to Musa. "Maybe thirty, kankoro sigu," said the officer to his viceroy.

"And we are only fifteen men strong." Musa removed his headdress and brushed his goatee in thought. "The barbarians outnumber us." He watched as the sand parted for the dark warriors advancing to within shouting distance. "The next time I insist on leaving additional men to guard the mines, feel free to kick me from my high place."

Fela grinned and nodded.

Musa returned the smile and calmed his horse with a

gentle stroke of its mane. He knew that facing the marauders warrior-to-warrior would end in his demise. If Allah watched over him and he was to prove victorious in battle, the fast-approaching storm would engulf the entire caravan. As the wind whistled past his ear, Musa contemplated his tactics. His father's early teachings resurfaced. Musa was a Mandingo warrior first and then a scholar. Regardless of his numerous teaching from the best universities in Timbuktu, Musa learned at a young age the art of taking another's life. It was a learned skill that he had not needed in the past.

"I will ride ahead to meet them before they reach us," firmly stated Musa.

"My lord, we could retreat to Taghaza," nonchalantly responded Fela, who knew all to well that retreating was never an option for his commander and lord.

"We are much closer to Niani-ba than from whence we came," retorted Musa, "No, we must not turn back. The storm grows and is moving closer." Musa began checking the sword in his scabbard to ensure that it was secure. He also removed the spear from his saddle and handed it to the officer. "I have a feeling that I will need to make a quick departure." Musa faced his officer. "Under no circumstances are you to stop this delivery."

"Your importance is immense, my lord. I cannot—"

"Every life is of importance to someone. Do not fret. If I am righteous, Allah will guide and protect me."

"I will accompany you," demanded Fela.

"No," said Musa, "I will personally hold you responsible if these wagons do not reach Niani." Musa untied several sacks from his saddle, and they dropped to desert floor. "I will take one horsemen in your place. Have another horsemen follow us in the distance, your best spearman."

The sofa warrior nodded. "Do not worry, my lord. Only death will stop our path." The officer reached underneath the protective cloth and removed a dagger still in its scabbard. "Please take this, my lord. The Tuareg are a conniving people." He reined his horse closer to Musa and handed the blade to him.

Musa graciously accepted the dagger and hid it on his person. "Perhaps death is the only choice we do have in life, old friend."

Musa and a youthful sofa warrior galloped steadfast until, moments later, they were mounted within a horse's length of their Tuareg assailants.

Nearly forty tattered Berber horsemen faced Musa. They all wore dark, soiled tunics that blended well with their bronze complexions, and their headdresses came with a veil that hid their lower face. Eager, they held tight to their sabers while licking their lips at the chance to slice the two Mandingoes into little brown pieces. Musa immediately distinguished the leader of the pack from the remaining tribesmen. He was heavyset with tree logs for legs. As he lowered his veil, Musa immediately saw the thick scar that ran across the hardened man's nose and finished at his left cheek.

"Land south of Taghaza is Mandingo land. Why have you entered, Berber?" hissed Musa in the Berber's native tongue, Tamarshak.

Hearing Musa speak the Berber language surprised the portly chief and his followers. The leader let out a hearty laugh, with the others following suit. Then he abruptly stopped. Silence pervaded the air and gave way to howling winds. The sound of metal shrieked across the dunes as the chief unsheathed his massive saber. Its blade glittered from the hazy sunlight that penetrated the clouds.

"Your use of our language will not sway our desires, Mandingo,"

bellowed the Tuareg leader.

"You cannot have what we carry, Tuareg," stated Musa with conviction.

The Tuareg chieftain's sunken eyes widened and gave Musa a stare filled with rage. In retribution for Musa's remark, the chieftain spat into the air, and the heavy wind carried it to within a few feet of the two Keita Mandingoes. Musa's brow arched in disgust, while the young sofa horsemen beside him held tightly to the hilt of his sword and detached a spear from his saddle.

"I have not asked for it, Mandingo!" said the chieftain as he motioned for his horsemen to unsheathe their sabers. The saber rattling began. "We are going to take your precious salt, after we disembowel the both of you and let your carcasses dry in the Saharan heat." His band of outlaws murmured in agreement.

Musa eyed the grotesque figure with contempt. "I am Kankan Musa of the Keita, son of Abubakari the First, brother to the crown of Mali, and kankoro sigu of this land." Musa paused to allow the horsemen to absorb what he had said, and their murmurs of trepidation signified that they had heard of the young Mandingo warrior. "You may attack us and our caravan, but by killing us and stripping us of our meager salt, you will never learn where the gold mines of Kangaba are located."

The Tuareg men became enthralled by the thought of learning Mali's most entrusted secret, information only known to Canco Palace's most trusted courtiers and the enslaved gold miners who never left the dark caverns alive. Of course, one of the chief's lieutenants had his doubts.

"Masudi, the more there is talk, the farther the salt moves away from us," whispered the horseman to his leader. "It is their normal trickery. Why would a prince surrender his empire's greatest fortune? He is Malian, able to tell lies with impunity."

"There is no trickery," countered Musa. "I wish only the desire to avoid needless bloodshed, which is why I have an offer for you."

Masudi's brimstone eyes darted back and forth as he scanned the horizon, searching for some mithkal of truth to Musa's claim. He relied on his instinct to determine whether a man spoke in half-truths. It mattered not. If the accused proved disingenuous, he would have them strapped to the back of a horse and dragged for several leagues through the desert; that is, until they bled to death and shredded limbs marked their path. But if Masudi could not decide whether a man was truthful, in his most merciful way, he would simply kill him. It is much better to be wrong now than to be proven wrong later. Yet Musa's confidence and status intrigued the chief. He could hear the trickle of potential gold overfilling his satchel. But then again, why risk the salt shipment that was quickly disappearing due to an enemy's promise? "It is your good fortune, Mandingo, that I will ensure you a quick

death," said Masudi as he pointed his saber directly as Musa.

The barbaric tribe closed in on the Malian pair, and the sofa horseman that accompanied Musa grew nervous. The young Mandingo warrior held tight to the hilt of his sword, withstanding the sweat that drenched his grip. Musa quickly reached within the folds of his tunic and presented a small cow skin satchel. The jingling of its contents gave pause to the encroaching Tuaregs. With just a flick of the wrist, Musa tossed the purse to the dry sands near the hooves of their horses. Its contents spilled gold coins of various sizes, a small fortune for the average vagabond. Several of the Tuareg horsemen hastily dismounted and dove headfirst into the sands in search of their share. Like undisciplined beasts fighting over a kill, there were growls and fierce tugging.

"Stop it you fools!" roared Masudi. "Besides, half of that belongs to me."

"There is more, if you hear my proposition," said Musa with a gratifying grin.

"What is your offer, Mandingo? My patience is at its end!"

"I will challenge one of your best warriors in combat. If I am victorious, you will spare our lives and forever discontinue your raids on Malian traders. But if I lose, you may have my life," continued Musa, "and I have instructed my guard to guide you to the gold mines of Kangaba." The sofa horseman was stunned by Musa's words, but gritted his teeth without saying a word. He knew very well that his kankoro sigui would never betray Mali and the Mandingoes.

Masudi's first thoughts were to kill Musa and then torture the sofa warrior into furnishing the valuable location. The salt caravan was no longer on the mind of the Berber. His shifty eyes could only focus on the gold pieces his men fumbled in their hands. In any event, if the Mandingo bested his man, he could always implement the plan of his original thoughts.

"Agreed," said Masudi as he corralled his men back to a more honorable manner. The Tuareg horsemen remounted their desert steeds with as many coins they could find.

"Do not draw your weapon, under any situation," said Musa to his horsemen. "Allah will not fail us," he whispered. Musa placed a consoling hand on the sofa's shoulder before removing his protective robe.

An uncomfortable silence allowed the eerie zephyr cascading across the ghostly dunes to permeate the air between the face-to-face opponents. The sky became gray as the clouds blocked out the sun once and for all. The air became wet to the skin and cold to the desert dwellers. Musa slowly dismounted and unsheathed his iron shortsword, made by the finest blacksmith in Niani. Indicative of its quality, his blade bore the emblem of the Keita family crest upon its golden hilt. "Who shall I face?" requested Musa.

The Tuareg chieftain smugly looked down at Musa. "Ah, that is where I must alter our agreement, Mandingo."

"You cannot alter an agreement!" snapped Musa.

"Oh yes. Yes I can. Words of glory travel very easily on the winds of the Sahara, Mandingo. I am very aware of your notorious skill in combat, Kankan Musa." Masudi took pleasure in his ability to disorient the Keita clan warrior. "You will battle three of my best warriors…to make it fair."

Three of the horsemen quickly alighted their horses and removed their chadors. The stout one to the left of Musa wielded a heavy saber. Before him stood an unusually pale Arab with sunken, cold eyes and a forked goatee, armed with a large broadsword. To Musa's right ambled a huge behemoth, whose face lay hidden behind bushels of hair. This monster chose to utilize the semicircle blade attached to each of the iron corselets that covered his forearms.

"Kankoro Sigui!" screeched the young sofa warrior from his horse. Before he could raise and propel his javelin, Musa glared at the young warrior, immediately causing the soldier to lower his spear. Satisfied, Musa returned his attention to the three men who formed a triangle around him.

"So be it," Musa remarked as he hunched in anticipation of an attack from any angle. His bright eyes expanded on his dark face and saliva trickled from the corner of his mouth. Musa scrutinized each opponent with disdain. The boyish features that remained from the days he and Abubakari sprinted through the channels of Canco Palace as children disappeared before the watchful eye of Masudi. "Who will be the first to stand before Allah and beg His forgiveness?" said Musa. At that moment, the Tuareg cheers around Musa became muffled, except for a heavy rhythmic beat of the deba drum that continuously thumped in his mind. Thus, he knew the battle had commenced.

The stout Tuareg with the large saber advanced from the right with an overhead downward strike, just as the beast with razor-sharp corselets launched himself at Musa from the right. In one fluid motion, Musa twisted to the right and crouched to parry the saber blow to his left. As the saber's heavy blade glanced off his sword, Musa followed through with a left-to-right slashing motion that connected with the stout man's left leg and severed the limb just below the knee. The stout man fell on his back in earsplitting agony; blood spurted into the air. Musa immediately pulled his sword over his back to deflect the ensuing forearm swing of the hairy behemoth. In catlike fashion, Musa rolled on the desert floor to elude the next corselet attack and came to his feet with the two remaining Tuareg combatants before him.

In a rage, the behemoth rushed Musa once again. Spittle dotted his unkempt beard as he cursed Musa in the Tamarshak language and crazily smashed his corselets together. Musa extended his sword forward and waited.

Slash.

Musa nonchalantly, elegantly, evaded the razor-sharp blades by crouching and shifting to his left. And with fluidity, Musa's sword dug into the Tuareg's flesh, dropping the giant into a pool of dripping blood. Instead of reveling in his easy victory, Musa spun and immediately focused on his last opponent. The other Tuareg tribesmen became uncomfortably silent as the blustery weather grew stronger. The sand grains rose into the sky between Musa and the figure before him. Musa felt absolute wickedness emanating from the ghostly man and knew that this one would not fall as easily as his comrades.

"Cut that Mandingo swine to pieces, Khalid," demanded Masudi of his tribesman.

"As you wish," said Khalid. The long-haired Arab twirled his large broadsword from left to right and tempted Musa with a maniacal smirk. He sprinted at Musa with the tip of his blade slicing into the sand.

The clangor of their blades chimed as darkness overtook the sky. Sparks flew as swords grazed each other. Musa knew that the storm was upon them, but his adversary was a worthy opponent. Back and forth, the melee switched from Musa's advantage to Khalid's. The Arab effortlessly manipulated the large broadsword, and for every move that Musa used in his arsenal, Khalid countered with lightning speed. Musa began to tire from the weight of Khalid's blade with each repelling maneuver, coupled with the fact that this was the Mandingo's third sword fight in so little time.

Clang.

Musa's sword flew from his hand and impaled itself into the ground. He found himself staring at the tip of Khalid's sword, inches from his nose. Unexpectedly, Musa's horsemen reacted with a swift hurl of his spear at Khalid. He missed the Arabian vagabond but distracted him long enough for Musa to unsheathe the dagger hidden in his tunic and move in on Khalid. Musa grabbed the wrist of the hand holding the broadsword and viciously slashed Khalid's face with the dagger. Khalid cried out as he covered his wound and blood poured down his hands. It worked to his benefit, but Musa did not want the sofa warrior to interfere, for he knew chaos would ensue. It did, simultaneously with jagged streaks of lightning brilliantly illuminating the dark skies.

"Cut them to pieces," roared Masudi to his men over the neighing of horses and the thunderclouds above.

"No!" Musa turned to the young sofa just as a Tuareg launched a spear into the horseman's chest. The young warrior exhaled crimson fluid and fell from his horse.

"Wait!" said Masudi. "Let us keep one of them alive to find the gold! Do not let the other escape!"

Several hurled spears whistled through the air until they found their mark. *Zip. Thump.* The Tuaregs were in disarray, unaware of the source of the projectiles. One after another, a Tuareg cried out from being run through and through. "It was a trick!" Masudi quickly dismounted and shielded himself behind the horse, followed by the other tribesmen who remained standing. "Grab him before the winds arrive!"

Musa dashed over to the wounded sofa in hopes that the spear attack was not fatal. His tunic flapped in the wind as he knelt beside the unconscious Mandingo. The warrior's chest was covered with blood, but he was alive—barely. With his remaining strength, Musa slung the Mandingo warrior over his shoulder and stumbled away from the Tuaregs, who were more concerned with the storm and the anonymous javelins falling from the sky. Musa smiled at the sight of a sofa horseman riding at full speed in their direction.

"Kankoro Sigui, we must find your horse!" muffled the Mandingo horsemen through his ivory chador.

Musa lifted the wounded warrior over the rear of the horse. "I will find my horse! Ride to safety and I will meet you at the Sahel! What is your name?"

"Basel, my lord."

"It is a good name. Now go!" Musa smacked the horse's rear and turned away.

"Yes, my lord!" The sofa horseman quickly galloped away.

By that time, Masudi and his clan began mounting their stallions and surrendered their hopes of gold. Their only concern was escaping the impending sandstorm. "Ride! Ride! Care less for the Mandingo! Ride for your lives!" furiously shouted Masudi to the scattered men. He needed his tree-log legs to prevent his large body from being tipped over by the heavy wind.

Musa found his sword and quickly sheathed it. It took a moment for him to squint through the haze of sand and locate his horse, but his well-trained steed remained where he had dismounted. He hurriedly made his way, relying on the animal's neighing for direction, until he reached the horse.

Suddenly, as Musa prepared to lift his fatigued frame into the saddle, two hands clutched his tunic and catapulted him to the desert floor. As lightning flashed and thunder rattled the landscape, Khalid towered above Musa. There he stood, with broadsword and a face of red. Dark, coagulated blood lined the scar that ran from his forehead to his chin.

"Look what you have done to me!" Khalid's eyes glowed and grew with madness. Before Musa could unsheathe his sword, Khalid gored Musa's left shoulder and held the blade tightly with both hands. The Arab pressed downward each time Musa screamed in agony. "I am going to kill you slowly, Mandingo," said Khalid within a sadistic chuckle, twisting the sword to inflict more pain. His haired flailed in the air, giving the Arab an unearthly guise.

Musa attempted to dislodge the sword by grasping the blade with his bare hands. The sharp double-edged weapon dug into his shivering hands. Blood trickled down his forearms and dripped onto his forehead. Whiteness surrounded his vision, and Khalid began to blur. Musa's thoughts of preserving his life had transformed into thoughts of the past. He had resigned himself to the days in Timbuktu. He had learned so much at the university. He whispered the passage that he had written on his Qur'anic writing tablet before returning to Niani. Thoughts of Abubakari and his father raced through his mind and conquered the searing pain.

"Allah, do not take me now," Musa muttered as darkness pervaded his sight. "There is so much more I want to do. But if it is your will…"

With the strength of a thousand rams, the two men were suddenly pummeled by a massive wall of sand, reaching nearly twenty men into the heavens and spanning the width of the Niger. Khalid was effortlessly thrown into the air and out of Musa's failing sight. Musa could offer no resistance, and the heavy force violently rolled the unconscious Mandingo several feet before the winds settled and the sandstorm passed.

There, Musa lay still, covered in the grit of the Sahara. Air still escaped his lungs, and the days once lived, and now remembered, crept into his subconscious. He was taken away from his reality, his pain, and thrown into the past.

"Say goodbye to your brother, Abu," said the teary-eyed

Mariama to her son as she stood behind the young Kankan Musa. "He will serve the Keita well as hostage to the King of Morocco."

"How long will he be gone?"

"For a long time, Brother," said Kankan Musa.

"For as long as Mali needs him," interjected Mariama. "Goodbye, Brother," softly and stoically whispered young

Abubakari, "May the ancestors watch over you." Without shedding a tear, the prince of fifteen years contemptuously wove his way through the many court well-wishers and left the royal stables with his two female attendants shadowing him. His sandals fell heavy on the ivory floor, and the cape that covered his tunic snapped behind him. He soon disappeared into the palace grounds.

"I will see you again, Abu," shouted Musa.

Abubakari did not respond. Musa was saddened by his brother's lack of response. He wondered if Abubakari blamed him for leaving. Although Musa begged his father to be the royal hostage, he did not wish to abandon Abubakari. It was Musa's dream to see the towering spires of North Africa, to walk into the very heart of Tunisia, and to learn what Islam truly represented. Coupled with the fact that the son of Mansa Abubakari would be a surrogate member of the Moroccan court and strengthen the two sovereign state's covenant, Musa knew that it was his destiny to leave his beloved Mali behind. "We must hurry, Kankan Musa," Mariama hinted as she gently placed her hand on the shoulders of the youth that had already grown beyond her height. "Your mother is waiting to see you off." Musa lowered his head. "How can I leave when Father is ill, Stepmother? Abu needs me more than ever. How can I be so selfish in thought?" A single tear escaped his notice and slowly trickled down his soft copper cheek.

Mariama stepped in front of Musa and came to her knees. The tender touch of a mother's empathy wiped away the tear and lifted the chin of the young Mandingo prince. Mariama gazed into the frightened, watery eyes of the self-effacing lad and recalled never seeing such a face on Musa. She understood very well the pain that accompanied the ruling of a people. Everyone must sacrifice a part of him or herself; give away the wraith within their soul. She loved Musa as though he was her natural born, and to see Musa in such anguish caused her to weep for him.

"You must remain strong, Kankan Musa. For you are the strong one." Mariama stood and gently caressed his face. "You are helping Abu more than you know, and one day you will understand." She gave Musa a beautiful smile. "This day has brought great joy to your father, the day that his son shall truly become a man and serve the Mandingo. It is a day of great celebration."

Young Musa grinned and his eyes lit up with the words of his stepmother. "I shall make my family proud of me, Stepmother."

"That you shall. That you shall," Mariama whispered softly.

Musa moved in and out of consciousness. He clenched the sands and crawled to safety from the whirling sandstorm. His thoughts remained hazy and his reason failed him. He lifted his sand-covered face and squinted for better vision. Through the swirl of dust and the high-pitched wind, Musa gazed at the shadowy figure trekking in his direction. He tried to remain conscious, but the blood that drained from his wound overpowered his constitution. As everything went black, Musa wondered if Mohammed could have withstood such a storm.

The approaching desert traveler made his way to the unconscious Musa. "It seems that Allah watches over you, Unfortunate One," said the guttural hooded figure as he lifted Musa and carefully laid him over one of the four camels tethered to one another. Before darkness covered the dry landscape, the tumultuous storm had continued on its path of destruction, leaving behind the serenity of blackbirds sailing overhead.

7.

"Aaarrrrrrrrrhhhh!" Musa launched himself from the cold cavern floor and stood barefoot in the darkness, dressed in only his hunter trousers.

"Welcome to the living," shouted the silhouette that sat near the small fire. "I began to wonder about your constitution to survive such a wound. You are of Mandingo blood, after all."

"Who are you?"

"Are you hungry?" The shadowy figure eyed the metal pot before him, as steam slowly rose from the red glow of the fire. He carefully stirred the contents of the container, with his face still hidden from Musa's view.

Musa slowly began to recall his immediate past. He remembered the battle. He saw the wickedness emanating from the face of his last opponent. He felt the storm smash into his frame, just as the sword dug into his shoulder. My shoulder! Musa jerked his hand upward for his left shoulder, producing excruciating pain and causing Musa to immediately drop his hand. Until the pain subsided, Musa studied the dressing that wrapped around his gash. His eyes then fell upon his extended palms that were also wrapped in bloodstained cotton cloth.

"Am I alive?" Musa stood there in a daze.

"Perhaps you thought you had crossed over and that I am Allah preparing a meal for his follower?" The man let out an amiable chuckle and continued to stir the pot.

Musa slowly ambled over to the fire, revealing more of the man's face with each step. The way the man spoke the Mande language was good, but he lacked the dialect of a native speaker. Nonetheless, Musa did not fathom that the man in the dark cave would be the grinning Arab sitting by the fire, one with unusually pale skin at that. Musa recalled the face of the earlier combatant, and there were some similarities in complexion and features to Khalid. Yet the man who sat before him was definitely not akin to his doppelganger in aura. Musa hazily knelt by the fire; his head throbbed as intensely as his shoulder. "It was you who saved my life," muttered Musa, "and I shall not forget. May I ask who you are?"

The stranger winked and chuckled at the request. "In my line of work, it is best that one remain unknown."

"What is your line of work?" asked Musa between a series of coughs.

"I am a merchant."

"Where is the danger in being a merchant?" Musa despised those who hid in the shadows. Secrets were the tools of the underworld in his pious beliefs. Musa became agitated by the man's refusal to answer clearly. Yet he was still grateful to his Arab savior.

The man pretended to ignore Musa's follow-up question and scooped a clay bowl into the boiling stew. He then handed the dripping bowl and a wooden spoon to Musa, nodding to the Mandingo to indulge. Musa studied the bowl's soupy contents carefully.

"Crocodile and the same baobab leaf that heals your shoulder," chuckled the stranger. "It is remarkable, is it not?" With a subtle hand jester, the Arab urged Musa on. "Please, eat."

Musa did not fear death, nor did he ever have royal tasters test his food before eating it. His life belonged to Allah, and no plot or trickery created by man could ever save him from his ultimate fate. And only Allah knew when this fate was dealt. Still, Musa felt that poisoning would be a dishonorable form of death. It would be better to die on the battlefield where he could truly glorify Allah. But a man does not heal a man only to kill him when he awakens. Musa ate the stew. He enjoyed the taste of the broth, especially. The baobab leaves were reminiscent of his childhood.

"Where did you come by baobab? That tree is not native to this region," said Musa as he slurped up the remaining stew in his bowl.

"I was introduced to it many years ago, while visiting Mali." "Your travels have taken you to Mali?"

"Now and then." The stranger slurped his portion of the bitter stew. Musa grunted as another sharp pain seethed through his shoulder

and arm. "I must take my leave. Many depend on my return." He regained his feet and stumbled over to where the stranger had piled Musa's belongings.

"It is better that you rest before your journey. Besides, many evil things run rampant in this desert at night." The Arab smacked his lips in appreciation of his meal and found a comfortable spot near the crackling fire to lie down. He covered himself with a wool blanket and turned away from

Musa.

Musa attempted to don his tunic, but immediately wrenched in agony, dropping the garb and falling to his knees. The sword that had been handed down many generations leaned against the near wall. Musa grabbed the scabbard and attached it to his belt. Countless thoughts ravaged his psyche. Did the caravan reach Niani? Did my men reach safe ground? How had this Arab come along at that time? Musa reclined against the cave's wall as his vision blurred from exhaustion.

"Allah sent you to help me," whispered Musa over the fire.

"Not every Arab believes in the ways of Islam, Mandingo," the stranger whispered back. "Consider it just your good fortune." He adjusted his position on the cold, dusty floor. "Nevertheless, I arrived too late."

"What do you mean 'too late'? You saved my life, and you will be repaid ten-fold for your generosity. I am—"

"Never mind. Repay me by sleeping, my friend." And with that, the stranger announced his retirement with loud snores that echoed through the dark chamber.

Unable to keep his head above his shoulders, Musa slouched down against the wall and nodded off into another dreamscape.

The next morning, Musa awoke to the ashy hiss of the diminished fire and the beams of sunlight that penetrated the rocky ceiling. Although his shoulder still ached, it had improved. Musa adjusted his sword, tied his boots, and donned his bloodstained tunic, careful not to disturb the bandage. After wrapping himself in his cloak, Musa scanned the cave for any signs of the stranger. There was no sign of him or his paraphernalia.

Musa mentally prepared for his long trek through the Sahara and exited the cavern. The storm had passed and the sky was golden with a hint of crimson, as the sun rose above the horizon. Musa was amazed to find his horse tied to a tree near the rocky embankment. He realized that he was some distance from where he originally thought, but ideally closer to the Sahel. He quickly mounted his steed with great discomfort and gently stroked the horse's mane.

"There, there, girl. All is well," said Musa to calm the neighing of the exuberant horse. He took a deep breath and welcomed the beautiful landscape before him.

Musa searched for a landmark to help him reach Mali as quickly as possible. To his left, he could make out the mountainous Songhai region, and behind him was desert. Considering that the sun rose from his right, Musa presumed that his path to Mali lay directly ahead of him. Soon, he was galloping southward, cutting a dusty trail through the whites sands.

For most of the morning, Musa rode at a feverish pace through the desert. Eventually, nearly fifty Mandingo horsemen coming the opposite direction met him. Fela, the graying sofa officer who had accompanied Musa from Taghaza, led the party. It brought tremendous joy to Musa to see his retainer once again. He greeted the group with an animalistic howl as they came closer.

Upon meeting, the entire unit of horsemen quickly alighted their mounts and prostrated themselves on the desert floor; they knelt with their foreheads touching the earth. The oldest warrior knelt lower than any of the horsemen.

"My lord, forgive me for abandoning you as I did." A tear ran down the cheek of the seasoned veteran. "I fear that I do not deserve to live and would ask that you take my life before my men for my disrespect."

Musa dismounted and quickly lifted his officer from the dirt. "There is nothing to forgive, my friend. You simply followed my commands." Musa used his good arm to hold tightly to the officer's shoulder. "You saved the shipment, and the spearman was there as promised. You are to be commended! Rise, please, and let us return home."

The comments of their kankoro sigui brought tears to the other men as they came to their feet. With a hearty smile, Musa went to each man and affectionately patted his shoulder. "Wassa wassa ayé!" cheered the sofa warriors for their commander and lord.

"I believe that the Birmindana Mosque is near," inquired Musa. "A half day's ride, my lord," responded Fela with a curious head tilt.

"We must stop there before returning to Niani." Musa mounted his horse and reined the horse's bit in the direction they would head.

Known to have been the first mosque constructed in Mali, the Islamic temple was created to honor the life of King Birmindana— the first Mandingo king to convert to Islam. The large, archaic structure stood at the edge of the Sahara, just north of Walata.

The contingent of sofa horsemen waited outside as Musa entered the white marbled building with ivory pillars at its entrance. Several marabouts led Musa to a fountain of cleansing, where Musa washed his hands, face, and feet before entering the main hall of the temple. The African muezzin, or head cleric of the mosque, chants echoed through the empty halls, for there were very few followers in prayer that day. Musa had never mentioned his rank in society whenever he prayed within a mosque, because in the eyes of Allah, he believed that all are able to serve equally.

Musa placed the prayer mat provided by the clerics and prostrated himself among twenty other unknown travelers. As his forehead and palms touched the cold, sandstone floor, Musa closed his eyes and recited the chant of the head cleric under his breath.

Fela allowed the sofa horsemen to rest their steeds and find shade from the burning sunlight. One of the junior officers, Basel, approached his senior officer and reported the healthy status of the men.

"Sir, the lord's piousness is truly heartening," proudly touted the junior officer. "If only I could be so faithful."

"He prays not strictly out of faith," replied the older one, "but out of respect for the dead."

"Fallen comrades, how honorable."

"And fallen enemies as well," quickly added Fela. "Most likely, those who fell under his blade."

Basel raised his eyebrows in bewilderment. "He is praying for slain Tuaregs?"

Fela nodded with a smile.

"What a great man," said the young officer in awe. "That he is, indeed."

8.

The young African marabout, dressed in his clerical robe, hurried down the well-lit, airy hallway of the Palace of Canco; his sandals clapped the porcelain floor beneath him. He stopped at a door guarded by two sofa warriors but hesitated to knock. It was the fifth time he was sent to remind the chamber's occupants that their presence was needed.

"Lady Mariama, the ceremony will soon begin," said the marabout with a nervous undertone.

"I see Es-Saheli is now sending his marabouts on his errands," sharply responded the female voice through the door. "Tell him that my daughter and I will be there as quickly as we can and not a moment sooner. Do you understand?"

"As you wish, my lady." The marabout nodded to the two stoic

sofa guards and cowardly scurried away.

On the other side of the door was an elaborately designed, spacious room with tribal masks, silk-woven blankets, and furs dating back generations. The two women within the chamber continued to laugh as they heard the marabout scamper away. They were both decorated in their most elaborate and colorful silk garments. Mariama released a sigh of satisfaction, as she had just completed plaiting Namandje's hair in time for the all-important ceremony.

"I am not sure why I find them so humorous." The radiant Mariama placed her piercing eyes on her newly crowned daughter-in-law and rejoiced in the young woman's beauty. Mariama carried her beauty well for a woman midway through life.

"Nor I, Queen Mother." Namandje, so much in her youth, carefully hid her mouth as she giggled. Though she became more voluptuous with age, Namandje's face remained that of the child who had ridden the carriage into Niani nine years ago.

They continued to chuckle as Mariama applied Namandje's colorful hijab to cover her head and surround her face, similar in color to the hijab Mariama wore as well.

"This is a very important day for Mali," said Mariama as she placed a caring hand on Namandje's forearm and offered a glowing smile.

"I know." Namandje's eyes dropped into her lap. "Yet I worry for Abubakari." Six years had passed since their second marriage ceremony and, in essence, the Malian court raised Namandje and Abubakari. Though they were husband and wife, they shared a sibling-like bond, love with very little intimacy. Abubakari never scolded her or praised her. He only communicated with Namandje in matters that required her presence—arranging entertainment for provincial lords, coordinating palace supplies, and giving birth to an heir. Yet once Abubakari was accepted as mansa, nearly a year after the death of his father, their relationship declined even further as husband and wife. They rarely saw each other and communicated to one another through their various retainers.

"After the ceremony, Abu will have the full support of the muezzins. There is nothing to worry about." Mariama empathized with the young empress. Everyday as a wife of a mansa rips into your own being. You soon forget who you are—who you were—and live only for your husband and the greater glory of the empire.

"I fear that I have disappointed him and the Keita clan, for I have yet to bear an heir. He looks at me with vexing stares," said the sulking Namandje.

Mariama gently caressed the young girl's face. "You are beautiful. Continue to be a beautiful wife to my son, and there is nothing to fear."

"Thank you for accepting me into your family, Queen Mother." Namandje blushed and became teary-eyed.

Mariama wiped her daughter-in-law's cheeks. "You will refer to me as N'na, for I consider you my daughter. I remember the day you and Abu were joined. We knew you would be a splendid wife for our son. You come from a very honorable family that you should be proud of, and I am proud to have a daughter such as you."

"N'na, may I ask you something?" "What is it, my daughter?"

"It is a very sensitive topic. Forgive me for my rudeness," humbly added Namandje.

"Do not hesitate to ask, Namandje. Our words belong to us both." Mariama was concerned for the trembling lass. She knew that whatever it was that Namandje would ask of her weighed for many moons on the young queen's mind.

"How did you feel when the Great Mansa married another?"

blurted Namandje.

Initially, Mariama chuckled at the question. She expected something much worse. But the fact was, Mariama had never thought about how it had made her feel when the late mansa took Kongo as his concubine. Very much like Namandje, Mariama was raised to be the wife of a mansa and married at a young age.

Mariama spoke inward, applying an emotional salve to her heart. "It is the way of the Mandingo. He did it to ensure that the bloodline of the Keita remained. He did it for Mali, and I supported him until his death. But there was never a moment that I thought he did not love me. One day, you will understand."

Her mother-in-law's response offered little conciliation to Namandje's churning emotions. Namandje lowered her head as she so often did.

"I believe there are many things I will never understand."

Hundreds gathered in the Great Hall located at the center of Canco Palace. Underneath the bejeweled ceiling supported by towering pillars, courtiers, provincial lords, village chiefs, and their respective consorts lined the walls to view the tribal dancers performing to the beat of the tabala and the repetitive strumming of the twenty-seven stringed kora. Servants darted from attendee to attendee, offering delicacies, such as rice cakes dipped in wosobula na sauce, fonio, and wine. Details of the anticipated ceremony were the subject of each group's conversation.

"Today will be a great day for our lord."

"It will definitely secure the bond with our Arab neighbors." "I cannot recall a religious ceremony having such vitality."

"I do not suppose it sits well with Es-Saheli." "Who cares? Es-Saheli is not our lord."

One sofa warrior particularly enjoyed the boisterous entertainment. It gave him the opportunity to display his hunter's tunic, which was adorned with items that celebrated his accomplishments—the bone spur of a rhinoceros, the feather from the headdress of a rival warlord, and other sacred items. He wove his way through the crowd to get a clear view of the man strumming the kora. He stood mesmerized by the musician that elegantly moved with each note. Someone shouting his name broke his concentration.

"Sulayman!"

"Kankan Musa!" responded Sulayman with joy.

Musa twiddled with his goatee, as he approached Sulayman with his normal charismatic and confident swagger. His long cape covered one shoulder and overlapped his hunter's tunic and trousers. He placed a strong hold upon Sulayman's shoulder.

"Sulayman, should you not be overseeing the guards in the anteroom?"

"Older Brother, when did you return?" Sulayman was happily surprised. He hugged his older brother, who grimaced from his wound that had not quite healed. The handsome and slender young man's heart had not hardened with age. Sulayman's face was clear of stubble, and his eyes remained that of a child's.

"I am only here for the ceremony. It is a pleasant break from the salt mines of Taghaza." Musa swiped away Sulayman's attempt to steal a look at the bandaged shoulder underneath the cape. "It is nothing to be concerned about."

Sulayman sympathetically raised his eyebrows. "It is very dangerous beyond the desert, is it not?"

Musa returned a reassuring smile. "Only if you lose your direction."

"It is good to see you, Older Brother." "As it is to see you, Younger Brother."

They both turned to the people that cheered the end of the melody and applauded the beginning of another. Musa smugly scanned the hundreds of gatherers. He was not pleased with the way the ceremony was being carried out and felt that it would have been more appropriately held in the royal mosque. Musa deduced that the idea for the ceremony to take place at a place of entertainment was at the behest of Abubakari. In the most arrogant manner, Musa ignored the many glances directed to him by the many unmarried female attendees that whispered his name.

"Is that Musa, brother to the mansa? He is more handsome than I assumed."

"Though it would be a tireless ordeal to be his bride. He is said to be more Muslim than the Arabs."

"He is a king among princes."

One woman far in the corner did attract Sulayman's gaze. She had a face of ginger, delicately wrapped in a cream-colored chador. Her full lips were the color of crimson wine. Sulayman estimated that she was of good status, by the way her chin always stayed parallel with the floor and the way she smiled to passersby, subtly, but with sincerity. "Does Abu know that you are here?" Sulayman broke from his trance.

"No, but I will see him after the ceremony is complete. I do not want to be a distraction in these important times," replied Musa.

"He has not been the same since becoming mansa," said

Sulayman as he shook his head with disappointment.

"Father's death weighs heavily on his soul, as with us all. We must support him and each other," sternly interjected Musa. Musa became the older brother and chastised Sulayman with his eyes as well as his words. Musa understood Sulayman's disdain, but the bond between brothers must rise above idle gossip.

Sulayman reluctantly nodded and again faced the kora player. "Look at the way he plays. How beautiful it is."

Musa watched the musician and then turned to his brother with a big grin. "If you wish to master the kora, Sulayman, perhaps you should spend more time with your lessons than with the daughters of the local kun-tigi."

"Perhaps you should spend more time with your lessons," replied Sulayman as he playfully mimicked a woman's voice. "You sound like Mother. As I explained to her, I will learn by letting the fine music enter my blood and heart, and it shall flow from my fingers." "Little Brother, whose feet never touch the sands of life," chuckled Musa. "Where is Mother, anyway?"

Within the confines of the palace dwelled an outdoor sanctuary filled with colorful flora and pristine waters, surrounded by decadent porcelain. Customarily a serene environment of sparrows chirping and fish splashing, the natural sounds of the royal garden gave way to the muffled tabala playing in the background.

The stoic, yet seductive, Kongo arrogantly strolled the garden with her head upright and one eyebrow raised. She was draped in ivory cotton from chador to dress and followed by an entourage of six young women—also dressed in white, with only their eyes visible through their silk veils. She waved her followers away and approached the lone, white-robed figure standing near the pond.

Es-Saheli's large eyes and thick, graying brow focused on the approaching queen. The bald Arab twiddled his mustache and sharp goatee and stood angrily with his arms folded.

"As salaam malakum, Es-Saheli," jeered Kongo.

"Malakum salaam, Lady Kongo." He gave a slight bow to Kongo but still appeared incensed.

Kongo took position next to the spiritual figure, watching the fish swim freely. "You seem…disconcerted."

"He is making a mockery of Allah and the entire Islamic faith," said the robed cleric as he slammed his fist on the ivory railing overlooking the pond. "Such a ceremony should take place at a mosque!" Es-Saheli moved away to regain his composure.

"My half-son is not a believer and is a fool," said the expressionless Kongo. "He wanted to stay close to the people of Niani. It is widely looked upon as an admirable deed."

"Is there not a mosque within the walls of Canco?" screamed Es- Saheli with shaking hands.

"Es-Saheli, you must learn to take the boy lightly."

"And yet your husband saw fit to make him mansa, despite my recommendations!"

"Everyone knows that my son, Musa, should have been named mansa, but the late mansa felt otherwise. You might say he had a certain affection for stray animals." Kongo allowed herself a slight smirk after her self-gratifying remark.

"When you requested my presence in your land, Lady Kongo, I came willingly. I crossed the vast Sahel to spread the word of Allah. The grand mosque in Timbuktu that I unselfishly constructed rivals those found in Arabia. I am starting to feel unappreciated." The head cleric lifted his nose into the sky and covered his upper lip with his bottom one.

"Silence!" spat Kongo with the sharpness of a dagger. She eventually relaxed the creases in her bronze face and calmed down to her normal monotone self. "Do not forget to whom you are speaking with, Es-Saheli. I have ensured your place as high priest. You have more power and more gold than the Sultan of Fez, himself. I suggest you remember who your allies are in this empire."

Es-Saheli had forgotten with whom he was releasing his frustration to. Experience had taught him never to test the patience of Lady Kongo, and he promised himself always to remember the hand that fed him. "I meant no disrespect, my lady, but it is well-known that Mansa Abubakari the Second is set on squashing Islam within Mali. And since he is in power…"

Kongo stepped behind the smaller cleric. "Power is fleeting, muezzin. I believe that the mistakes one makes can be costly…very costly."

Es-Saheli revealed a sinister smile as he faced Kongo. "Sometimes, Allah chooses a beautiful woman to bring me center, for he understands what helps me open my eyes and ears to his words."

Kongo was unimpressed by Es-Saheli's compliment. "Rest assured, to let Abubakari remain as mansa would bring great joy to my late husband's other wife. And that, I cannot allow."

Sulayman waited until the court musicians completed their performance and approached the kora player, who was methodically wrapping his instrument for travel. The court musician bowed, obviously recognizing the status of the sofa officer.

"Please, let us dispense with such formalities," said Sulayman while waving the man upward.

The musician straightened himself but continued to look downward. The musician was about the same age as Sulayman, maybe a little older. He was significantly smaller in stature than Sulayman and rather shy for a court performer. The musician's smooth complexion and fine clothing relayed to Sulayman that the nervous man before him came from good upbringing.

"Do you know who I am?" chortled Sulayman in an attempt to calm the musician down.

The musician nodded.

Sulayman also nodded in hope that the young man would respond verbally. After a few awkward seconds of silence, Sulayman offered praise to warm the conversation. "You play the kora with excellent skill. Perhaps you can teach me?"

The musician remained still and silent.

Sulayman looked around as though he was a victim of a

prank. Often, Sulayman saw his royal blood as an impediment to really understanding what it meant to live as the common citizen. Though musicians, as with other artisans, held high status in the Malian kingdom, they were still below the standing of the warrior.

"Will you set aside who I am, for a moment, and speak to me as a fellow lover of music?" Sulayman was growing impatient, yet he managed another laugh to relax the frozen figure before him. "Even more brilliant, a kora player that is mute. That should save me many hours of scolding for my poor play."

"If it pleases my lord, may I ask why he wishes to learn to play the kora?" suddenly responded the musician in a soft, melodic hiss. His eyes continued looking downward.

"I have practiced it in the past, but I have never heard it played with the ease and beauty in which you play it."

"I see, my lord."

"So, you will instruct me?" "No, my lord."

Sulayman mouth dropped and his almond-shaped eyes became wide circles. What did he say? Did he decline a member of Keita royalty? Often, Sulayman appreciated his bloodline, which allowed him access to what others could never have.

"How dare you decline my request!" snapped Sulayman.

The musician lowered his head further. "I do not mean to offend you, my lord. But you are a warrior prince. Your duties to the land and people would never allow you the time needed to master the kora."

"Are you being presumptuous with me? Of course, I have free moments to spare. I do not require mastery, just improvement."

"It is just uncommon for a warrior to show interest in the

94

ways of the kora," replied the musician.

"Cast away class, will you?"

The self-effacing musician thought for a moment. "My clan has performed before the royal court for eight generations, since the days of the Old Kingdom. It is very unorthodox to instruct someone outside of our bloodline. You would become the first."

"So, you will teach me?" eagerly inquired Sulayman. "It would be my pleasure, my lord."

Sulayman smiled and patted the man on the shoulder. "You will not be disappointed. I am not as bad as others may say. Where do you stay?"

"I reside in the wooden house next to the Inn of Daka in the artisan district. It was the former home of a merchant who sold nafiola in abundance. So you will find that it still smells of nafiola."

"I have smelled worse. I am a warrior, remember?" Sulayman saw the man grin for the first time and was pleased to know that the musician was capable of emotion. "My guard duty ends every evening at the Hour of the Lion. We can began lessons from that time, in three days?"

"That would be fine. If you would excuse me, my lord, I must depart since we travel together as musicians." He gave Sulayman another quick bow, grabbed his kora, and prepared to leave.

"Oh, what is your name?"

"I am Camara, my lord," said the musician before disappearing into the crowd.

"What a strange man you are, Camara," muttered Sulayman as he continued scanning the patrons.

As the sun disappeared from the sky, the ceremony began

within the Great Hall. The slow, heavy beat of the tabala announced the immensity of the day. The attendees stood in their sections on each side of the long walk space leading to the statue of Nama-tigi, the werewolf god of the Bambara people. There waited Es-Saheli in robe, with Koran in hand. The muezzin began his chant, singing verses of the Koran in a tone similar to that of a sharp humming sound.

Musa observed the ceremony from his rightful position near the front of the audience. The whole event made him uncomfortable.

Everything seemed impure, unholy. Musa understood that the gathering was necessary for Abubakari to grab a firm hold of the religious zealots within Mali, but it appeared fabricated to the faithful Islamic follower. It had been two years since he had seen his elder brother. Musa wondered if Sulayman's words about Abubakari held any truth.

The light within the large atrium diminished as the golden lamps that lined the walls now served as the only source of illumination. In the same way an ocean wave crossed the great waters, everyone in the room fell to their knees, paying homage to the man in the red velvet tunic promenading down the path leading to the altar. No one risked having their eyes meet with those of their immortal mansa.

The slender Abubakari the Second had discarded his boyish features over the last nine years. His face was handsomely chiseled, yet his eyes still held a gentle beauty. If one had lifted his head as the mansa walked, he would have seen how Abubakari arrogantly scanned the obedient crowd. He would have witnessed Abubakari's impertinent snarl as the mansa ascended the steps leading to the waiting muezzin.

With one hand, Es-Saheli motioned Abubakari downward, and Abubakari slowly fell to his knees with hands resting in his lap and palms extended. The Mandingo king closed his eyes and lowered his head as the tabala simultaneously ceased, whereupon Es-Saheli placed a palm on Abubakari's head and began his hymn.

"Praise belongs to God, the Lord of the worlds, He the merciful, the compassionate, He, the ruler of the Day of Judgment! Thee we serve and Thee we ask for aid. Guide us in the right path, the path of those Thou art gracious to, not those Thou art wroth with, nor of those who err."

Es-Saheli released his hold on Abubakari and turned his back to the onlookers. The cleric fell to his knees and lowered his head towards the eastern wall of the chamber. The audience followed and prostrated themselves in the same direction.

As Es-Saheli's chant of the Fatiha faded into the air, Abubakari's mouth trembled and his closed eyes flickered. Saliva flowed down the corner of his mouth, for he was taken to another place, another time, where white sands met vivid blue oceans.

His dark feet trekked through the chalky earth, contrasting the bright setting of a place he had never perceived. Occasionally, the tide came to gently cleanse his feet, which pleased him. It all appeared real to Abubakari. But his eyes…If only he could command his eyes to open a little wider; he knew that he would be dreaming of paradise— his paradise.

Is this your paradise? I blame everyone.

It is you who are to blame.

The world seemed ambiguous for Abubakari when his mind returned to the ceremony. He endured kneeling before the muezzin as sweat soaked his entire body. His thoughts were of his father, wondering if he was watching his son from the heavens. Abubakari also remembered the late Azikiwe, wishing that he could lean on his old advisor's wisdom in the troubling days ahead.

After the ceremony was complete, Abubakari was escorted to his private chambers and the guests courteously dispersed. Anticipating thousands from various villages around the kingdom, the servants prepared for the huge festivities scheduled for the upcoming five days of celebration.

9.

The Days of Feasting began the morning after the religious ceremony. The tam tam drums and xylophone-like balafons played as villagers gorged and ceremoniously danced in celebration. The large fires that were stoked for roasting buffalo generated enough smoke to be seen for miles. People throughout Mali came to honor Mansa Abubakari with song and dance. Merchants and artisans set up shop around the Palace of Canco in the hopes of selling their goods.

Namandje gently tapped Abubakari to regain his attention before the ritual performance began. Abubakari, with Namandje and Mamadou behind him, sat on the same three-tiered pavilion just outside the palace's gate. Sofa guards provided a well-armed shield at the base of the pavilion.

"I grow weary of these tedious moments." As Abubakari gazed at the towering silk-cotton tree, he happily reminisced of the days when his father shared his deepest feelings to his sons. He thought of other places he would have rather been. The previous evening, he shared several flasks of Moroccan wine with a few of his most trusted court administrators.

Having never partaken in the ecstasy that is libation, his inexperience manifested itself in the forms of massive headaches and slight nausea. The tight turban atop his head only heightened the pain.

"My lord, we come to you to pay homage to you and your great ancestors!" came a bellowing voice from below.

Abubakari finally focused on the celebrators before him. He squinted through the glare of the sun. Frustrated, he called for a servant to adjust the large umbrella above him. Once done, Abubakari smiled down to the three figures peculiarly adorned in colorful feathers, wooden heads that were shaped as those of birds with red beaks, and body paint to complement their ensemble.

The mansa erupted with a boisterous laugh. "Who are you? Or should I say, what are you?" Soon, the gathered subjects joined Abubakari in laughter.

"We are the Songbirds of Dioma, Great Mansa, and have come to sing a poem to honor this grand occasion." All three men, or so it was assumed since their heads were that of birds, fell to one knee and bowed before their emperor.

"Well, it seems that you have flown very far. How can I not let you perform?" Abubakari smiled to Namandje, who smiled back.

"As you command, my lord." The three performers rose and began their song. In synchronized motion, each dancing bird sang his or her verse in a high-pitched tone, one after another.

Take your bow, Abubakari the Second, Take your bow on such a beautiful day, Allah Almighty has created a beautiful day, Great ancestor, Sundiata, take your bow!

The performers let their bodies twirl into the air and their feathers flicker in the breeze. Their passionate voices held the crowd in awe. Abubakari was pleased with the performance to that point. The song, on the other hand, vexed Mamadou.

"The 'Hymn to the Bow'? That is a forbidden song, only a privilege of the djeliba!" argued Mamadou as he adjusted the belt of his robe.

"They have excellent voices. Why be concerned with archaic traditions?" responded Abubakari in a nonchalant manner, purposely teasing his old guardian and friend. He grinned as Mamadou heavily lamented over Abubakari's boyish thoughts.

The way of the antelope will guide you, Great Mansa,
Listen to those before you, Great Mansa,
  A beautiful day it will be,
  Take a bow, Mansa Abubakari the Second

The performers completed their song and bowed. The audience waited for Abubakari to raise his palm before they cheered the performers. Abubakari stood, inducing everyone around him to kneel in his presence.

"You may rise. I was very impressed with the way you men honor me and my father." Hearing Abubakari's words, the three performers stood. "Now, remove your masks so that I might see the faces behind these wonderful voices."

One by one, they removed the wooden bird heads. The third songbird surprised everyone in attendance, for underneath the mask was a beautiful woman. Sulayman, who was patrolling the crowd with several guards, recalled having seen the young woman before, but did not recollect the place or time. Mm, perhaps I courted her and cannot remember?

"Have you hidden a jewel from the eyes of your mansa? What form of insolence is this?" joked Abubakari at the sight of the female performer.

"As it is said, my lord, a jewel in one's hand tempts all thieves. It is better to leave it in one's purse," said the older male performer while bowing even lower than before.

Abubakari laughed at the jovial manner in which the man replied. "N'ko, I am intrigued! On another occasion, you are invited to dine with me within the palace. Please, call on me again when I am not so weighed by my duties."

"We are most grateful, my lord," exclaimed the three performers in unison. They prostrated themselves once more and departed.

A line of people had assembled to pay homage to the newly recognized Mansa Abubakari the Second.

"Thus, I continue," groaned Abubakari as he sat down.

One elderly man and ten women carrying baskets of grain and vegetables approached and fell to their knees.

"I pay homage to you, Mansa Abubakari," humbly said the man. "I am Batil, mochrif and kun-tigi of Kumbi Saleh. A truly auspicious day it is, indeed. On this glorious day, in celebration of a united Mali, I present to you blessings from the ever-providing land...rice, taro, yams, calabashes, peanuts..."

Mamadou leaned over to Abubakari. "I do believe he said those exact words at your coronation." Mamadou repressed laugh sounded like a smothered toad.

Abubakari yawned. By the tenth gift, his aches quickly moved from his head to his neck, and the scorching sun drilled a hole through his forehead. This was not the discomfort of ambrosia. It was an agony he had suffered through on occasion.

Another man and an entourage of soldiers, all dressed in dawn- tinted African garments, approached, raised their spears before Abubakari, and took a knee. Twenty or so horses stood behind them. "I, Bokhari, fama of the Gao province, offer these mighty steeds

to convey my loyalty to Mansa Abubakari the Second. I swear upon my ancestors to offer continued support to Mali." The visiting governor bowed as Abubakari listlessly raised his palm in acknowledgment.

As Abubakari rubbed his head from the pain, Namandje looked on with concern. One after another, people stood before him, women with cotton, farmers followed by cattle, sheep, goats, and more stock. Before long, the throbbing of his temples won the day. He began coughing profusely until and single line of blood streaked from the corner of his mouth. Suddenly, Abubakari clung to his chair and stood.

"Enough! Mamadou, continue in my absence." Abubakari rose to his feet and was assisted down the pavilion by his two female attendants, who were now young women clothed in white cloaks and headdresses.

Before he could leave, Namandje grasped his tunic. "Are you well, my love?"

"The pain has returned." Abubakari then pulled away and left the pavilion, escorted by several sofa guards. The people all came to their knees as he left, and soon, they whispered to each other their reasoning as to his early departure.

Mamadou and Namandje welcomed the remaining visitors and accepted their gifts on behalf of the mansa and the Keita.

Several candles illuminated the private chamber of

Abubakari as he slept upon his bedding. Mariama wiped Abubakari's brow with a wet cloth and massaged his brow that tightened from the pain. She dipped the cloth into a golden bowl filled with water and pressed it gently against his forehead.

"My son," whispered Mariama as she looked upon her son with motherly eyes.

"N'na," mumbled Abubakari. He slowly awoke to the sound of her voice, but was still slightly woozy.

Mariama gave him a reassuring smile. "Rest." She pulled the silk cover over his bare chest.

"I dreamt of the monkey-bread tree in the courtyard. I remember the days that Kankan Musa and I would see who could grab the most baobab leaves before darkness. Then Father would count them and reward us with hippopotamus steak. Those were happy days."

"Yes, they were, my son."

"Days long passed." Abubakari turned away and dredged up loving memories of his father, if only for a brief moment.

A certain sadness overcame Mariama, and she remained silent. Thoughts of her late husband frequently invaded her consciousness. Yet Mariama's inner strength would not allow her to mourn Abubakari the First's death after his burial. There came a point near the end of the mansa's life when the king and queen discussed the reality of his fatal ailment. Heart consumption had no known cure, and only rest would offer any comfort. Death was inevitable, but life could be prolonged if one did not constantly become exhausted. The daily administration of Mali and the continual attacks on Djenné hastened his sickness. That was the mansa's wish. It was Mariama's duty to ensure that his last days were peaceful and that Abubakari the Second inherited the throne with no conflict from upstarts vying for power. Mariama never had the time to mourn. She only had time for her son.

Moments later, a servant entered to announce the arrival of a guest requesting an audience with the mansa. Abubakari eagerly approved and lifted himself onto his elbows. The young ruler anticipated who the visitor could be, thanks to Sulayman.

"Abu?" said Musa as he entered the dimly lit room.

Abubakari was excited to see his brother. "Musa! When did you return?"

"I was at the ceremony, but I did not want to disturb you on such an important day," said Musa with a smile before turning to Mariama. "Peace be with you, Queen Mother."

"A visit from my brother is never a disturbance," said Abubakari. "What has it been, two years?"

"Yes, I would say so," Musa responded.

Mariama stood and held tight to Musa's leather-corselet covered forearms. "Musa, it is good to see you. Are you doing well in those trying conditions?"

"One learns to befriend the desert," reassured Musa.

"I scolded Abubakari for making his brother the kankoro sigui of such a dreadful place," Mariama gave Abubakari an admonishing glare.

"N'na, the salt mines are important to Mali," said a coughing

Abubakari as he sat up.

"Perhaps, but you could have sent another. Musa, how are your mother and Sulayman?"

"They are well." Musa was cordial, but it was obvious by his body language that he wanted to discuss more pressing matters with Abubakari.

"We see little of each other since your father's

passing," continued Mariama.

"Musa, tell me of the mines," said Abubakari with excitement. He was able to sit up and wipe his brow with the cloth.

"I will leave now." Mariama bent down and kissed Abubakari's pate. "Rest and regain your strength. Rest your heart."

As she left, Musa gave her a slight bow. He then faced Abubakari. "The pain continues?"

"It is nothing of great concern." Abubakari dismissed the earlier pleasantries and responded in the tone of one who was being badgered.

Musa sauntered to the other side of the chamber and peered through the window. "You should listen to your body. It is a message sent from Allah." Musa's eyes followed the glowing candles of the surrounding villagers, appearing as fireflies floating above the black landscape. When Musa listened carefully, he could hear the chirping of crickets from below and the call of an owl.

Abubakari let out a haughty laugh, as he made his way to a table with a carafe and slowly poured fresh water into a small wooden bowl. He drank slowly, allowing the liquid to swish in his dry mouth. The taste of his own blood clung to the walls of his throat as he swallowed.

Abubakari wiped his mouth with his bare hand and set the bowl down. "It is required that a mansa is recognized by the muezzins, but do not believe for one moment that I follow a religion that fears what it is to truly live...a religion that covers its women as though beauty is to be ashamed of." Abubakari eyes fell on his brother across the dim chamber. "Have you forgotten the way of the Bambaras, Kankan Musa?" Abubakari smiled.

"If you could hear their words, Abu, you too would believe. No, you would know," bluntly stated Musa.

Abubakari chuckled once more. "I hear them often…the muezzins praying from their mosques. They remind me of savannah crickets crying into the night." He grunted to himself with satisfaction.

Musa gritted his teeth and restrained himself from lashing out at his brother. He knew that Abubakari was simply antagonizing the pious Musa, goading him into another challenge of power. Why Abubakari felt the need, he could not fathom.

"You called me back from Taghaza for a reason," asked Musa after taking a deep breath.

"Yes, I want you to lead the attack on Djenné."

"Djenné?" Musa was dejected. Had he forgotten the promise he made to his father so long ago? He had not. Musa had only hoped that such a dream died with the man.

"Yes, I will fulfill our promise," reminded Abubakari of their oath to their father and each other.

"Why now? Mali has expanded beyond our ancestors' dreams. We are the rulers Africa, from the Sahara to Egypt. Why should we concern ourselves with a simple village like Djenné?"

"Did you know that they are said to have the most beautiful temples and the finest scholars, even rivaling Timbuktu?" Abubakari spoke with great passion. "They can clear one's vision with the stroke of a blade. Perhaps, their knowledge can rid me of my pain." "Abu, Djenné has been attacked countless times by Niani, and at every siege, we have failed," replied Musa. "They will not be subjugated."

Abubakari snatched the wooden bowl he drank from and slammed it on the floor. "They will fall before me, and they will kneel to the will of Mali! They belong to a united Mali!" The light of the lamps flickered in Abubakari's fiery eyes.

Musa watched the bowl rumble until it became still. He lifted his eyes to meet the scorching glare of his brother and king. Musa moved closer to Abubakari as one does when deciphering what is real and what is made to look real.

"What has happened to you, Abu?" whispered Musa for their ears only. "When did you become such a bitter soul? You were not this way when I left for the university."

"Yes, and while you were frolicking away in Timbuktu, I was here ruling a kingdom! I had not the luxury of freedom that you enjoyed. Be careful whom you judge, oh brother of mine."

"Father chose you as mansa, not I," shouted Musa.

"That is correct." Abubakari moved to within a few steps of Musa and stared him down. "And as mansa, I would ask that you not question my decisions. Therefore, as my man-at-arms, you will prepare the sofas for the siege on Djenné after harvest."

"Who will serve as kankoro sigui in Taghaza?"

"You need not concern yourself with such matters, Younger Brother. I shall have council seven moons from today with yourself and our southern commander to discuss strategy." Abubakari contemptuously lifted his chin. "Once the harvest is complete, we will have Djenné and a unified Mali. Father's dream will come to pass."

Silence pervaded the chamber.

Musa condescendingly backed away from his brother; his eyes never left Abubakari. Musa reached down and grabbed the bowl. He handed it to Abubakari, who quickly snatched it from his grasp. Musa gave a sarcastic bow and left the room to the scornful glare of Abubakari.

In his heart, Abubakari believed that the ancestors gazed favorably upon him for his decision to invade Djenné. Yet he knew that his decision came with harsh consequences. Blood would flow down the Niger and spill into the villages that lined its shores. Mandingoes would die by the thousands, creating twice as many widows and orphans. The realities of war mattered not. Abubakari was determined to assimilate the very people who hastened his father's entry into the afterlife, one death at a time.

The owl had taken flight and swooped down to the dark plains within the palace's walls. Mercilessly, the winged carnivore sank its claws into the prairie dog it had observed for some time and lifted it into the dark skies. Only the crickets heeded the screams that echoed from the prey and floated across the savannah.

10.

1308 C.E.

The large village of Djenné was constructed on marshy land located between the Niger and its tributary, the Bani. Its walls of solidified mud had withstood countless attacks since the time of the ancients and had remained impenetrable for a thousand years. The inhabitants even repelled the powerful Ghana Dynasty, the predecessors of Malian rule. The natural moat created by the marsh created a damp stench under the spring sun.

Zip. Thump.

Waves of arrows flew over the walls and impaled the invading Malian foot soldiers, as they attempted to scale the high walls of the towering village of Djenné with futility. The spires at its gates provided an advantageous view for the spear-hurling Djenné defenders, as projectiles from every angle pummeled the Mandingo warriors from above. The warriors shouted menacing war cries down to their Malian invaders. Their long, plaited hair, midnight skin, and colorful feathers around their heads, waists, and knees only accentuated their fierceness.

Sofas who survived crossing the eastern river and wading the sludge of the marsh ascended wicker-like ladders, their long buffalo- skinned shields raised and their spears drawn. Spears whistled downward and embedded themselves into the chests, heads, and necks of Mandingo warriors. Blood poured from the fallen. "An gnewa! An gnewa!" Cries of fortitude sounded on both sides as smoke flowed from the ramparts.

In the distance, Musa and Sulayman sat atop their steeds, dressed in tunic, headgear with colorful plumes, painted face, sword, and leather attachments as armor. Their advisors and officers surrounded them, watching the wounded stumble to the safety of the river's edge. The Malian bandaris, flags identifying each tribe, flickered in the wind, and the screams of the dying filled the air.

A scarred, mud-spattered junior officer sprinted up and took a knee before Musa. "General, it is useless! Every place is guarded well, and my warriors are dying where they stand!"

"What of the rearguard?"

"Half their warriors have fallen. All is lost!" cried the war-torn

sofa officer.

"We need one of their gates to fall for our cavalry to easily trample them! Until then, our horsemen are of no use."

Musa sighed and stared into the faces of his mounted officers. "We are Mandingo! Are you telling me that we cannot seize a single gate?" The remonstrated officers remained silent with their heads lowered.

"Yes. They fight like a lioness protecting her cubs," fearlessly interjected the kneeling officer.

"Brother, let us set it afire and draw them out," beseeched Sulayman. "That is the only way we can be victorious. If we position our archers—"

"Are you mad?" barked Musa. "To obliterate what we hope to possess?" Musa stroked the mane of his steed, his ritual of good fortune before entering into battle. Musa shook his head in disgust. "Withdraw the men and tend to the wounded. Prepare camp for the night." Musa faced Sulayman. "There are other strategies we have not considered."

Moments later, Musa sent a messenger to the southern commander on the north side of Djenné with orders to halt the attack.

Later that evening, Musa sent an envoy to the chieftain of Djenné with terms for peace. The special envoy returned in the dead of night with a reply from the leader of the fortified village. It wasn't such an inconvenience since Musa was never able to sleep during military campaigns.

"It is true, my lord. Chief Abayomi requests only you," said the aging diplomat. Proper etiquette would normally demand that he knelt before the Mandingo prince, but due to Musa's great respect for the elderly statesman, they sat as equals within the general's tent.

"I see." Musa contemplated the proposal as his eyes glimmered from the glowing lamp. "The fact that he prefers to negotiate with me alone is disconcerting, indeed. I will return to the palace and inform my brother of the situation at dawn."

"That may not be possible, my lord." The envoy cleared his throat before speaking. "Chief Abayomi requests that you go before sunrise at the Hour of the Serpent."

Musa stole away from the Malian camp with only two horsemen to accompany him. In the darkness they galloped away, riding hard across the dew-covered plain. Upon reaching the wall of Djenné, an iron bridge was lowered over the marshland, and a small contingent of torch-bearing Djenné warriors escorted Musa to Chief Abayomi's home.

The rustic home was modest in appearance for an aristocrat. The two-story residence had very few attendant dwellings surrounding it, and its gate had nearly weathered away into nothing. There was an auspicious garden in the rear that added a pleasant scent in the air for Musa. Though it was not the grand castle that Musa had anticipated, Musa felt honored simply to be a guest in the infamous village, for he was the first Keita allowed entry into Djenné since Sundiata's reign. "I am most grateful that you accepted my invitation." Chief Abayomi was uncharacteristically stouter than most natives of Djenné. His graying, scruffy beard, colorful smile, and fleshy cheeks gave him an unimposing demeanor. The robed chieftain lowered his head in a respectful manner and sat cross-legged on the mat before Musa.

"I am the grateful one." Musa knelt before the unassuming man and lowered his head.

"Would you join me in having some tea?" Abayomi raised his hand, and a male servant brought in a tray with two bowls and poured the steaming baobab-bark drink. He place one bowl before each man and quickly departed, leaving the ceramic pot. Without any hesitation, Musa sipped the bitter brew.

Abayomi let out a boisterous laugh. "I had heard that you are a man of great honor, but not until I saw it before my very eyes had I believed it to be true." After sipping his own, Abayomi grabbed the teapot and ladle and refilled Musa's bowl.

"I am afraid that you have caught me by surprise, Chief Abayomi,"

responded Musa as he accepted the village leader's kind gesture. "You did not hesitate to drink the tea I offered you, before I had my fill. Did you ever consider that I commanded my servants to poison the tea to which you have completely swallowed? You are a trusting man, Musa."

Musa smiled. "You think too highly of a pitiful person such as me, Chief Abayomi. Besides, I know that such trickery is not the way of the Djenné."

"You are correct, young warrior. If I wanted you dead, a thousand arrows would now protrude from your lifeless body," suddenly hissed the chieftain.

"There is a new day in Mali, Chief Abayomi. No longer will petty warlords vying for more of its precious land govern it. Mali belongs to the Keita." Musa finished his tea. "Its sky, land, and waters are protected by Allah and controlled by the mansa."

Chief Abayomi stood in defiance, spilling the contents of his bowl upon the wooden floor. His chest heaved in and out and his brow wrinkled in anger. There was silence between the two men as the bowl toppled back and forth until clinking to a halt.

Musa gazed upward, but his head remained lowered.

"Nothing is served by your refusal to submit."

"We will never allow you to conquer us as you have so many! You tell your snake of a brother that if he is determined to take hold of my beloved Djenné, his hands will be covered in Mandingo blood. You tell him that!" The jolly figure who once stood before Musa had transformed into a raging buffalo that was poised to charge. "Abubakari the Second will fail, just as your father did!"

"I have come to you in the darkness with the hope that there may be a peaceful resolution to this matter," said Musa as he lifted his head.

Chief Abayomi heavy breathing ceased and he soon opened his ears to Musa.

"I am a young man, and yet, I have grown weary of battle," Musa continued as he shook his head in disgust. "Though our clans share the same roots, we continue to spill each other's blood in squander." A single tear streamed the cheek of the vexed Mandingo warrior. "Perhaps our children will find reason in our foolishness."

"Perhaps." Chief Abayomi was taken by Musa's sincerity, enough to lower his guard. The old man sat once again, across from his formidable adversary. "Unless, we, as men, can find a common belief in peace and live together as equals."

"N'ko, every man is equal before Allah." Musa nodded, almost whispering to his inner self.

"We are peaceful villagers who refuse to be ruled by anyone, but we can learn to be steadfast allies of the Keita." Chief Abayomi leaned over and placed his hand on Musa's shoulder. "For we too share the blood of the Mandingo."

"If you would share your thoughts, your minds, I am sure that we can find common ground," enthusiastically replied Musa.

"I believe you and I have on this glorious night."

"I will present our discussion to the mansa at sunrise."

"On another occasion, let us drink wine and speak as Africans." Abayomi gleefully nodded and refilled his bowl with pinkish-gray baobab tea. After taking a sip, "You remind me of my son. He also had your candor."

They talked until the savannah crickets no longer sang in the night, and the sky above transformed into a sea of violet and mist. Musa learned that Abayomi's son was killed during a battle with Mansa Abubakari the First. And although the sofa warriors under his father cut down the Djenné youth, Musa felt no animosity from the chief. Chief Abayomi reminisced about the superior qualities of his only son as though he and Musa were lifelong comrades. The old man was also drained from the countless Malian invasions and wanted the peace necessary to coexist as two nations. Nonetheless, he refused to allow his proud people to bow and serve another lord. He would never surrender the walled city but would open its gates in friendship.

"I've enjoyed our conversation, General Musa."

"As have I. When we meet again, I will return with open hands filled with peace." Musa gave a respectful bow and quickly rode back to camp.

Several leagues from the battle for Djenné the day before, on the grassy plain near a Niger tributary, Abubakari sat cross-legged atop a small pavilion and pempi, surrounded by Malian bandari rising from the earth. His face was painted and feathers protruded from his head. He sat without flinching in buffalo-hide armor, laced with gold trimming—the same armor worn by his father during his campaigns. Below Abubakari, nearly three hundred well-armed sofa warriors stood frozen with spears extended, and behind him sat his two stoic female attendants studying all those who approached with reports from the battle. As always, Mamadou sat near his mansa with sound advice.

"I believe that is Musa approaching," said Mamadou as he pointed at the four dusty trails crossing the plains west of the Bani.

Abubakari acknowledged his djeliba with a stern glare and a tight jaw as the four Mandingo horsemen rapidly approached the main camp. "I hope he is returning with news of victory," grunted Abubakari.

Musa and three sofa officers galloped up and quickly alighted their horses. They simultaneously took a knee and placed their fists to the earth.

"Mansa, I return to report our progress," said Musa with his face pointed downward.

"Commence," stated Abubakari with a snarl.

"Djenné cannot be taken by force. The losses are too great and our attacks are futile. They are a proud people."

"I see." A strong breeze passed as Abubakari sat still at a ninety- degree angle, with no expression. The silence could be cut with a knife.

"But they are open to peace," interjected Musa. "A treaty?" said Abubakari with eyebrows raised. "Yes."

"How foolish," laughed Abubakari. "Would the lion form a treaty with the antelope?" He continued to bellow as his military advisors below soon joined in the amusement. "Is this what their envoys are offering?"

Musa lowered himself even further. "No. This comes directly from Chief Abayomi. I had the opportunity to speak with him directly."

"Is that so?" Abubakari ceased laughing and an abrupt

silence permeated through the camp. The mansa slowly rose to his feet with a stare that shot daggers at his commander and brother. "Tell me, you met personally with the enemy…?"

"They are not our enemy," Musa responded sharply as he lifted his head to face his brother. Unpleasant thoughts echoed through his mind. Musa understood and respected the importance of protocol. Every man had his position in life, for it maintained stability and order in the kingdom. As someone once said, A nail that sticks out gets hammered.

"Without my knowledge?" continued Abubakari. "Yes."

"Who gave you the authority to attempt such a thing?" screamed

Abubakari. All who were present shivered at his abrasive state.

Musa replied in a casual manner, refusing to match Abubakari's tirade. "The chieftain would have it no other way. As I said, they are a proud people."

"They are my people! They cannot be proud, for I have not told them to be!" After taking a deep breath, Abubakari sat in his previous spot. "There will be no peace treaty. I want to hear other options."

Musa trembled in his kneeling position. His men looked on and witnessed the anguish in their commander's eyes.

"Well?" demanded Abubakari.

"I recommend that we surround their village and starve them into yielding," mumbled Musa through his clenched teeth. Beads of sweat raced from his brow to his chin.

"Tell me, General, when did Mandingoes become such cowards?"

"You misunderstand—"

"I understand that you're avoiding destiny," smugly

116

snapped Abubakari. "General, you must fight like a Mandingo who understands that this one village belongs to Mali! It is a prize to be had. If its cost demands Mandingo blood, so be it."

"As you wish." Musa glowered at Abubakari.

"Yes, it is as I wish," replied Abubakari, emphasizing the word I. Musa rose, and his officers followed suit. He defiantly mounted his horse, and they galloped away.

After the mansa once again took his place on the pempi, Mamadou faced Abubakari. "Young Mansa, you should not be so unforgiving of your brother."

"Do not meddle, Mamadou."

"I am only concerned with your legacy, my lord."

"I would rather have your concern for how Djenné will fall." "Some legacies are not guaranteed. I have much work to do," said the disgruntled Mamadou, just as a sofa sprinted to the bottom of the pavilion and took a knee.

"Mansa, a traveler from across the Sahel requests an audience." "From across the Sahel?"

"Yes, Mansa. He claims to be of Moroccan blood." Abubakari pondered for a moment. "Allow him entry."

The sofa sprinted away, and soon he returned with a pale-skinned

Arab with long black hair and a sharp beard, mounted on a camel.

The Arab bore a permanent swagger in his actions and was dressed in dark tunic with trousers. Behind him were four camels with sacks draped over their backs, all tied together at their bridles. The young man dismounted and gave a half bow as Abubakari's guards slowly moved closer to the Moroccan.

"Greetings, Great Mansa, leader of the Mandingo," said

the Arab in Mande.

Abubakari waited until the visitor raised his head. "I am impressed, Arab. How have you learned the language that is clear like the open savannahs?"

"A childhood friend from long ago."

"I see," countered Abubakari with a false smile. "Tell me, what has given you the courage to travel so far and disturb me while I am in the midst of battle?"

The Arab returned the false smile as guards held tightly to their spears. "I travel the Angila Passage and the Drar. I am here to trade the finest goods. I bring ivory, honey, jewelry, rare birds, and the rarest metals. All but only a mithkal to your kingdom, mansa."

Abubakari chuckled. "It is said that Arabs often slip their god in with their silks, perfumes, and amulets. I am a follower of Mohammed, but not necessarily a believer."

The Arabian traveler laughed along with Abubakari's officers. "You cannot always believe what is said, Great Mansa. For example, it is said that travelers from Mali can tell lies with impunity."

The Arab now laughed alone.

Murmurs from the officers and military advisors only increased the anger in Abubakari's face. Abubakari rose as one of the attendants, on one knee and head down, quickly handed him his decorative long spear. The guards grabbed a tight hold of the traveler, with their blades threatening his neck.

"Was it something I said?" The Moroccan continued to grin as Abubakari slowly descended the pavilion. With a wave of his hand, Abubakari ordered his men to release him. They did and moved back as Abubakari came face to face with the stranger.

As Abubakari stared into the man's eyes and clenched his long spear, his face slowly softened and his eyes lit up. "Ibn? Ibn? Ibn Battuta!"

"It has been too long, Abu, my friend."

They embraced, holding each other's elbows. The attendants smiled once they realized that it was a friendly engagement.

"You, forever the jester," said Abubakari while nudging Ibn on the shoulder. "I was going to have your head and offer it to the village witch."

"It is one of my better qualities," replied Ibn, who without much thought nudged the mansa back.

Abubakari's guards immediately placed their blades to Ibn's throat. "Sheath your weapons!" ordered Abubakari. The men complied and returned to their places, away but not far. "Never do that."

"Words to live by." Ibn swallowed deeply as he gently caressed the nape of his neck. "Ah, but I knew you could not forget a face such as this."

"Tell me, have you improved at wori?" Abubakari recalled the days he and Ibn would play the game of strategy as children, well into the night.

"I am always ready to partake in a game," answered Ibn.

"Good. Stay here for a moment, rest your caravan, and let us have a game." Abubakari placed an affectionate hand on the Arab's shoulder.

"That would be good."

They continued to exchange warm smiles. Afterwards, Abubakari ordered the retirement of the camp. Soon, reports from the battle ceased and only the cicadas buzzed within the Malian headquarters.

That night, just outside Djenné, tents and campfires scattered the savannah and the sofas prepared their meals in large pots and open fires. Tam tams played as several soldiers exchanged pleasantries, their lanky shadows waving back and forth. Musa stood among them, speaking with his officers. He took a moment to espy Abubakari's large tent atop the hill and contemplated what his brother and Ibn were discussing. Musa had the opportunity to reunite with his childhood friend after returning from the Malian blockade to discuss strategy with Abubakari's military council. He thought of their conversation and the revelation he experienced.

"Musa, Ibn has returned," announced Abubakari to his sibling. "It has been a long time since you have seen each other."

Musa's heart stopped after realizing that Ibn was the stranger who had rescued him from the unforgiving sandstorm over a year ago. Not surprising, since they had never viewed each other as strong young men. Musa was speechless as Ibn hugged his limp body.

"Actually, our destinies crossed not too long ago," Ibn said happily.

Abubakari and Ibn were always closer than Musa and the royal hostage of Niani ever were. Not long after his arrival, Musa's education had begun, sending the Mandingo prince away from the palace for most of his youth. By the time Musa returned, Mali's alliance with Morocco was thus strong enough for Ibn's release.

"How is the shoulder?"

"It has healed well, all praise to Allah," replied Musa. "I am in your debt."

"It was no bother. I only wish I knew that you were an old friend," thoughtfully remarked Ibn.

"The fact that you didn't know who I was exemplifies your humanity." Musa appeared gracious. But deep within, a cold rush of wariness overcame him while standing near the Arabian prince, as it did that night in the cave.

As the smoke from the campfires dissipated into the azure night sky, Musa turned his attention from the tent and focused on uplifting the spirits of his warriors. Soon, ancient songs from the past poured from their lips, and thoughts of returning to battle curled in their bellies.

Within the young mansa's spacious tent, which was decorated with elaborate silks and furs and heavily guarded on the exterior, Abubakari and Ibn Battuta played wori—a game like draughts that involved moving small stones around bored holes in a tree trunk. It was a game of strategy and deception.

Both men comfortably sat upon mats with sly grins, obviously anticipating the next one's move. As always, Abubakari's two female attendants waited patiently on their knees behind him. They were his ivory-cloth shadows, and only Abubakari had ever heard the voices of the motionless and soundless royal servants.

"Are you prepared to surrender?" offered Abubakari.

"Never. I am not one who gives up so easily," countered Ibn as he waved his index finger from side to side.

"I am thirsty," Abubakari said over his shoulder.

One attendant hurriedly brought Abubakari a small ceramic bowl and poured dark wine from the carafe. With a nod from the mansa, the attendant did the same for Ibn. The two men raised their bowls to the gods and sipped joyously.

"I look forward to seeing the Palace of Canco." Ibn took

a long swallow, smiling afterwards from the wine's delicious taste. "I have not seen it since we played as children. Ah, you told me of your beautiful queen, but when will you have an heir to the throne?"

"In time," Abubakari said as he smiled at his wine. The young mansa could not explain his lack of physical contact with Namandje. For the most part, his duties did not permit him the luxury of intimacy. Privacy was short-lived, yet the murmurs of courtiers floated through the palace. The queen has yet to give birth to an heir, one said. Perhaps, the mansa is displeased with his choice, whispered another. These conversations were far from the truth. Abubakari loved Namandje. He envied the purity of her soul, to the extent that he shunned Namandje in fear of defiling that innocence. Abubakari's world was one of lies, treachery, and merciless decisions. He decided to walk that path alone.

"Well, here is to her beauty and the beauty of all women. The children can wait." Ibn raised his bowl to the sky and sipped his wine. "I remember the day we slipped into the royal granary and caused a complete mess." Abubakari laughed and exhaled. "Father was so angry, but you took the blame for us all. Father had taken you away and told Musa and me that he had you crucified like the ancient Carthaginians. We cried and cried." Abubakari could barely speak as laughter intermingled with his storytelling. "And then, he carried us to show you where he had you crucified. And there you were, dangling by your trousers on the hook where my father rested his helm." Abubakari simulated a limp body in his drunken stupor. Ibn laughed, almost to the point of tears.

Once the laughter dissipated, a sincere smile radiated from Ibn. "Abu, although my father sent me here as a royal hostage to maintain peace between our two lands, I had always considered you and Musa as my brothers."

"I too." Abubakari remembered Ibn as his only friend throughout his childhood. Since the moment he left his wet nurses, Abubakari was secluded from an ordinary upbringing. He had not enjoyed the privileges of play and socialization granted to the children of common villagers. So were the tribulations of being a royal descendant of the Keita, thought Abubakari. To avoid his tears, Abubakari slightly changed the subject. "So tell me. Your father, he is well, is he not?"

The intoxicated Ibn slapped his knee. "You jest? He is as strong as an annoyed elephant. That bitter man is going to live forever." Ibn sighed deeply at the likelihood.

Abubakari chuckled as he sipped. "When will you return to Morocco?"

"I will not return."

"Is that so?" Abubakari considered the possibility that a son of a king would feel estranged after his father willingly surrendered him as a token of peace. Yet Abubakari saw it as a prince's responsibility to protect the sovereignty, regardless of the duty or humiliation.

"I have given up my right to the throne and have chosen my own path," Ibn added bitterly.

"How can you give up your birthright?" Abubakari chortled as one does of a fool's dance. "One cannot surrender such things so easily."

"Then I shall be the first," snapped Ibn. "What did your father—?"

"My father is a fool! Moreover, my destiny does not belong to my father. It belongs to another."

Abubakari finally saw the turmoil in his old friend's heart and motioned to his attendants. "Leave us." The two attendants lowered their heads and departed. Abubakari stood and peered out the opening in the tent, viewing the guards standing nearby and ensuring that his words were not heard. He gazed at the many tribal banners streaming down the embankment, silhouetted by the starry sky. The sounds of the celebratory drums from the soldiers made their way to his tent. "I envy you, Ibn," whispered Abubakari.

"Envy me?" Ibn asked in bewilderment, nearly spilling the contents of his ceramic bowl.

"You followed your path in life. You have rejected your worldly possessions. You have the strength to search for yourself." The glowing dots created by the campfires below appeared as fireflies to Abubakari. "I do not have that strength." He closed the tent.

"It is not that simple or what it appears to be. Besides, our situations are different, Abu." Ibn hiccupped and took another drink to clear his throat. "You have the richest empire in the civilized world in your control." He used one hand to balance himself as he turned to face Abubakari.

"Empire?" hissed Abubakari. "This empire is a dungeon, and I am a prisoner of it. What I desire…No one cares what I desire." In the end, Abubakari desired peace. He wanted to escape his life and all that surrounded it. His father's death began his inner turmoil. Will I suffer the same fate, to die a young man? I have not forgotten you,

Oni. I will avenge your death. The sands of time are against me. I must find happiness before I enter the afterlife. The worn king buckled to the ground near Ibn and rested his head in his hands. "I will die the ruler of a dungeon, sooner than I would like."

"What do you mean with such a foolish proclamation?" replied Ibn in comical fashion.

Abubakari did not answer.

Ibn slid over and placed both hands on Abubakari's shoulders. "You have not changed at all, my friend. Even when we were but lads, you recklessly held your thoughts for your own."

"I have never shared who I truly am with anyone. Such information would tear Mali apart. Neither the Keita elders or my wife knows what fills my every waking moment." Abubakari finished his wine and carefully lowered the bowl to the floor.

"But you are not sharing it with fellow clansman," retorted Ibn. "You are simply entertaining a drunken traveler who easily forgets where he leaves his camels hitched, let alone the dreams of a king." Abubakari stood and then methodically searched through his various writings piled inside the chest near his bedding. "The writings of Abu Zaid and Istakhri tell the story. Many years ago, Mansa Sakura welcomed Moroccan court officials, and they spoke of the lands beyond the waters." After briefly sifting through the parchment, he eventually discovered the large document he was looking for.

"Across the Green Sea of Darkness?" This was a sobering revelation for Ibn. He quickly straightened himself. "Of course, there have been many theories that such a place exists, but no one has ever returned. It is a gourd that drowns ships and man alike."

"There is no proof of that!" Abubakari suddenly wrenched in agony, clasping his head with one hand and the document in another.

"Abu, what is wrong?" Ibn nearly rose to assist his friend. Abubakari held him off with a raised hand. "An ache I often get.

It is nothing."

"Should I call a medicine man?"

"No. Tell me more of what you know of the sea."

Observing that Abubakari's pain was easing, Ibn relaxed once again. "The waters to the west are tumultuous and unforgiving. Any knowledge we do have comes from the many fishermen and traders trapped in its currents and never seen again. It is suicide."

"That is because they have relied on sail." Abubakari rushed over to Ibn and placed the nautical map he was holding on the floor before his friend. "Tell me, what if such a vessel also had oars, much like the *dua la mtepe* that sail the seas to the north? They are strong and easy to maneuver. They can make the westward journey."

"When did you become an expert of the waters?" remarked Ibn as he scanned the ink-drawn map. As a seasoned trader, Ibn immediately determined that the coordinates and sketches of Africa in comparison to Europe were of good quality and most likely precise. The Arabic writing and the signatures of several recognizable court officials showed that the map was clearly made by Moroccans. Though the parchment was discolored, it was still a sturdy, well-kept historical document. With numbers for each line throughout the atlas, Ibn followed one line leading westward from Africa to one large landmass covered with trees.

"It is something that I have considered for many years, but have hidden it deep within, until now. This was the map given to Sakura. I believe that my ancestors had preserved it in hopes that a future mansa would have the courage to fulfill the destiny of Mali."

"What are you going to do, Abu?" nervously requested

Ibn.

"I shall build and send a fleet to find what I have dreamt of since childhood. That is my path. As you said, Ibn, I control the richest empire today. My army is one hundred thousand men strong. It is time I used its wealth to bring its leader happiness as well."

"Knowing the corruption that often flow through the blood of courtiers, there are those who will surely try to dissuade you."

"Let them try. I have the power of the ancestors on my side." Abubakari folded the map and quickly returned it to the chest, as though he was a child concealing treats from his elders.

"It will heavily tax your resources and riches," countered Ibn. "How will the common villager react when the added sweat he bears on his farm is being assessed to pay for the dream of a mad mansa? You do know they will call you a madman, right?"

"As my father lay dying in my arms, he told me to always remember your dreams, but never forget the hearts of the people." Before he continued, Abubakari paused in remembrance of Abubakari the First. His eyes watered for a brief moment. "Now I understand his feelings. As I said, I have contemplated this moment for most of my life. But it was not until this very moment that I truly understood what he was telling me."

"And that is?"

"To know. Are my vivid dreams that of a madman? Or, are my thoughts real? Does such a place exist? I must know. For if I do not, I will go mad."

With a grin of one who has resigned to verbal defeat, Ibn sighed, grabbed the carafe, and poured more of the plum elixir into their bowls. He then handed Abubakari his share and cupped his wine bowl in the other hand. Abubakari cordially accepted the bowl.

"Then let us drink to that happiness," offered Ibn as he placed a hand on Abu's shoulder. The two simultaneously drank and exchanged smiles. "Yet I cannot let you escape this game of wori," joked Ibn.

"Indeed." Abubakari caressed his bowl and raised it with a smile.

11.

The lone horse-drawn carriage left the walls of Canco and penetrated the shadowy forest just north of Niani. Several leagues along the winding road, the carriage turned off the main road and down a narrow path where the moonlight did not penetrate the brush. Malians believed that the forest was where spirits dwelled and where magic held its highest power. The forest was a place of spiritual knowledge, but only the regal carriage occupant knew of the path to the nine Great Witches of Mali.

Kongo, known as the mother of Musa, stepmother to Abubakari, and arch-nemesis of Mariama, ordered the carriage to a halt. She stepped comfortably out and inhaled the bitter night air.

"Alas, I have returned to where my blood runs deep." Two sofa warriors in black chain mail helped Kongo down. She commanded her driver to wait at that spot as she and her two guards walked deeper into the wooded area, disappearing into the darkness as an owl called out from above.

A windswept shrine was nestled next to the small creek that served as an eerie habitat to toads, crocodiles, and many other forms of wildlife. Their various mating calls did not rattle Kongo's icy stare as she entered the holy place built to worship Chi Wara, the God of Agriculture and the entity that taught man to farm, also known as the "Animal of Tillage." The decrepit stone building was constructed during the times of Sundiata, and the vines that wrapped around the stonework accentuated its antiquity.

"Ah, it is the Lady Kongo," hissed a woman's voice.

Kongo stood before the nine Great Witches of Mali. The evil spell casters were gathered around the remains of a lamb whose belly had been slit. The animal's blood drained from the stone slab into a metallic bowl as eight of the nine hags sang incantations. Many candles lined the dimly lit chamber, and giant shadows climbed the walls from their lanky frames.

"Soumosso Konkomba, it is good to see that you are well," responded Kongo in her monotone voice.

The leader of the witches, Soumosso, had outlived many generations of African kings, beginning with Sundiata, Father of the Bright Country. Some local villagers placed her at around one hundred fifty years of age. Soumosso's brown skin appeared as leather, contrasted against her stark white hair. As Soumosso's small, robed frame separated from the other witches of similar stature, Kongo ordered her guards to move away from the anticipated conversation.

"How may we serve you, my lady?"

"There is a thorn in the bush," replied Kongo.

"A thorn in need of immediate removal, I assume," added

Soumosso. "Yes."

"Who is this thorn, my lady?" "It is Abubakari the Second."

Soumosso's eyes widened. "The mansa? How may I ask

is our lord a thorn in my lady's existence?"

"That I cannot answer," responded Kongo.

"Your reverence, our lord has not caused us enough disdain to cut him down. It would greatly upset the ancestors to do such a dreadful deed." Soumosso emphatically shook her head. "I am afraid that we cannot be of service to my lady."

Kongo lifted her signature single eyebrow. "I have arranged for several bushels of rice and millet to serve as my gratitude, if you could find it in your heart."

"Several bushels?" This peaked the witch's interest.

"I will also arrange for the creation of a more suitable shrine for your noteworthy ancestral beliefs."

"You are of one god, my lady. Why would you want our witchery on a grander scale?" Soumosso replied cynically.

"My beliefs are irrelevant at this moment. What you have to think of is how you and your sisters will benefit from our arrangement," countered Kongo.

"A troublesome situation indeed," sighed Soumosso. "We have no cause to harm our lord. Therefore he is untouchable." Then she raised her finger with a sudden idea. "But it will only vex the ancestors if we harm the mansa. What if we focused on someone close to our lord? Would that not cause enough grief to satisfy your dark request?"

Kongo had not anticipated Soumosso's suggestion, but now she saw the value in the idea. The question was whom would she choose. Who should suddenly fall deathly ill from disease or suffer madness before taking their own life? It would take some deep thought, since there were many names that passed through her mind. Mariama was her ideal choice, but not necessarily effective. It had to be someone who would serve her ultimate goal.

"That will be satisfactory. Once I decide who will be your victim, I will notify you. In the meantime, I will have the rice and millet brought to you immediately." Kongo turned to leave.

"Excuse me, my lady," asked Soumosso. "Why do you wish for the demise of our lord?"

"I do not. It is destiny that requires his fall." With that, she departed the dwelling filled with gloom and doom.

As the various African fauna retreated into their holes during the Month of Agwunsi, it was a time for celebration within the walls of Niani. Abubakari surprised his entire court when he agreed to a Mali and Djenné peace treaty just before the New Year. So as Niani farmers prepared for Ekenta mbu, or New Year's Day, by harvesting their crops for the upcoming New Yam Festival, another celebration was taking place in the palace.

Neither sovereignty relinquished offerings of good will. There was only the agreement that Djenné would remain autonomous, yet recognize the mansa as one sent from the heavens and honored as such. This recognition fell short of the city-state's complete obedience. So in honor of this momentous event, Abubakari held an evening revelry for his courtiers and the Djenné royal family.

Within the Great Hall of the palace, servants fervently gave rice cakes and wosobula na sauce with potato leaves. Court musicians played their kontingo lutes, similar to the kora except that it has only five strings. Nearly a hundred attendees watched as Malian female dancers flowed up and down, like the torches that surrounded them.

"What a wonderful performance," said Chief Abayomi to one of his retainers. "We lack such performers in Djenné."

"Ah, it seems that we have much to learn from each other after all, Abayomi," laughed Abubakari from across the mansa's table.

It was forbidden for commoners to witness the mansa eat. Therefore, Abubakari had eaten his evening meal in the privacy of his chambers, before the celebration could begin. Few had the privilege of sharing the mansa's table: Abubakari's two attendants, Musa, Lady Namandje, Lady Mariama, Lady Kongo, Djeliba Mamadou, Sulayman, Ibn, Chief Abayomi and his four courtiers, and the Songbirds of Dioma—the poets that performed for Abubakari one year ago.

Ignoring the dreary conversation around him, Sulayman could not take his eyes off the poetic thrush before him. He had learned from Musa that her name was Isa. It was at that moment that he remembered from whence he first saw the stunning bronze beauty. *I saw you at the religious ceremony for Abubakari.* He just needed the light of the torches to remind him. Occasionally, Sulayman witnessed the young lady espy the warrior prince and quickly look the other way. He smiled with satisfaction.

"Forgive me, my lord," interrupted Isa. "I am afraid that the festivities have made me slightly feverish. I ask that his lordship excuse me so that I may step outside for some fresh, savannah air." "Of course," replied Abubakari as Isa stood and hurriedly departed. "Perhaps you should accompany her, Ibn, to ensure that she is of good health."

"I will!" said Sulayman. Realizing his enthusiastic tone, the embarrassed Commander-of-the-Guards added subtlety to his voice. "I have had my fill, and I see that Ibn has not. What an inconvenience that would be."

Abubakari knew how flirtatious Sulayman was with any

woman that entered into his gaze, so he decided to have fun with his younger half-brother. He turned to Ibn. "Oh, I am sure that it would not be of great inconvenience to Ibn."

"As you wish, my lord," said a grinning Ibn as he rose from his seat.

Sulayman sprinted over to Ibn and forced the Arab back into his seat. "How can I watch as a guest of my older brother is not allowed the honor of finishing his meal? Surely the ancestors would never forgive such a deed." Sulayman placed his hand over his heart. "It is I who will make such a sacrifice." He stayed in that position while looking upon Abubakari with begging eyes.

"So be it." Abubakari waved him away, as he and Ibn smiled to one another.

"Thank you, my lord." Having showed his gratitude, Sulayman flew out of their sight in search of Isa.

The evening continued, and Abubakari soon fell victim to the effects of the Moroccan wine provided by Ibn. The casual questions asked of his Djenné guests could have easily been misconstrued as insults. Abayomi, in turn, refused to back down and countered by listing several faults of the Malian kingdom. Though the two leaders laughed away the tense conversation, others at the table worried that the situation could erupt into war once again.

"What my lord meant to suggest is that once you share your science with the people of Mali, we are more than eager to offer military support to defend Djenné. This is normal sharing between stout allies," Musa proposed in an attempt to soften Abubakari's threats.

"Mansa Abubakari offers what we need the least. Our defenses are superior to any attack." Abayomi's big cheeks swelled with an amiable grin. "We are in high spirits to open our gates to the Keita, but it will take time to soothe old wounds."

"The wounds of a dying father," spat Abubakari as he drank from his goblet.

"As those of a dying son, Mansa Abubakari," retorted Abayomi. "I will pray for your son's wraith, Chief Abayomi," said Namandje. Mariama placed a hand on the young queen's lap in hopes of silencing her.

"Thank you, Lady Namandje." Abayomi stood, bowed to her, and raised his goblet to the sky. "Let us not dwell on past events. This is the beginning of a historic alliance that will benefit my people as well as the Keita."

Abubakari slowly came to his feet and raised his goblet to the chieftain's. "To the benefit of both our people. May this alliance put an end to fruitless deaths."

Abayomi's eyes watered from Abubakari's generous words. The chieftain skirted the oblong table and came face to face with Abubakari. With their eyes never leaving each other's glare, they drank simultaneously. After finishing their wines, Abayomi gave Abubakari an approving nod and motioned to his court escorts to rise. "I have enjoyed this moment, Mansa Abubakari, but my administrative duties have forced me to now return to Djenné." "The walls of Canco Palace will always welcome you," replied Abubakari. "In three moons, I will send emissaries to ratify our agreement."

"I look forward to it." Abayomi and his men bowed to Abubakari and departed the Great Hall.

Abubakari's smile dissipated as he sat once again. He leaned over to Namandje and whispered, "A queen must know when to keep her mouth shut."

Namandje momentarily sat in astonishment. "Forgive me,

my lord. I was just—"

"You were just out of your place. Do not err again," hissed Abubakari as he leaned back in his chair. "Perhaps I have indulged in too much wine." He stood. "I will retire to the veranda. Musa, would you join me?" Followed by his attendants, Abubakari stumbled out of his chair and abandoned his guests without another word.

Abubakari and Musa, followed by the attendants, casually strolled the balustrade-protected veranda overlooking the large inner garden. The air was cold enough to snap the appendages off any man. Yet the brothers did not concern themselves with trivial matters such as keeping warm. The steam from their noses and mouths trailed behind them as they stopped at the edge.

"It seems that you are not as intoxicated as you wanted us to believe, Abu." Musa had observed how Abubakari quickly straightened his walk once he was no longer in sight of the celebratory event.

"You are very observant, Kankan Musa," replied Abubakari as he listened to the howling wind whisk through the gum trees. "A snake travels sideways but attacks straightforward." The cracking of the branches as they swayed back and forth served as his soother in the past. From his tunic, Abubakari removed an item from that past, a small wolf's tooth necklace that was still covered in dry blood. The dark clouds approached, hiding the full moon in the midnight sky.

"Thank you, Abu, for finally bringing peace to the region. Djenné was our last obstacle, and now, Mali is complete."

"Not quite," murmured Abubakari as he inserted the necklace back into his tunic. "I have dispatched some of my most trusted horsemen to follow Chief Abayomi." Abubakari faced Musa. "He will never reach the walls of Djenné alive."

"What?"

"My great-grandfather, Sundiata, would be proud of my craftiness."

"What have you done?" Defeated, Musa's mouth dropped, and his hands fell to his side.

"The people of Djenné will assume that he was attacked by Tuaregs. After they find that their leader is no longer, they will open their arms to their mansa."

"This is madness, Abu! They will rise up and call for war. What have you done?"

"N'ko, I have done what Father asked of me! Have you forgotten your promise to our father, Kankan Musa? We swore to take Djenné. To take, not bargain for!"

"Why did you even bother accepting the treaty?" cried Musa. Abubakari personified confidence with his arrogant snarl. "I actually considered withdrawing the men before the peace offer. New events have transpired that will require the full attention of Mali. But I must be grateful to you for delivering an alternate plan for Djenné. Now I can delay the conquest without fear of attack. You have done well."

"I have done nothing! Abayomi trusted me, and I made the mistake of trusting my brother."

"You are observant, Musa, but far too gullible. That is your greatest weakness. Your faith in your one god has blinded you." As Abubakari approached Musa, his velvet robe and silk tunic flapped in the wind. "I am only striking before Abayomi does. What you are unaware of is that, two moons ago, my agents captured several Djenné spies plotting my assassination. Of course, they were immediately gutted and fed to the crocodiles."

"Assassins?" This information took Musa by surprise.

"Why wasn't I informed of this?"

"You would soon tire of hearing the many plots throughout the day." Abubakari extended his palms before him. "There are many who conspire my demise. As mansa, I must always be aware of such treachery." Abubakari rested a hand on Musa's shoulder. "I do not have your luxury of trust. I must trust no one to succeed in administering the people."

Musa showed his approval by nodding. Although he despised the dishonorable method at which Abubakari orchestrated the subsequent death of Chief Abayomi, Musa could sympathize with his brother's plight. Regardless, Musa felt betrayed. His own heart fooled him. Musa had always relied on Allah's guidance and his faith in humanity to determine the intentions of the people he encountered. It had never failed him until that moment. Perhaps he was naïve to believe in the goodness of man.

"I understand, Brother," said Musa as he placed his hand on Abubakari's shoulder. "But what will killing Abayomi accomplish? I told you before. They are a proud people. They will strike against us in anger."

"Never has Djenné launched an offensive. They are only concerned with defending that pitiful village." Abubakari took a deep breath and let it fill his lungs, before exhaling with a huge smile. "With Abayomi gone, they will be in complete chaos, giving me time to set my goals elsewhere."

"Where is 'elsewhere'?" inquired Musa.

"In time, Kankan Musa." Abubakari folded his arms and walked away, followed by his attendants. "For now, enjoy the festivities." Abubakari faded into the dark corridor leading back to the Great Hall.

Musa was frozen on the veranda as ice pumped through his veins and into his head. This was not caused by the winter air, but by the coldness that suddenly overcame his heart. He wanted to believe his brother about the conspiracy, but Abayomi did not appear to lack honor. Such contemplation wore on Musa, sending him directly to his quarters to rest. Before closing his eyes to sleep, he knelt upon his prayer mat and pleaded for Abayomi's soul.

Sulayman finally found Isa wondering near the royal stables. To his surprise, she allowed him to accompany her on a stroll of the palace grounds. After spending a substantial amount of time touring the various gardens, they decided to find warmth within Canco's walls.

How can someone so beautiful be a simple artisan? Sulayman did not necessarily sneer at the status of artisans. In fact, artisans were viewed in Mandingo culture as the voice of the ancestral gods, whether by hand, tongue, or dance. What intrigued, as well as relieved Sulayman the most was when she informed him that she was actually the daughter of a blacksmith from Krina. Blacksmiths held the next highest status, obviously below the royal court. Referred to as "The First Sons of the Land," blacksmiths were thought to have the ability to harness the energy of nature, known as nyama. Blacksmiths also held great political power within Mali, having won control of the empire's komos—associations with strong political, social, religious, and judicial ties.

Sulayman and Isa passed guard after guard until they reached the corridor leading to the inner chambers of the complex.

"What is there?" asked Isa as she stood on her toes to peek over the taller Sulayman. Several sofa guards lined the corridor in the distance. "Those are the inner chambers. There you will find our lord's personal chambers, his battle chamber, the royal kitchen, and…" Feeling that he may have said too much, Sulayman stopped his description. "Only the mansa, his personal guards, and those who share his Keita bloodline are allowed entry." Sulayman comically stepped in her way to block her view.

"Are you allowed entry?" seductively asked Isa with a perfect smile. "You are his brother."

"Yes, but I rarely go, well, except for the battle chamber, which I use to practice my swordsmanship in the late hours of the night. As Commander-of-the-Guards, I hold the keys to the locks throughout the palace," stated Sulayman in a braggart manner.

"I believe you are a well-skilled warrior, my lord." Isa's eyes glittered under the elegant lamps that hung on the walls.

Sulayman became liquid within a carafe; to be dispensed however suited Isa. He had courted many women in his years, but there was something about Isa that his emotions had never encountered. He moved closer, but she stepped back. He tried to caress her shoulders, but she evaded his grasp.

"Am I displeasing to your gaze?" softly solicited Sulayman. "Are you sworn to another, or am I but an unfortunate soul?"

"No, my lord," responded Isa with her head down. "It is best that I return now." Isa slightly lifted her silk hijab from her feet to allow for a hurried departure.

"Wait, I will escort you back." Sulayman chased after her and blocked her path. "But first, I have one request."

"I really must return to my brethren." Isa attempted to circumvent Sulayman, but he would just counter her movements.

"Would you recite to me one of your poems?" Sulayman held her hand and looked deeply into her opal eyes. "Tell me a poem just for me."

Isa stopped and returned his gaze. She beamed from his modest request and gently moved her lips next to his ear, tantalizing the Mandingo warrior with her white flower scent. With a whispery intonation, allowing only for their ears to share her words, Isa spoke:

Only the wind knows,
What the rains washed away, Only the butterfly knows,
From where it came,
Only the clouds above know, Where our destinies lie

Lost in her words, Sulayman instinctively moved his lips to hers. They touched briefly, before Isa slowly moved away, holding on to Sulayman's hand. She led him as one leads a pet or a small child, back to the Great Hall.

Chief Abayomi, three Djenné officials, and his small party of ten horsemen had reached the western edge of the serene Bani River, near the village of Koulikoro. At full gallop, they had made good time and hoped to reach Djenné by dawn. The Hour of the Hare drew near. Frost that settled on the arid grasslands glittered under the clear moon that was now free of storm clouds.

"Whoa! Let us rest the horses!" commanded Abayomi of his men. "That may delay our arrival, my lord!" shouted the closest courtier. "If our steeds collapse from thirst, we may never see Djenné!" They came to a halt and galloped over to the free-flowing Bani.

Abayomi immediately dismounted, as did the others, and he cleansed his hands and face in the waterway. He noticed that the water was clearer in the late months than in the summer months. Abayomi thought of the wife as his horse slurped from the riverbed. He was eager to tell her of the treaty and that Djenné could finally enjoy peace.

"Musa, I trusted you and not my heart. Surely the gods bless even the most foolish." Abayomi chuckled to himself. Musa had convinced him that Abubakari's offer of peace was sincere and not a ploy by the Mandingo king. Abayomi had his doubts, but he trusted in a man who, until only a few moons ago, was his bitter enemy. "This is just a beginning," murmured Abayomi as a reminder to not get ahead of his ambitions. Whenever he became overeager, he remembered the day his son had died on the battlefield. It was a very sobering thought. At least, Abayomi thought, I will not have to bury another child.

Suddenly, the horses became restless and began wildly neighing, alerting the men. The Djenné warriors came to their feet and unsheathed their shortswords from the belts of their tunics. They formed a semi-circle with the river at their backs as they stared into the blackness before them.

"Does anyone see anything?" shouted Abayomi.

"No, my lord." All of his men consecutively had the same response. The men with plaited hair began nervously shouting at each other. Confusion as to the source of the horses' neighing was invading the hearts of Abayomi's men.

"Over there!" screamed one of the men.

Abayomi could see nothing. "Silence! Silence!" The men listened and the chaos eventually subsided. Within moments, the heavy trembling of hooves grew louder and louder. Abayomi recognized the sound. "Mount your steeds!" ordered the chieftain.

"Bandits, my lord?" asked a courtier as he settled in his saddle. "No." Abayomi grabbed the reins of his horse and turned it around to face the approaching assailants. "They are Mandingo! We have been betrayed!"

Out of the darkness poured forty sofa horsemen, dressed not in their normal black chain mail but in dark tunics and veils. Waving sabers above their heads, they appeared as Tuaregs to Abayomi's men. But Abayomi had fought the Keita for many years, and he had grown accustomed to their fighting techniques and their paraphernalia. He also knew that the Keita had mastered horse combat and that he and his men were at a disadvantage, not to mention outnumbered. Malian steeds were practiced in warfare, while Djenné warriors rode horses bred for farm work. Sofa horsemen were highly skilled in open field battle, while Djenné warriors were skilled in defending walls.

"Into the river," shouted Abayomi. "That should nullify their speed." They shifted their horses towards the river as the Mandingoes closed in. Many grew nervous and turned back around to battle the Mandingoes one on one. They were fiercely cut down. Blade after blade struck the Djenné warriors from all angles. Blood spewed onto the riverbank.

"Abayomi must not escape!" screeched a sofa horseman.

Only five men entered the dark waters of the Bani with Abayomi. The horses panicked with the splashing of water that came to their knees. Soon, the Malian horsemen surrounded the desperate Djenné men. The clangor of swords and the splash of screaming bodies that plummeted into the river filled the night air.

Abayomi found that he was now alone. He extended his sword to fend off the enemy that encircled him. He thought of the wife who waited for his return.

Zip. Thump.

The hurled saber embedded itself in Abayomi's abdomen.

Blood flowed down his midsection. As one sofa horseman charged, Abayomi slashed the man across his throat, felling him from his horse. Another attacked his rear, but the veteran warrior chief evaded the blow and countered with a fluid backswing to the man's chest. The sofa horseman screamed as he fell into the shallow water.

Abayomi kicked his horse into full gallop, cutting his way through the barricade of Malian horsemen. A mist was created as his horse's powerful hooves struck the river. The chieftain attempted to pull the blade from his abdomen, but he needed both hands to maintain his grip on the reins.

"Do not let him escape!" The horsemen gave chase, riding full speed at the heels of Abayomi.

Thoughts of his wife, children, and the son who died at the hands of the Keita raced through Abayomi's mind. He wanted to live. For Djenné, he had to live. He begged his ancestors to allow him to live. How could I be so foolish as to trust a Keita clansman? Abayomi coughed profusely, and blood poured from his mouth. Too weak to maintain his balance, Abayomi's limp frame plummeted into the Bani. He waded across to the riverbed and crawled up the slight embankment.

Abayomi stumbled to his feet and forcibly removed the saber from his midsection. He cried out and let the blade fall to the muddy slope. The pursuing sofa horsemen reached their prey and took turns slashing the defenseless Abayomi from all sides. The final blow severed Abayomi's throat, forcing him to fall backwards into the river.

Just before he closed his eyes and departed the world, as he floated away, Djenné appeared to him. At its gates stood the son he had grieved over for so many years.

12.

1309 C.E.

Within the throne room of Canco, the large portals of the spacious chamber allowed the autumn sun of the third month to warm the Niani inhabitants. A murmuring crowd of courtiers had eagerly gathered to hear Abubakari's sudden announcement.

The marabouts stood shoulder to shoulder in their cloaks, with Es-Saheli up front. Mariama and Kongo were there with their respective entourages. Several Mandingoes from neighboring villages looked on as well.

Abubakari entered and sat with his legs crossed upon his pempi, with his two stoic attendants kneeling behind him. Next to him sat Mamadou and Namandje. Musa and Ibn sat beneath him in an advisory position, with sofa warriors guarding beneath. Sulayman stood strong with the warriors.

Musa leaned over to Ibn. "Are you aware of his intent?"

"Yes, but he had me promise to not disclose it."

Musa recalled the few days he and Ibn shared as children and expressed an even more cynical look.

"N'ko!" said Abubakari as he came to his feet. The crowd became quiet and still. "People of Niani, as leader of the Keita, I come to you without fear from our ancestors, for I know that they would be honored! I have postponed our aggression of Djenné and promise you something grander than a mere city! I offer the people of Mali another world, one that we share with the unknown! I speak of the Westward Sea!"

Abubakari pointed over the heads of the onlookers. "There lies the future of Mali! It is not ending! Beyond the sea, the ancestors have foretold to me that a land with plentiful crop and metals brighter than the sun above!"

There was a look of surprise among the people, especially from Musa. Es-Saheli, on the other hand, grumbled to his fellow clerics at the news.

"I call upon the boatmen of Niger, Gambia, and Senegal!" continued Abubakari. "I call upon the Bozo and the Somono! At harvest's end, construction of one hundred ships shall begin on the Senegambia!"

Es-Saheli separated from his marabouts and approached the royal pempi. "Mansa, perhaps we should have a gathering of minds before embarking on such a rash decision." The head cleric humbly bowed to show his good intention.

"As always, I welcome the clerics who serve Allah," calmly responded Abubakari. "But it is not a rash decision I have made."

Es-Saheli became impatient. "We were not consulted in this decision, my lord, and we cannot offer our approval."

Frustrated, Es-Saheli turned his back on Abubakari and waved his marabouts to leave. The whispers quickly moved through the crowd at such a disrespectful act. One should never turn his back on the mansa. Only the fact that Muslim clerics held substantial power under the Malian government prevented Es-Saheli's head from rolling immediately.

With a nod from Abubakari, sofas surrounded the Muslims, stopping them where they stood. The clerics held their breath as they watched the soldiers hold firmly to their long spears.

"I ask not for your approval, Es-Saheli, but for your obedience,"

said Abubakari, "And I shall not ask again."

Es-Saheli cheeks quivered with Abubakari's words. There

the clerics remained, frozen with spears pointed their direction. His face filled itself red with anger, but he was not so foolish as to challenge Abubakari's resolve.

Once satisfied that the clerics were controlled, Abubakari returned his gaze to the gathering. "I have spoken as your mansa. The ancestors have heard my wishes. Now my wishes will come to light." Without as much as a simple glance, Abubakari exited the chamber, followed by his attendants, Namandje, and Mamadou.

Musa could only close his eyes and look upward for some unearthly guidance as perspiration poured down his brow. He saw darkness stalking the Keita, and now it had arrived to destroy his clan. Though he stated it many times in passing to Abubakari, it was not until that moment he felt within his heart the madness that pervaded his brother's spirit.

"Omniscient One, Most Beneficent, Most Merciful, I ask for your guidance."

Musa prayed with a hundred other followers, as Arabic chants filled the candle-lit, white-pillared room of the Niani mosque. Dressed in white robe, Musa's forehead and knees touched the mat beneath him, and then he rose with palms extended, absorbing the marabouts' words from the Qur'an.

And the chiefs of those who disbelieved from among his people said: *He is nothing but a mortal like you*

Who desires that he may have superiority over you

And if Allah had pleased, He could certainly have sent down angels

We have not heard of this among our fathers of yore

He is only a madman, so bear with him for a time

As Musa meditated, he was taken into the past. Within the depths of his memory, flashes of himself and Abubakari standing on the Gambia after their rite of passage flooded his consciousness. He envisioned their youthful innocence at that moment and the words they shared.

"Ever wonder what is out there?" "The sea."

"No, there…beyond the sea." "Nothing is there, Abu."

He also remembered the words his father had said to them before he fell ill, that night on the pempi.

"What else should he have done? That was his duty as your brother. And as long as you are brothers, you must stay united, for each of you possess a gift. There are those that will try to divide you, but you must not let them. You will be mansa, Abu, and you will one day rule the greatest empire. Do you understand?"

"Musa, always be there by your brother's side. He will need you in the darkest moments, as will Sulayman."

Musa finished his prayer and exited the gold mosaic, ivory- bricked mosque. He welcomed the gentle breeze after spending several hours within the humid place of worship. The air smelled of the sweet, ovoid-shaped baobab fruit that normally flourished in spring.

Braziers lined the dark path of the palace grounds, illuminating the way for Musa. He sauntered beyond the occasional courtier. As he passed, they lowered their heads to acknowledge his status. He acknowledged them with a slight nod and continued walking. It was the Hour of the Owl, and most people had already retired for the night.

"Kankan Musa."

"N'na?" Musa looked over his shoulder and espied Kongo standing and admiring a statue of a giant emerald serpent. Its translucent scaly skin glittered from the moonlight. Musa slowly approached his mother. Her lanky fingers caressed the belly of the large grotesque creature.

"Tell me, my son, why does Abubakari find such beauty in the deities long vanquished by the One God?"

"The Serpent-Bida has not been vanquished in Abu's eyes, nor has the Nama-tigi." Musa looked over her shoulders. "You should not wander the courtyard without your escort, Mother."

"I appreciate your concern, Kankan Musa, but I wandered this courtyard long before your conception, and I do not fear darkness." The corners of Kongo's lips curled slightly for the benefit of her son, the closest expression to a smile for her.

"You have nothing to fear from the people of Niani, but we are at war, Mother," said Musa sternly. "Assassins of Djenné could lurk in that darkness you seem to be so fond of."

Kongo took Musa's hand. "Your concern would be better served if you directed it at your brother, the mansa. He has made many enemies among the merchant class. The heavy taxes imposed for his frivolous journey have become a great burden. Many believe that he has lost touch with the wishes of the common people."

"I believe that Mali should build our relation with the East. Abu envisions a land to the west, beyond the unknown." Musa's head sunk into his chest. "Although I feel he is being irresponsible as mansa, I will support him as any brother would."

"As I said, he has made many enemies. Your support worries me as your mother."

"Abu has nothing to fear." Musa felt a little uncomfortable, as he routinely did around his mother.

"How can you be so certain?"

"Because I am his brother, and I am here to ensure no harm will befall him."

"My son, the protector, although it is well known that the people would have you as mansa, if you were to rightfully claim it as yours." "I have claim to nothing." Musa jerked his hand away from her grasp. He could kill a man with the swiftness of lightning, but in the presence of his mother, he became restless and uncertain. Love and fear, they were her power over him.

"Abubakari has never considered you his brother," said Kongo as she gently stroked Musa's face. "He despises your beauty."

Musa grabbed his mother's wrists and clenched them tightly. "You are my mother, and a portion of my heart belongs to you. But never forget, I understand who you are and that power is very important to you. I know that it is you who felt cheated and vexed by my father, your husband. I can see your unending desire to see Abu fail. I will never betray my brother, not even for you!"

"Betrayal is such a severe word. It is Allah's will. You would simply be fulfilling your destiny."

"I will never betray my brother, not even for Allah," whispered

Musa as he released Kongo and kissed her on the pate of her head.

Without raising his head, Musa departed, ignoring the ominous smirk on Kongo's face.

Abubakari gazed at the cloudless blue skies from the vantage point of the portal in his private chamber. He had finally had a chance to rest after spending the entire day coordinating and discussing the empire's finances with his key advisors. He was unable to hide the pleasant mood he was in. It had been a long time since Abubakari had a positive outlook for the future.

"You requested me, my lord?" greeted Mamadou upon entering the chamber.

"Yes, old friend. Come in." Abubakari waved the djeliba in without taking his eyes from the flock of blackbirds that sailed over the courtyard towards the setting sun. "Tell me, what are the feelings of the people about my decision?"

Mamadou tilted his head and rubbed his scruffy beard, somewhat perplexed. "The people will heed the mansa's command, my lord," the storyteller stated firmly in his deep, gritty voice.

"Yes, I know," replied Abubakari. "But what do they say about their mansa?"

"Forgive me, my lord, but does it matter what the people feel about your decision to explore the Great Sea? Would you change your decision to do so?"

"I depend on my djeliba to know the hearts of the people and also answer my questions in a direct manner and not speak in overtones!" The agitated Abubakari faced the mystic teacher. "Is that too much to require from my djeliba?"

"Very well." Mamadou stepped to within a few feet of the young man he helped raise. In a way, Mamadou blamed himself for the man that Abubakari had become. Some time after Mansa Abubakari the First's death, his son emotionally secluded himself from everyone. The teller of tales wished he had intervened more, but every man must mourn the death of his father in his own way. "The people are unsure of your motives and are uneasy with the heavy taxes that you have burdened them with. Yet they will unconditionally support your wishes, for you are God of the Land, and they are your loyal servants."

"I see." Mamadou's words returned a smile to Abubakari.

"I do this not only for myself. I do this for the Maninkakan, the Mandingo people."

Mamadou continued. "After so many years of war and death, they find a certain amount of joy in your cause. The farmers sing as they are raising crops, craftsmen are more diligent, and villagers have more spirit."

"Then I have made the right decision, have I not?"

"It is hard to say, my lord," sighed Mamadou. "It is always the people closest to you who can cause you more harm. Just remember, an enemy defeated by truth will never return, but an enemy defeated by weapons is certain to return. If you are correct in your beliefs, and there is land beyond the Great Sea, you will be heralded as the next Sundiata. But if you are wrong, you will be despised for generations as the mansa who destroyed Mali."

Abubakari was amused by his djeliba's forthrightness. "I am sure that your thoughtful words will not leave my legacy as one to be despised." He turned away and looked out the window once more. "No man in his right state of mind would attempt what I know I will accomplish. That is why I know that I am guided by the hands of our ancestors."

"Your health should be your chief concern, my lord," said Mamadou with a paternal tone to his suggestion. "You have not looked well for some time. Do you consult the medicine man as I had recommended?"

"I am of good health. What ailed me before has now subsided. Do not concern yourself with me."

Mamadou's brow crinkled in confusion. "That is not possible since I am only here to ensure your place in Malian lore. Otherwise, I serve no purpose." With his hands nestled in his heavy robe, Mamadou spoke to the air above him. "I see that your age has not allowed you to relinquish the foolish thoughts of a boy," said Mamadou with much disdain in his voice.

Abubakari chortled for the entire palace to hear. "Only you would be so bold to speak to me in that manner. You are quite an auspicious man, old friend." The mansa continued to laugh loudly, and before long, Mamadou joined him in his joy. After their laughter dissipated, Abubakari placed his hands on the shoulders of the djeliba. "All shall see what I have dreamt of since I was that foolish boy you speak of. Do not worry. The gods will not fail me."

13.

1310 C.E.

Eight months had passed since the massive ship construction began on the Senegambia seacoast. Huge numbers of trees from inland forests were cut down and floated down the Senegal River. The best craftsmen and the most knowledgeable men throughout Mali participated in the endeavor—carpenters, blacksmiths, navigators who normally used the stars to guide caravans through the Sahara. The construction had reached its final stages. Fifty thousand Mandingo natives climbed high planks to hammer and attach the final sails to the dua la mtepes in port. Supplies of grains and livestock were loaded into the ships' bellies. Atop their decks protruded lengthy oars numbering thirty or so. As they raised the Keita clan bandaris high up the mast of each vessel, drums played for the enjoyment of the women and children who had gathered to inspire the men.

Upon the crest of an ancient ivory tower overlooking the shipbuilding endeavor stood Abubakari, confidently observing his dream unfold before his eyes. He had not visited the region in many moons, yet his thoughts were always of the forgotten Ghana Kingdom and their fall. Did they view the Great Sea as I do? Did they see the beauty beyond its tumultuous waters? The invading Almoravids had constructed the ancient tower nearly three hundred years before the Keita took power.

Whilst the sun moved closer to the horizon, generating an orange and purplish sky, Namandje appeared from the stairs behind Abubakari. She slowly moved to him, placing her gentle hands on the railing. Her eyes followed the path of his gaze and back to the smile on his face.

"I have never seen you so overjoyed, my lord," the young queen of Mali whispered softly. "It also brings me joy to see you this way."

"It is more than a glorious day for Mali," Abubakari replied cheerfully. "It is my chance to fulfill my destiny, as prophesied in my thoughts."

Namandje smiled. "Mamadou is beside himself with your decision, but he often tells me that you are only being true to yourself. He understands."

"Mamadou refers to me as the second birth of Kalabi Dauman, the ancestor of adventure and not government. He insists that it will also be my legacy as mansa."

"My lord, in the dream you speak of…am I ever there?" Namandje inquired fretfully as she lowered her head.

"I am not sure if I am really there, Namandje. But my innermost feelings tell me that it is another land far from home…far from Niani. The warm sand beneath my feet is washed away by cool waters."

"I am neither here nor there," sighed Namandje.

"Have I not put your heart at ease?" Abubakari became

perturbed by her remark. "Despite my ancestral right as mansa, I have not taken another wife. And yet you persist"

"I am with child."

Abubakari's eyes became complete circles and his mouth was unable to open. His hands shook as they slowly moved closer to her midsection. Namandje held his hands and guided them to the belly under her robe. Her almond-shaped, brown eyes looked up at his.

"Namandje." Abubakari closed his eyes and kissed her on the forehead. A tear trickled down his cheek.

"Are you pleased, my husband?"

"Very much so. I thought nothing could equal the joy that I felt by my endeavor to explore the Great Sea. I was wrong. This is greater."

"That is good."

Abubakari held on to her stomach once again. "Please bear me a healthy child, my wife. If it is a son, I shall name him Kalabi, for good fortune."

"That is a good name, one worthy to be your heir." "Yes, Kalabi Naman."

Tears streamed down Namandje's face. "I will ask for a healthy son to carry the Keita blood." She embraced Abubakari tightly.

"Ah, that is good, but I will love a princess just as well." Abubakari gently lifted her chin and smiled down at her. "What is important is that he or she will know that they are loved and that life is theirs to be lived."

They gazed into each other's eyes as the torches from the docks below increased with the passing of the sun, like fireflies in the backdrop of the dark-blue waters.

A fleet of nearly two hundred ships, accompanied by two

hundred supply boats filled with provisions and gold, disembarked that winter; their bandaris flapped in the wind as salutations to Abubakari and what they had accomplished. The seamen were treated as heroic giants facing the hands of fate. Women and children waved farewells to their husbands and fathers, as thousands of Malians sent the fleet off with screams of joy.

Abubakari proudly stood on the pavilion positioned along the riverbank. Mamadou, Namandje, Ibn, and his two attendants were also there for the glorious event. Abubakari was disappointed that his mother could not attend the ceremony. She was being cared for at the palace, due to a high fever. He took comfort in knowing that several ladies-in-waiting worked tirelessly to bring her back to good health. "Silence! N'ko!" shouted Mamadou as he moved forward and raised his golden staff to the sky. Eventually the crowd simmered down and faced the pavilion to hear his words.

"Once more, Mansa Abubakari the Second has shown his greatness in the eyes of the Keita and the people of Mali!

Remember this day always. Remember the joy that you harbor within your soul…the excitement of discovery! Abubakari the Second made this possible. He searches for the Sahel westward. It is the calling from the ancestors! Remember this for future children, and their descendants! Remember this momentous day!" Mamadou paused for a moment in dramatic fashion. "Because once the chain is broken, every link that holds a truth are scattered and discovered by those who choose not to see the whole. Wassa wassa ayé!"

The villagers wore big white smiles and they sang in celebration:

Great Mansa of Mali, leader of Niani, Holder of the Great Bow of Mali! Great Mansa of Mali, leader of Niani, Holder of the Great Bow of Mali!

Discoverer of new lands beyond the dark sea! Lead us! Lead us!

As the villagers continued, Abubakari exchanged smiles with Namandje and Ibn. Their eyes followed the dua la mtepes that floated away and disappeared into the golden horizon.

That evening, Abubakari dreamt:

His feet continued trekking through the white sand with the blue ocean water occasionally rinsing them. He stumbled along in tattered cotton trousers and he was bare-chested. His dark, lean frame glowed from the bright sunrays above, their beams powerful enough to cause him to squint.

Abubakari's eyes adjusted to see the blurry, human silhouettes approaching from far down the coast. He paused momentarily to allow his sporadic breathing to decrease. Suddenly, the cackling of blackbirds drew his attention upward. Abubakari's eyes followed the flock of birds flying overhead. It pleased Abubakari, though his smile quickly contorted to a look of grave concern.

Abubakari stepped back as one bird crashed before his feet into the sand. Abubakari fell to his knees with a tear in his eye. He reached down to stroke the trembling bird, which had suffered a broken wing from its fall. The bird squealed in pain just as he touched it. Unexpectedly, the blackbird shattered like glass, gushing salt-water covered in white froth.

When the blackbird gave one last squeal, Abubakari could feel the sunrays scorch his back, causing him to convulse in agony.

Abubakari quickly threw his fur blanket off and rose from his bedding. Gasping and sweating, he espied the candle that had exhausted itself and left dried wax. He panned his private chamber to ensure that no one was observing his erratic behavior.

"Father, I am lost. I ask for your guidance."

Unable to return to slumber, he lay awake until daylight. The next morning he returned to the Palace of Canco and proceeded with the droning work of administration.

14.

From the advantage of the mosque's veranda, in the shadows, Es- Saheli and Kongo overlooked the many Africans praying to the east. A single torch burned feverishly; its light reflected in Es-Saheli's frightening stare.

"Nearly six months have passed, and the Great Mansa is left with nothing."

"The people are in an uproar," joyfully added Kongo. "My agents have informed me that Abubakari's expedition to his land of fantasy has come at the expense of the villagers. The kun-tigi whisper for his demise and riots in various villages run rampant."

"As well they should," hissed the cleric. "He tossed a massive amount of resources into the sea. Resources that, mind you, would have been better spent in Allah's service."

"Then everything has fallen into place. Are you prepared?" asked

Kongo.

Es-Saheli contemplated their malevolent options. "It is a difficult task. The people still regard him as a god. He is guarded from dawn until he sleeps. Every chamber in the palace requires a special key for entry. Whether they are angry with the mansa or not, the Muslims would be the first ones accused, if it occurred outside the palace." He sighed in disgust. "We would be stoned in the middle of Niani. No, it must occur within the walls of Canco."

"I have limited access to the inner chambers, but I have someone who will serve our purpose," said Kongo with confidence.

"Lady Namandje is now with child. Mali will soon have an heir." "Which is of little concern, your eminence."

"We must be patient and wait for an opportunity to reveal itself. Lady Kongo, please do not precipitate the matter. We have much to lose."

Kongo placed her hand upon his. "Patience has always been my strength."

Es-Saheli smiled in anticipation of the days ahead.

In the battle practice chamber of the palace, Abubakari skillfully swung his long wooden staff from one end of the chamber to the other. Sweat enveloped his face and tunic. With every slice through the air, he grunted aggressively to show his strength.

This was relaxing for Abubakari. Wielding his staff released tension as well as reminded him of his youth. He remembered the countless hours he and Musa were rigorously trained in the martial arts. They both sought to be as strong as their father, the warrior- king. Typically, Abubakari enjoyed the isolation from his duties and courtiers unscrupulously attempting to gain his favor. But, he needed to confer with someone he trusted the most to expose his deep thoughts.

Ibn observed from the floor in the corner. His eyes

followed every strike, every thrust, and every evasive stance. He watched as Abubakari twirled the weapon above him and came to rest with a downward blow.

"Spectacular!" applauded Ibn.

Abubakari smiled with satisfaction as one attendant fetched him a cloth to wipe his brow, and the other brought water in a porcelain bowl. He dried himself and drank. He waited until the attendants left before speaking with his childhood friend.

"I practice as much as I can. Father always believed that a ruler must always be prepared to go to battle with his warriors. You should also learn the ways of combat. It may prove useful in your travels."

"I'd rather outwit my opponent with clever words," replied Ibn while stroking his goatee. "I do not remember you as left-handed."

"The left hand is evil, but it is the best."

Ibn chuckled and approached Abubakari. "I am not what you would refer to as a religious zealot, but I do know the difference between good and evil. Besides, these are joyous days. You must be pleased that Lady Namandje is with child."

"Yes, very much so. It somehow brings peace to my soul." Abubakari took a deep breath and exhaled with a smile. "Knowing that Mali will have an heir is wonderful. I have prayed every night for a son, though a daughter would also bring me great joy. If I am fortunate enough to have a son, I shall name him Kalabi Naman."

"That is a great name for a prince," replied Ibn.

Abubakari placed the pole on the wall rack where the other staves hung, many with blades attached. "Is it possible to be both?" said Abubakari as though speaking to himself.

"Both?"

"Both, good and evil," said Abubakari.

Ibn tilted his head and searched for a response. "At times, I suppose we are all both…and neither."

Abubakari head sunk into his chest in disappointment. "So many moons have passed, for naught! No ships. No message of triumph. Perhaps I sentenced them all to their doom. What do you believe, Ibn?"

"Abu, it is not my place to—"

"I ask for the truth, something I rarely receive," interjected

Abubakari. "Give me that."

Ibn hesitated for a moment. "I am a traveler. My only concerns are the cloak on my body and the goods strapped on the backs of my camels. I go where I want. I do what I please. I chose that path. You have not that luxury."

"Meaning?"

"Meaning that the people must come first, always. That is the first rule for any good leader."

"So many depend on me…the villagers that till the land, my wife, my soon-to-be-born child." Abubakari sat on the floor and sighed. "To dream is why we live as men, but dreams are often engulfed by the shadow of responsibility. One cannot have both."

"It appears not," said Ibn as he joined him on the floor. Abubakari clenched his fist and pounded his knee. "I must believe that word will soon arrive."

"If they have not returned so far, Abu, they most likely will not," said Ibn with a stern glare. "You must prepare yourself for that inevitability." "There is a land beyond the waters. It resides in my dreams. Yet there it will remain as I continue to rule." Abubakari continued with an uneasy grin. "Good and evil. There are times, my friend, that I want to be pure at heart, but the weight becomes overwhelming. And then it becomes much easier to retreat into the darkness."

In the tenth month of year 1310, riots erupted in Kidal, a village located in the northern most corner of the Songhai Province. The small number of protesters were primarily farmers, agitated by the higher taxes imposed on them. Armed with agricultural tools, they proceeded with setting the merchant district afire and looting every goldsmith, coppersmith, jeweler, weaver, and craftsman business that dealt directly with the Niani government. Several owners were dragged from their homes, had their heads shaved, and then were mortally slashed across the throat.

Sulayman was dispatched to Kidal with five hundred warriors to quash the rebellion and bring the insurgents before the Niani court. Prior to entering the modest village, the young Commander-of-the- Guards was perched on his steed, patiently watching the scorching flames and smoke darken the afternoon sky. His war-painted and feather-adorned foot soldiers waited in formation behind him.

"Nothing good can come of this," said Sulayman under his breath. He adjusted his chain mail and secured his sword in its scabbard. He turned in his saddle and waved the warriors forward.

The deba resounded and the lines of sofa warriors slowly marched towards the outskirts of the village. Sulayman found it difficult to concentrate on the task at hand. He could only think of seeing Isa again.

Sulayman had convinced Isa to leave her native village of Krina and remain in Niani. Eventually, they began courting one another in secrecy. Sulayman would dash from his military duties and rush his kora lesson with Camara at the

Inn of Daka. After washing the nafiola scent from his person, he hurried to the dwelling he had set up for Isa in the artisan district, near Camara's home.

It was Isa's decision to keep their relationship a private matter. She chose to protect Sulayman from the gossip that routinely echoed the halls of the palace. Regardless, Sulayman planned to have Isa as his wife once he returned from crushing the riot. For the moment, he removed her violet, translucent veil from the pouch of his tunic and inhaled her white flower fragrance.

Sulayman pressed forward. Once within the village, Sulayman found himself surrounded by utter devastation and suffering. Flames leaped from dwelling to dwelling, ruthlessly incinerating anything or anyone that crossed their paths. Native Kidalians fought to contain the fire with a short supply of water from their reservoir, but the fire outgrew each bucket they tossed at the inferno.

Charred bodies lay dead in the streets—children and the elderly, for the most part. Sulayman quickly brought his horse to a slow trot. Kidalians eventually saw the Niani soldiers and cheered their arrival.

Sulayman alighted and swiftly ordered several of his men to disperse and help contain the roaring flames. He also stationed warriors at the outskirts of the village in order to detain any insurgents attempting to escape. One hundred sofa warriors remained with him.

"Where is the kun-tigi of this village?" Sulayman snagged the arm of a passing old man.

The old man responded in a Songhai dialect that allowed Sulayman to only decipher a few of his words. Regardless, from the Mande words the man used, Sulayman was able to gather that the initial rioters had taken the kun-tigi and his family hostage and threatened to behead the entire lot.

After remounting his horse, Sulayman followed the old man's directions and led his warriors to the residence of the village chief, outside the market area and away from the fires. The well-kept and large mud-constructed home was surrounded by twenty or so men wearing soiled and tattered tunics.

Sulayman scanned the weapons of the ragtag group—rusty picks, pole arms, and axes. He made sure the Keita bandaris waved high for the insurgents to see.

"Who commands your group?" shouted Sulayman.

"And who are you?" said an anonymous voice in a Songhai dialect. The man speaking was in the home.

"I am Commander Sulayman, and I carry the will of the mansa, the will of your lord!"

"The mansa is a madman, and we no longer consider him our lord. Now be gone with you, before more blood is shed."

Sulayman dismounted and handed the reins of his horse to a nearby page. "You have taken the kun-tigi hostage. Surely you have some demands!"

"There are no demands, only vengeance!" replied the muffled voice from within. "Take your leave, Keita!"

"Only after we have resolved this matter in the most amiable way possible. Those are the words of our kind lord." It was at that moment that Sulayman knew that the village chief was already killed. What atrocities were being committed against the kun-tigi's wife and children was another matter. He was done negotiating.

With the rapidity of a charging rhinoceros, the Mandingoes stormed the home. Without mercy, their blades fell any farmer that resisted being captured. Blood splattered the walls, and wails of the dying echoed through the cavernous dwelling.

In time, the insurgents were subdued with few casualties to the sofa warriors. Most of the Songhai farmers were mortally wounded, except for the eleven men who were captured.

Covered in blood, Sulayman breathed heavily to overcome his queasiness, for he had discovered the bodies of the chief, his wife, and their three small children. They had been disemboweled in ritualistic fashion. Their insides were offered as spiritual fertilizer by the Master of the Land, the high priest of the village, said to be the descendant of the first man to make the land arable and create the first village.

The Commander-of-the-Guards tunneled his way through his men until he reached fresh air outside. The children affected Sulayman the most. In his nineteen years among the living, he had never experienced the massacre of children.

Afraid that his men would discover him exhibiting weakness, Sulayman hid behind nearby brush. He hastily unfastened his chain mail to allow his chest more room to expand and then collapsed to his knees. Coughing profusely, he vomited onto the ground.

Later, the young Mandingo commander removed Isa's veil from his pouched and inhaled its white flower fragrance. At the same time, Sulayman prayed for the salvation of the children who would remain embedded in his memory for many moons.

15.

Abubakari, his attendants, Sulayman, and Musa walked the velvet carpet and reached the pavilion just beyond the walls of Canco Palace. As Abubakari sat upon his pempi, his sunken eyes looked upward to appreciate the sunlight penetrating the silk- cotton tree. The rainy season was fast approaching, and he felt as though that may have been his last glimpse of Sol.

Waiting. It had worn a hole in Abubakari's soul, and it showed in his health. He had lost considerable weight since the boats first sailed from the Senegambia Coast. Having yet to hear any word from the expedition, Abubakari found it difficult to continue his other duties as mansa, like bringing rioters to justice.

Sofa warriors led eleven bound Songhai rebels and their kin— men, women, and children—to the edge of the pavilion. A substantial crowd of Niani onlookers gathered along the path and shouted vulgar language at the captured, while the sofa warriors circling the scene held them back.

"Traitors to the mansa!"

"There is no place in Mali for those who kill their own brethren!"

"What do you expect from the Songhai?"

The dust kicked up from the ruckus and mixed with the dried blood of the shaved and beaten prisoners. All eleven men were placed in a line in front and brought to their knees as their children cried out for their fathers.

Namandje looked on from a palace tower with Mamadou and Mariama at her side. Namandje rested her hands on her protruding belly. Finding it difficult to sit in her pregnant state, Namandje preferred to stand.

"I must request that you not witness this. Consider your health. Please, Lady Namandje, I beg of you!" Mamadou turned to Mariama in hopes of support for his concern.

"Mamadou, though I am with child, I am still the wife of Mansa Abubakari and queen. Whatever pains my husband, I too must endure," responded Namandje. "Our lord needs us most in these trying times."

The crowd soon settled down, and Musa stood to address all those watching. Holding a ceremonial staff, Musa pointed it at the captured.

"These are the Songhai of the Kidal Riots, brought to justice for their attempt to rise above the mansa, true ruler of Mali! As punishment for their disobedience, they will be put to death."

In unison, the sofa warriors standing next to the prisoners unsheathed their swords. The villagers exploded with more Mande slurs directed at the moaning captured, cheering for the execution of the prisoners. Satisfied that the people supported Abubakari's decision, Musa returned to Abubakari.

"You are certain that they are the instigators, Sulayman?"

whispered Abubakari to his half-brother.

"I am certain," replied Sulayman with confidence. "I would not punish an innocent man."

"Innocent," muttered Abubakari to himself. "In any case, well done." "I understand that deciding who lives and dies is not an easy matter," said Musa as he knelt beside Abubakari. "Why not have the court resolve this matter? Let the Council of Elders determine their

guilt or innocence."

"No, but they are not innocent, are they?" Darkness emanated from Abubakari's demeanor, surprising even Musa. "They raised their arms against the mansa, and for that, their punishment is death. Commence."

Musa reluctantly nodded to his brother and slowly retreated to the edge of the pavilion. "The mansa is prepared to now hear your pleas for mercy."

An elderly man with graying scruffy beard and hair defiantly stood with his arms tied behind his back. Unafraid, he shouted his vexation.

"Your taxes destroyed our land! We have nothing left to sow! And for what? Take our lives if you must, and enslave our women and children, but we know what you are. We deem you monster, Abubakari the Second, not worthy as our leader!"

There were soft grumbles in the crowd as Musa approached Abubakari, once again. Musa's heart was with Abubakari, but he sympathized with the farmers' strife. He also understood how quickly the dead could rise among the living and grow in power.

"Brother, if you spare the lives of these men, the people would look favorably upon you," begged Musa. "Kill them, and they become martyrs."

Abubakari mumbled to himself and rubbed his temples in discomfort. "No one understands. I know what is real." Abubakari was disoriented and spoke to the empty space before him.

"Brother?" Musa grabbed his shoulder and stared deeply into his eyes. "Have there not been enough needless deaths?"

"Will they understand when my day has passed?" "Abu!" grunted Musa in a low voice.

"Kankan, you are here?" said Abubakari with a freakish smile. The mansa's stare no longer carried the glaze of one non-respondent and he returned to the matter at hand. "Commence," commanded Abubakari.

"Perhaps you should rest, Brother, and decide their fate in the morning." Musa attempted one last time to save the lives of those who would see his brother killed in their place. He felt that sparing their pitiful lives would do more for

Abubakari's soul than the condemned Songhai farmers.

"I do not want my child to inherit my miscalculations. No, they must die in order to preserve our great kingdom. It is just another wonderful duty that was bestowed upon me," sarcastically responded Abubakari as he leaned back.

Musa unenthusiastically stepped away and extended his palm for the sofa warriors to see. The old man was thrown to his knees and the eleven Songhai men soon had two sofas' swords at their necks; the blades were crossed at their necks.

The beat of the deba filled the air.

Namandje caressed her belly and felt the child within move. Anguish engulfed her, and she was filled with tears. Since she arrived in Niani and became the queen of Mali, death surrounded Namandje. Thoughts of her own clan in Burkina Faso raced through Namandje's mind.

"N'na, why do men yearn for blood so?" she asked of her mother- in-law.

"It is the Mandingo way," simply replied Mariama. "Come, you must rest."

Namandje moved away from viewing the execution, followed by Mariama. The robed figure, Mamadou, closed his eyes and offered words of wisdom to the pristine sky above.

His heart, no longer part of this world
Sought the blood of others
To refill what had been drained
Abubakari the Second gave in to his inner demons on that
day

Musa clenched his raised fist and quickly let it drop.

The swords at the captured men's throats screeched and

instantly severed the men's throats. Blood splattered to the earth below as each man fell face-first into his own pool. Everyone watched in silence as their final gurgles remained until they lay still.

Screams erupted from the wives and children of the executed, as they temporarily broke free of their captors' grasps and ran to the sides of their fallen fathers and husbands. Musa quickly waved the sofas to remove the women and children.

"Wait!" said Abubakari as he stood. "What are you doing?" "It is done," responded Musa.

"No, they too must suffer the same fate. They are to be executed!" The sofas paused. It was customary for the family of the captured
to be sold into servitude. Their lives were spared, except for unforeseen circumstances.

"Why must they die?" demanded Musa.

"To discourage future uprisings against Mali," hissed Abubakari. "I do not want to battle an embittered son in the future."

The sofas followed their lord's command and pried the women and children from the dead. Ruthlessly, the guards shoved the helpless Songhai to the ground.

"No," whispered Musa. His eyes shifted from Abubakari to the women and children, who numbered nearly twenty.

"Commence!" screamed Abubakari.

The sofa guards placed their blades at the necks of the bound and defenseless captives. The brawny deba drum player began pounding the cow-skinned instrument. The guards waited for the order to draw blood once more.

"Stop!" Musa leaped from the pavilion and entered the realm of the execution grounds. "Ignore the mansa's command! I will not allow this!" To everyone's surprise, including the guards, Musa moved from captive to captive and pushed the swords from their necks.

"How dare you challenge me!"

"As farin, I challenge your decision in this matter!" spat Musa, reminding Abubakari of his status as military governor.

The sofa guards trembled in a confused state. They looked to one another for guidance, unsure of which order to follow. Mansa Abubakari was their true lord, yet every man held a deep loyalty to Musa, the general of past campaigns.

"Do as I command!"

"Disregard the mansa's order! He is not well today!"

Sulayman quickly approached Musa. "Brother, what are you doing?"

Abubakari slowly moved towards Musa, followed by his attendants. "Musa, listen to Sulayman. He may save you from a treasonous death."

"Then I shall die in their place!" Musa pushed Sulayman away. The crowd became silent as Musa ran down the pavilion and fell to his knees before the sofa guards. He unsheathed his sword and embedded it into the dirt. He ripped his tunic off and exposed his bare chest.

"Spare their lives, Great Mansa, and offer my blood to our ancestors, for Allah watches over me! I, Kankan Musa, await my fate!"

The captives and the crowd admired the bravery of Musa; some were overcome with tears. The situation was unprecedented. Never had anyone publicly defied the mansa's order, especially a sibling of the ruler.

"Do you believe that I am incapable of executing a brother who disobeys my laws?" Abubakari scanned the scene before him with gritted-teeth, until his eyes found Musa.

"Abu'?" whispered Sulayman. "You cannot be serious."

"I await my fate," said Musa as he lowered his head.

Though the deba drum continued to beat in Abubakari's heart, it had ceased playing for the audience. Silence engulfed the warm spring setting, and the chirping of blackbirds marked every second that passed. Hearts paused in anticipation of what would happen next.

"Enough! They will be spared." Several exhaled in the crowd after Abubakari's words. "Not because of your utter disrespect for Mali, but because I have had a change of heart," continued the mansa.

"Your kindness, I would never question, my lord." Musa humbly bowed his head until it touched the ground.

"As for you, brother, I cannot ignore your disobedience. Guards, he is to be restricted to quarters as I contemplate a proper punishment." Abubakari stepped down from the pavilion and stepped to within inches of his brother. He knelt down so only Musa could hear his parting words. "You never cease to disappoint me, brother."

Abubakari immediately departed with his attendants. Musa continued to stare into the ground below. A tear trickled down his cheek as the guards carefully lifted the drained Musa to his feet and escorted him back to the palace.

The remaining Songhai prisoners were spared certain death, though they were condemned to slavery for life. Tied at the hands and waist, they followed the sofa guards to the merchant who dealt with people. They were sold to neighboring tribes and banished from the kingdom.

Later that evening, Abubakari admired the full moon that

floated in the indigo-blue sky. The bathing chambers were for his enjoyment alone, and that he did. Though the large steaming bath was within the palace, Turkish in design with porcelain flooring, its open ceiling allowed for the dry savannah air to permeate the misty room.

Several scantily clad female servants, or royal bathers to be more precise, stood waist-high around the nude mansa and methodically rubbed the soils of the day from his lean, muscular body. Abubakari leaned against the pool's sloped inside, unaffected by the ecstasy that surrounded him. He thought of what transpired between himself and Musa, until his trance was broken by the rush of boiling water poured from a wooden bucket into the bath. The youngest of the royal bathers did this every two minutes to ensure that the water stayed comfortable for her lord.

"That is not necessary," said Abubakari to the submissive girl, "I will soon retire."

She bowed with a timid smile. "As long as my lord remains, the warmth must be replenished. Forgive me for my disobedience." The female servant hurried to the corner of the room where an enormous metal pot bubbled with a bustling fire beneath it. She hurriedly used the ladle to refill the bucket.

The warmth must be replenished. For whatever reason, her words vibrated in Abubakari's heart. His pool also needed replenishing. Long gone were the days that Azikiwe chuckled at the young mansa's naivety and guided Abubakari to the right decisions. Mamadou was at times helpful, but Abubakari often viewed his djeliba as an observer, with the mansa's best interest at heart. The loneliness did not creep up as he had predicted to himself. No, it engulfed him as quickly as the Niger does its banks during itum.

Namandje entered, prompting the servants to exit the bath and bow before their queen. She ignored their presence and stepped to within a few feet of her husband.

"My wife, should you not be resting for the sake of our child?"

asked Abubakari with his eyes on the ripples of the clear water. "I have come to beg for the release of Musa, my lord." Abubakari eyes darted her direction and his lip curled at its end.

"Leave us!" he shouted to the servants, who immediately obeyed and fled the tense engagement.

As Abubakari rose from the water and donned his loincloth, Namandje gently knelt with her head pointed downward. He approached the small fire near the bath to warm his dripping frame. "Musa is of no concern," casually remarked Abubakari as he

wrapped himself in a cotton robe. "He is your brother."

"I know this is true!" Abubakari took a deep breath, sorrowful for the explosion of emotion. He hovered over Namandje and reduced his tone. "Musa, brother or not, publicly defied my command. He left me no choice."

"What will become of him?"

"I could no more order his death than I could order yours."

"I am sure he regrets his disobedience, my lord," offered Namandje. "Can you not see it in your heart to forgive him?"

"A woman should not dabble in political affairs." Abubakari knelt beside her and caressed her waist. "How is our child coming along?" he said with a smile.

"Very energetic," Namandje said while meeting his caring eyes. "With everything that is happening, it is good to know that these tumultuous times are unable to taint this part of my life."

In the Month of Anyanwu, heavy spring rain drenched the Malian landscape, forcing Malian merchants to close their doors and hope that the dark sky would brighten the next day. Rain fell for eight days straight, and the streets of Niani became gushing rivers, devoid of inhabitants.

Musa watched the storm from the portal of his palace chamber, or at that point, his prison. The rain did not bother Musa. In fact, he enjoyed the way it cleansed the land and its people, purifying the evil done by his fellow man. Eleven days had passed since Musa had been confined by order of the mansa. He spent his days praying to Mecca and copying chapters of the Qur'an with ink and papyrus provided him.

One of the three male servants assigned to him knelt behind the entrance's drape. His muffled voice announced that Fela, Musa's most loyal officer, has come to pay a visit to his lord. This made the veteran warrior the fourth visitor for Musa.

"Ah, Fela, it is good to see you in good health." Musa bowed while sitting cross-legged on a cotton pillow. "As salaam malakum." "Malakum salaam, my lord," the graying officer replied as he prostrated himself before Musa. He wore a tunic that had seen many a battle. His chain mail was dented from the blows of edged weapons. Fela's eyes began to water, tormented by witnessing Musa in such an uncomfortable situation. "Disgust fills the ranks of the men at how unjustly you have been treated, my lord. Forgive me for my appearance. The vexation is wearing on me so."

"It is good to see my most trusted officer," said Musa, "but do not concern yourself with me. Your duty is to your men and our lord, Mansa Abubakari."

Musa clapped his hands and ordered that dinner be brought for him and his guest. Before long, servants scampered in and served the pair bean fritters and fonio. They also dined on boiled gnousgous, a vegetable that had just come into season. After commiserating over dinner, they sipped baobab tea and discussed the situation in whispers, fearing the ears of a spy.

"What is the situation of the men?" inquired Musa.

"They are of low morale, my lord. Many have never faced the Mossi in combat, but they fight on as though you were there." Fela explained to Musa the conflict that had transpired since his confinement. The Mossi of the Southern Forest had entered Malian territory, harassing border villages. In response, Abubakari sent a contingent of foot soldiers to squelch the Mossi. Skirmishes broke out, but full-scale battle had not erupted.

The dead have risen among the living. Keita spies reported that Chief Abayomi of Djenné had betrothed his daughter to a Mossi prince, thus forming an alliance between the city-state and forest dwellers. Abayomi's death angered the Mossi king, and he blamed Malian conspirators for his demise. Furthermore, the Mossi king learned of Musa's unfavorable situation and determined that he would take the opportunity by the throat. Rival tribes knew of Musa's past exploits, and they feared him. Learning that he was confined, the mouths of the tribal lords watered to battle Mali.

"We must never battle the Mossi," Musa stated firmly. "They are trying to provoke us into a rash attack. If we are foolish, we may see the end of the Keita!" Musa leaned forward and clenched Fela's tunic. "You must not allow this to happen. Swear to me that you will not let this happen, as long as I am confined."

"I swear, my lord," said a teary Fela. "As Commander of the Southern Armies, I will stake my life on convincing the mansa to reconsider engaging the Mossi." At first, he was too bashful to ask, but Fela forced himself to blurt it out. "When will our lord release you from this madness?"

"I am not certain, my friend." Musa sipped his tea and heaved a sigh. "He is just in his beliefs. No one must rise above the mansa, no matter how strong his conviction may be. If I am to die, I take delight in knowing that I am also capable of giving life."

On the other side of the palace, the showers outside her chambers did not disturb Namandje from her slumber. As she lay on her side, her face twitched from a horrific dream.

Namandje ambled through the misty forest, lost from the world. The cold air caused white smoke to pour from her nostrils and mouth. The gawking of large birds pierced the crisp, desolate air. Mud covered her tiny bare feet, and the strong wind nearly removed her scanty robe. She was not with child in her dreams.

In the distance, a hooded-figure knelt with his head down. Namandje hesitantly stumbled closer. The mist cleared and revealed nine other dark robes standing around the man on his knees. She was dreaming; she knew this. But Namandje was unable to separate the reality from the fantasy. The feelings of suffering and sorrow overtook her and caused her to weep.

A standing figure removed the kneeling man's hood. His pale skin began to flake, and tears rolled from his opaque eyes.

"Abubakari!" Namandje sprinted towards the unholy

gathering. As she moved closer, the grotesque faces of the Great Witches of Mali came into view.

Soumosso unsheathed her stained scythe and lifted it above her head, towering over a wavering Abubakari. The other witches formed a circle around Abubakari and began chanting prose from ancient mystical tomes. Soumosso's eyes widened in frightening proportions, and her mouth gaped open to reveal her discolored fangs. While she swung the scythe downward in hopes of removing the mansa's head, Namandje forced her will through into the inner circle.

"No!" Namandje was quick enough to put herself between Soumosso's blade and Abubakari. Namandje trembled as she looked down to see dark red blood flowing from her chest. Leaning on Abubakari's back, she peeked over her shoulder at her husband who remained on his knees and frozen. "Abu?" There was no answer. As the blood spewed from her mouth, she slowly looked upward to the wicked glare of Soumosso.

"Such a foolish girl," giggled the ugly witch.

With no hesitation, Soumosso swung again. The sharp blade of her scythe whistled towards Namandje's screaming face.

Namandje abruptly awoke from her dream and sat up. Her hands twisted the fabric of her robe as she searched for the wound in her chest. Reassured that she had awoken from a nightmare, Namandje exhaled. Yet she felt a deep pain emanating from her midsection. Her hands felt warm and wet in the dark room.

"Light!" shouted Namandje.

"Yes, my lady." Three of her most trusted female-servants rushed in with lamps to illuminate the chamber. The servants suddenly screamed at the sight of their mistress.

Shivering, Namandje gazed at her blood-covered hands and then downwards. Blood soaked her robe from the waist down and enveloped her bedding. Namandje could almost hear the cackling of Kongo once she realized that the heir to the Malian throne was dead.

16.

Abubakari was not immediately informed of the details before he hurried to her private chamber. He was told while meeting with several senior members of the council that the queen was experiencing problems. Knocking down any item or person that entered his path, Abubakari flung himself to her bedside. The soothsayers and medicine men moved away and prostrated themselves in his wake.

Namandje lay supine as she rested her head in the lap of Mariama, sobbing incoherently. Mariama also wept for Namandje and Abubakari's loss. Most importantly to her, she cried for the loss to Mali. Mamadou observed everyone from the corner of the chamber.

"It was a prince, my lord," cried Namandje. "Forgive me." Abubakari fell to his knees and slid down the side of the bedding.

His body contorted as he released a silent scream before his lament filled the entire chamber. Eventually, he gathered himself and stumbled over to his wife. Their eyes met, and it was apparent to Abubakari that she felt shame. Abubakari clasped Namandje's hand and rested his head in her chest, unable to utter a consoling word. He then incomprehensibly jumped to his feet and his eyes darted from attendant to attendant.

"Where is my son?" stoically requested Abubakari as he wiped his tears.

"Abubakari, please do not torture yourself any further," begged Mariama.

"WHERE IS MY SON?" screeched Abubakari. "GIVE HIM TO ME, NOW!"

Never had the servants or attendants seen their lord as furious as that moment. They scurried to grant his wish. In seconds, Abubakari gently held the son who might have been. Abubakari unwrapped the silk cloth that surrounded the infant's minute frame. Upon seeing the face of the fragile, blue newborn, tears once again flowed.

"I shall name you Kalabi Naman," explained Abubakari to the motionless infant. "I will explain to you the importance of your name, Kalabi." Ignoring all in the room, Abubakari paced the chamber, speaking only to the child. "Bilali Bounama, ancestor of the Keita and servant of the prophet Muhammad, had Lawalo, the first king of Mali." Abubakari suddenly turned to his djeliba. "Am I correct thus far, Mamadou?"

Mamadou nodded. "Yes, my lord."

Abubakari smiled and his eyes were brightened by his achievement. He continued. "Lawalo had Latal Kalabi, who had Damul Kalabi, who had Lahilatoul Kalabi, who had Kalabi Bomba, who had Mamadi Kani. The first hunter king was Mamadi, and the hunting god, Kondolon Ni Sané, loved Mamadi as a father loves a son."

"My lord, please." Mamadou approached Abubakari and held his hands out with sympathetic eyes.

Abubakari kissed Kalabi Naman. "Ensure that he receives the burial worthy of a prince, Mamadou," demanded the mansa before handing the infant to Mamadou.

Mamadou nodded and departed the chamber with the child. Abubakari then ordered everyone out so that he and his wife could share their grief alone. The medicine men and attendants removed themselves. Mariama rested her forehead on Abubakari's forehead for a brief moment, cupping his worn face with her hands. She then departed.

Abubakari sat next to Namandje and slowly stroked her brow, rearranging stray hairs from her soft, red eyes. Her auburn skin was pale and appeared weak to him. "You must rest and heal yourself."

"I only want to die," whimpered Namandje. She then lifted herself into Abubakari's arms and shoved her face into his chest. She sobbed once again.

"We will have another son," consoled Abubakari. He did not blame Namandje for losing his son. The ancestral gods had failed him. They were angry at his ways. Abubakari internalized his anguish and hid it in the deep crevices of his spirit. He questioned his purpose in life and how long he had to endure it. The death of Kalabi strengthened his desire to make the most of his life and the ones he loved. Abubakari abandoned fate and resolved to create his own path and achieve his dream.

Namandje slowly drifted in and out of consciousness. "My lord," she mumbled. Namandje pulled Abubakari closer to her lips. "The wraiths came to me. I now know that they are after you, my love." She took a deep swallow. "They tell me that only a love as old as the evil that pursues you can save you." Namandje then passed out; Abubakari's firm hold supported her limp body.

"It is the mansa, my lord," said the male servant. "He wishes to speak with you."

"I see." Musa nodded and immediately prostrated as Abubakari arrogantly flung the drape open and entered the nondescript chamber. "My lord," said Musa without lifting his head.

Abubakari sat across from his brother, carefully folding his red velvet tunic under him to prevent wrinkling. He scanned the parchments filled with Qur'an scriptures along the walls of the room. An uncomfortable silence warmed the room as well as the sunbeams that cascaded from the open portal. Several days had passed since the death of Kalabi Naman.

"I have not forgotten your disobedience, Kankan Musa."

Musa remained still. Then suddenly, he began chuckling uncontrollably, to the point where he was unable to stay in his submissive position. Musa lifted his head to the ceiling as he chortled loudly.

"Do not take me lightly," snapped Abubakari. "I could have you executed before the sun reaches the Senegal."

"Forgive me, Brother. I just find it amusing that while the kingdom is on the brink of war with the Mossi, you are concerned with me. Should you not be meeting with the war council at this very moment? Have you even properly mourned the death of your son? Lady Namandje must be overcome with grief. Why do you not concern yourself with her?"

Abubakari sprouted to his feet and clenched the collar of Musa's cotton tunic. He shook Musa robustly. "I was going to simply expel you from Niani! I even considered giving you your own palace somewhere far away!" spat Abubakari. "But I can no longer bear your insults!"

Musa did nothing. He did not even look his brother in the eye when speaking to him. "I suppose I should thank you,

Abu," softly remarked Musa. "When one is confined to solitude, he is able to look within and rediscover the man he had always wished to be. I have come to terms with where I belong."

"Save your scriptures for the marabouts, Kankan," chuckled Abubakari. "We both know that you have never agreed with Father's decision. You have always been jealous of my power. I am a god among men, and you are just a common soldier, no different from the young sofa who dies for the greater glory of his mansa."

"You see the lands with your eyes closed, Abu. What power does a god have if the people do not believe in him?"

"Enough!" Abubakari slung Musa to the floor and towered above his younger sibling. "You pretend to be a greater man than I, but I will show you that you are nothing more than another subject in my lands. It is a shame that you forced my hand in such a way."

Musa glared at his Abubakari. "Kill me if you must, or banish me to Taghaza."

"First, there is a matter that we must resolve," snarled Abubakari.

Abubakari and Musa had once again returned to the battle- practice chamber from whence they competed as children. The two brothers uneasily faced each other, separated by no more than a few steps. With only their white cloth trousers and bare chests, they stood with their long, wooden staves, poised for melee. Abubakari's attendants bowed and exited the dimly lit and airy chamber, leaving the competing brothers alone.

"I will help you remember whose word is the voice of the ancestors." Abubakari twirled his staff and brought it still with an aggressive grunt.

"This is foolish, Abu." Musa remained in a wide stance, following Abubakari with his eyes only. His chest muscles rippled as he raised his staff.

"Since we were children, you have always sought my demise, Brother."

"I have only shown you a brother's love. Evil spirits have twisted your mind, Abu. You cater to the witches of a religion long forgotten. Seek the protection of Allah and follow Mohammed to salvation."

"Allah?" laughed Abubakari. "Allah will be the downfall of Mali. I seek new lands never imagined, and you pander to what is already known."

"You have failed, Abu! You have gone mad! This dream you carry has killed thousands of Mandingo warriors and nearly broken the will of the people! Let me help you, Abu."

"I do not desire your help!"

Abubakari launched himself towards Musa, shouting Keita war cries along the way. He twirled his staff on his side and followed with a downward strike. With his left hand, Musa used his staff to deflect the blow and thrust Abubakari back. Abubakari was startled for a moment by the ease of which he was propelled backwards. He gritted his teeth and his jaw tightened in frustration.

"A daffeké, you are not." For Musa to call Abubakari "less than a fine charger" was a great insult from one combatant to another.

Abubakari slammed his staff to the ivory floor and hurried to the wall. He detached a halberd-type weapon. "I will slice that swagger in half!" Hunched over and breathing heavily, Abubakari waited for Musa.

"You draw your blade against me?" Musa's heart

imploded from grief. Never before had they threatened mortal harm to one another.

"You have forced me to take such action!"

Abubakari launched himself again, this time twirling the weapon before him. Musa effortlessly evaded the blows, with each strike whistling through the air before him. The nimble Musa used his staff to defend himself, holding it on both ends. Inevitably, Abubakari's heavy blade snapped Musa's staff in half, leaving him holding two five-foot poles.

Abubakari waited with a smile as sweat poured down the crevices in his face. The two brothers exchanged threatening looks, anticipating the next move of the other.

"My warrior skills are superior to yours," pleaded Musa. "Put down your weapon and let us dismiss such childish behavior."

"I am not the weak sibling you remember!"

"If you were not my sibling, I would have already taken your life,"

countered Musa.

"You have my permission to try," said Abubakari with confidence.

Abubakari charged Musa with the blade of his weapon extended. Musa evaded the sharp edge and deflected the pole with his two staff pieces. Abubakari was thrown slightly off balance, but quickly regained his stance. Musa turned and faced Abubakari with his poles crossed.

"Tell me, Brother. Can you hear the deba?" Musa asked softly. Musa charged with lightning speed. Before Abubakari could defend himself, Musa whacked him once in the abdomen and again across the chin. As Abubakari fell, Musa snatched the halberd from his hand. Abubakari turned onto his back with a blood-smeared chin. Musa hovered above

Abubakari with the halberd's blade at his throat. Abubakari cowered like a wounded animal.

"You are an evil soul and a fool. I have asked Allah for forgiveness, for I allowed you to send men needlessly to their doom. From this day forward, I cease to be farin…and your brother." Musa let the halberd fall to the floor, and metal met stone and echoed through the giant chamber. After shaking his head in disgust, Musa headed towards the massive chamber door.

Abubakari regained his feet. "Kankan! You are mistaken, Kankan! None of you can see what I see!"

Musa continued without looking back. Just as he was near the doorway, Sulayman burst through the door, with two sofa guards not far behind. After taking a moment to regain his breath, Sulayman grabbed Musa's shoulders with great joy.

"Abu! Abu! A ship has returned! A ship has returned from the Great Abyss!"

"What did you say?" said Musa in disbelief.

"A messenger has reported that a boat returned to Senegambia from the expedition, and its commander is en route to Niani as we speak!"

Musa and Abubakari's wide eyes conveyed their surprise. In an instant, they had forgotten their bitter dispute from only moments before. A smile pervaded Abubakari's face as he eagerly raced to Sulayman.

"This is a sign from the ancestors that Kalabi's death was for naught. I knew that they would not fail me." Abubakari hugged Sulayman, unable to control his enthusiasm. "Where is this boat's commander? I must waste no time to speak with him."

17.

"A boat has returned?"

"Yes, my lady," replied the lady-in-waiting as she helped
Namandje sit up in her bedding.

Many days had passed before Namandje's regained her strength, both physically and emotionally. Depression overwhelmed her innocence, and she no longer knew how to find the goodness in life. Yet hearing the news from her attendant warmed her heart. She wanted to be by her husband's side when the boat's commander entered Niani.

"I wonder has the queen mother heard of this," inquired Namandje to herself. She was grateful to Mariama for staying by her bedside day after day as she recovered. Namandje struggled to stand, but she eventually ambled to the window of the queen's quarters.

"My lady!" The attendant rushed over to Namandje and helped the young queen stand. "You are not well. Please return to bed."

Namandje gently fanned her away. "Leave me be. I am much stronger than most would believe."

Early summer left the baobab and silk-cotton trees that dotted the palace in full bloom. Under the bright sun, Namandje gazed downward as palace workers prepared the courtyard for the expected celebration. Keita banners hung from every spire of Canco Palace, and a line of wagons filled with yams, onions, poultry, and braised cattle reached beyond the palace's walls.

Ibn spent the morning in the royal stables, caring for his

camels. After feeding them and checking their large frames and hooves for tsetse flies—blood-sucking insects known to bring down the mightiest of steeds with several bites—the Arabian traveler stopped at the mosque.

The ivory place of worship was uncharacteristically empty. Ibn assumed that most of the faithful and clerics were at the palace awaiting the arrival of the sea captain. It had been years since he had stepped foot in any mosque. He felt uncomfortable at the site of the massive Qur'anic writing tablets and the horned torons protruding from the walls of the main prayer hall. Ibn did not come to meditate. He had hopes of speaking with Es-Saheli, especially since the head cleric requested to see him.

"As salaam malakum," came a voice from over Ibn's shoulder. Es-Saheli slowly approached Ibn with his hands clasped before him. "I thank you for accepting my invitation." Es-Saheli gave a slight bow. "It has been a long time."

"You will forgive me if I pass over a happy greeting," sarcastically said Ibn. "I knew you were here, but how did you know I was in Niani?"

"Very little occurs within this city without my knowledge. For example, I suppose you are contemplating why I have decided not to foolishly wait for the sea captain's arrival. Am I correct?"

"Well, you were never one to miss an opportunity to stay near a king in his moment of triumph, Es-Saheli."

"Ah," replied the cleric with a smile, "as I said, very little occurs within Niani without my knowledge." Es-Saheli's huge eyes scanned the hall, searching for anyone hiding behind its pillars. "Let us go to a more discreet location."

Ibn and Es-Saheli went to the mosque's library, which

was located on the top level and housed tomes that were nearly a millennium old. Es-Saheli dismissed the library's keeper and the two men stood at the center of the massive annals of Malian and Arabian history.

"It was wise of you to flee Morocco," said Ibn. "Some believe you had a hand in the death of the Ethiopian envoy."

"Outright lies!" barked Es-Saheli. "After staying loyal to your father for so many years, it burns my heart to know that he would not support me."

"Do not take it to heart. My father trusts no one."

Es-Saheli forced a slight chortle from his pointy lips. "Ibn, it is good to see you. Rarely do I have a chance to meet my brethren." Es- Saheli sighed. "Africans are a different lot from us Arabs. I have made many adjustments just to survive."

"You seem to be surviving very well," commented Ibn.

"Do not misunderstand my words," said Es-Saheli as he raised his palm. "I have lived very comfortably by the graciousness of the Keita, all praise due to Allah. But my lips do miss the delightful flavors of Fèsian cuisine."

"What is it that you want of me?" retorted Ibn.

"You have spent many days in Niani. It seems that you and Mansa Abubakari are very close. It appears that you are prepared to remain here for a very long time." Es-Saheli approached Ibn with a serious expression. "For a trader to remain in one place for long periods of time is destined to be ruined."

"Goodbye, muezzin." Ibn turned to exit the building.

"That is unless someone made the trader's time worth more." Es-Saheli raised his voice to get Ibn's attention before he exited the arched doorway. "In the end, you are a shrewd man, are you not?"

Ibn stopped and faced Es-Saheli. "Meaning?"

Es-Saheli felt the blood rush to his head, for he took pleasure in manipulating the minds of the unsuspecting. Once he gave Ibn reason to pause, Es-Saheli knew that he could convince his fellow Moroccan to do his will. The cleric understood that the seeds of every fruit, even the sweetest fruits, are planted in darkness. Greed was in the hearts of every man.

"I possess a large fortune, but it is nothing compared to the riches I...we could amass, with your assistance, of course." Es-Saheli then turned his back on Ibn and approached the altar. "Though, I do wonder how your deep loyalty for the mansa might interfere with matters."

Ibn stood beside Es-Saheli with arms folded. "I am a very shrewd man who requires a very large amount of riches." Ibn checked over his shoulder. "That is my only loyalty."

Pleased, Es-Saheli grinned and nodded. "Very good." His bright eyes engaged Ibn and did not blink before the Moroccan. "In time, after I know where your loyalties lie, I will need information."

"Information?" asked a startled Ibn. "What kind of information?" "In time, my friend, you will be a very wealthy trader. That is all you need to know at this moment." Es-Saheli inserted his hands in the opposite sleeves and wandered away from the motionless Moroccan.

"You were always wiser than your brother."

"So, you have noticed an improvement," asked Sulayman. "Certainly, my lord. You now play with the elegance of one wh belongs to the Musician's Guild," cheered Camara.

Three years of constant study had finally taken form.

Under the tutelage of Camara, Sulayman soared in the art of the kora, and he had reached the skill level that enabled him to make his own twenty-one stringed musical instrument. Under the cloudy sky, behind the wooden house next to the Inn of Daka in the artisan district, Sulayman and Camara spent the next month making his personal kora. The warrior had grown accustomed to the nafiola fragrance.

Sulayman chose a large gourd calabash that was also deep. After slicing the calabash in half, he then inserted a dry, hardwood post through it in preparation for his strings and bridge. Not wanting to hunt, Sulayman purchased the finest heavy cowhide for his instrument.

Combining their strength, Sulayman and Camara stretched the cowhide over the open side of the half calabash, which was a difficult task. Camara then rubbed a liquid mixture on the cowhide skin to remove the cow hair.

On the fifteenth day of letting the skin sun dry tight on the calabash, thus holding the wooden post in place, the two artisans sipped fresh water while sitting under the warm sunrays that sliced through the fluffy clouds.

"I apologize for serving you only water, my lord," said Camara. "Will you cease with that!" replied Sulayman in good nature. "We have known each other for nearly three years now, and you continue to refer to me as 'my lord.' When I am here for my lessons,

you are the teacher, and I am the student." "I will try to remember that, my lord."

Sulayman nodded and reclined against the beaten wooden frame of Camara's home. They were separated from the inn's grounds by a high sandstone wall, which surrounded the musician's inner keep. Sulayman's eyes trailed the wispy, cotton-like clouds as they drifted over the tip of the single baobab tree on his property.

"You should try to improve this place. You might attract a wife that way." Sulayman chuckled in response to his own humor.

The slender, brown-faced Camara only smiled at the poke. They had become Sanakhou, "banter brothers," a privilege normally afforded between clans that were allowed to tease the other. Except Camara would never make fun of Sulayman.

"The skin is dry. We should prepare your strings," said Camara. "I picked these up from the merchant district three days ago." Camara opened a copper pot near him and pulled out strings of braided antelope hide. "It will not give you the clear sound for performing alone, but it will do just fine under song for any kumbengo performance."

Camara then mounted the tall bridge on the skin face of the kora, securing it with a repugnant wax only found within the trees of the Southern Forest. Once stable, Camara attached twenty-one necessary strings, tuning them to his desired sound along the way.

Occasionally, Camara hummed a tune from long ago as he plucked and tapped the base of the completed kora.

"Treat it with the care one shares with the heavens." Camara bowed and gave Sulayman the instrument with both hands.

Sulayman kindly accepted it and found a small stool to sit on. As he was taught, he held the base with his third, fourth, and fifth finger and plucked the kora with his forefinger and thumb. Each note that he played, with no particular tune in mind, launched Sulayman deeper and deeper into his emotions. The beautiful yet simplistic strumming brought the reality of his life to front. He was torn

191

between two brothers.

The young Commander-of-the-Guards felt his loyalty should only be for the mansa and the common villager. However, Kankan Musa was the brother who shared the same mother. Like Musa, Sulayman harbored a certain amount of resentment for being considered the outcast bloodline, even if the view was formed by fictitious undertones. Until recently, Sulayman could endure the friction between his older siblings.

Musa informed Sulayman that he was preparing to leave Niani, never to return. Though Abubakari had not ordered his banishment, Musa did not desire to stay in his beloved city. He would cut all ties with the Keita and his family.

Against Musa's wishes, Sulayman went to Abubakari and informed the mansa of Musa's plans. The young warrior pleaded for his half-brother to go to Musa and convince him to stay in Niani. Sulayman even introduced logic into the equation, stating that Musa was his best general and most trusted supporter.

Abubakari pondered Sulayman's request, more so out of appreciation for Sulayman and his enthusiasm. But it was obvious to Sulayman that Abubakari was only concerned with the anticipated arrival of the sea captain and not the Mossi engagements. After two days of contemplation, the mansa responded, "If that is his wish, so be it." The dejected Sulayman left it at that.

Sulayman's thoughts then focused, once again, on Isa. He had hoped to see her for the evening, but she had fallen victim to a slight ailment and requested time alone to recover. He wanted so desperately to go to her nearby residence anyway, but the sun now rested on the hills, and he did not want to upset her.

Camara shyly handed Sulayman a thin vest, constructed of the cowhide used on the base of the string instrument. "There was additional hide, so I made you this." As Sulayman accepted it and compared it for fit, Camara continued. "It is thin enough to wear under your tunic and armor."

"What is this?"

"It is a vest that I had enchanted by the village witch doctor. It will protect you."

Sulayman laughed. "A simple vest that is constructed of hide will not protect me from the blades of my enemies."

"Perhaps, it was not charmed to protect you from your enemies, my lord. I believe the witch doctor..."

"Never mind. Thank you," said Sulayman. "Are you now a member of the Tailor Guild?"

"No!" softly chuckled Camara. "As musicians, there are times that we make our own clothing for a performance. And since you are a warrior..."

"Shall I don it?" interrupted Sulayman as Camara tossed the vest to the warrior. Sulayman suddenly stood and removed the top of his tunic, unveiling his strapping, ebony chest and arms. He extended his chiseled arms behind him.

The sky took on a golden hue as day slowly became night. "It should serve as another line of armor." Camara positioned Sulayman's arms through the holes of the vest and gradually slid the vest over Sulayman's shoulders.

"Not as comfortable as my hunter's tunic, but it fits nicely. Thank you." Sulayman secured the vest with the ties in front. Sulayman peeked over his shoulder. "Camara, you have always been kind to me, chiefly for your instruction." Sulayman cleared his throat to fend off the rush of emotion. "I am grateful."

"You are a talented musician, my lord, but you do require further instruction."

Sulayman turned around again with a sarcastic glare. "Was that really necessary, or do you find pleasure in pointing out my every shortcoming?"

A huge smile pervaded Camara's face. They both let out a boisterous laugh before continuing Sulayman's lesson for the night.

The sea captain and the fifty sofa horsemen who accompanied his carriage had finally reached Niani in the sixth month at the Hour of the Boar. Ten members of Abubakari's administration gathered in the throne room of Canco Palace to hear firsthand the words of the returning expeditionary. Many of Abubakari's court officials were elder members retained from his father's reign. They lined themselves five on each side of the path leading to Abubakari's pempi. Seated behind the pempi were Mamadou, Sulayman, and Namandje.

Namandje silently prayed for auspicious news. Though her devoutness to Allah only surfaced now and then, she had learned the entire Qur'an as a child. Namandje's father, the Dogon noble, believed that the future of their clan's success lay in the following the god of Malian emperors.

In front of the pempi knelt the Mandingo sea captain with a scruffy beard and thick eyebrows. His soiled tunic was torn at the edges, and the limpness of his emaciated arms and legs denoted the fatigue that seized his entire body.

The sea captain's yellow eyes closed, and everyone lowered their heads as Abubakari plunged in past the guards. His female attendants took their place on either side of the pempi, but Abubakari abandoned protocol and took a knee by the captain instead. He gently held the man's shoulders.

"Forgive, my lord, for appearing before you as unclean as I am," said the captain without lifting his head. "I have not had the opportunity to bathe as commanded by your loyal retainers. I was overcome with bringing news of the expedition directly to you as soon as possible."

"Let your head rise, brave Maninkakan." Abubakari gleefully shook the man. "It is a blessing from the ancestors to have you before me. Tell me of your journey. What did you find? How many ships have you returned with?"

The sea captain slowly lifted his head to reveal tears and the face of a man who had seen a nightmare unfold before his forty years. His lips fluttered as he spoke.

"My lord?"

"Yes, I am here."

"What you see before you is all that remains of the expedition." "What did you say?"

"Only my boat survived."

Abubakari brow crinkled as he shook his head, praying that the words he had just heard were just a passing breeze. "What? This is not possible. The ancestors have spoken to me."

"But it is true, my lord." The captain's tears flowed. "We sailed west for many moons, nearly falling off the horizon with no sight of rock or soil. At that point, the other captains and I chose to return to Mali. Our rations were dwindling and the livestock had become infested with sickness. We had no choice."

"I see." Abubakari moved from his knee and flopped on his buttocks in delirium.

"As we changed directions, the waters continued to pull westward. Our sails, our rowers were helpless at the sea's power. I was able to break its hold, but the others were drawn into the abyss. Many drowned in hopes of swimming to safety…such horror."

Abubakari suddenly lunged at the captain and clenched his tunic. He shook the weakened man like a doll. "Liar! Why are you still alive if what you say is true? Why must I hear you breathe? Liar!"

"My lord!" cried one of Abubakari's retainers.

"Abu!" Sulayman rushed over and peeled Abubakari off the whimpering captain.

Abubakari howled in anger and pain as his retainers assisted Sulayman in trying to control the rage of the mansa. Bright red blood spurted from Abubakari's mouth. He fell to his side, gasping for air.

Abubakari gripped his temples to relieve the pulsating beats within his head, paralyzing him into a silent scream. The vision had returned just as the young king lost consciousness.

Abubakari stood frozen upon the white sands of the shore. There were only the sounds of a slight breeze and his trousers flapping. The dark, ghostly figures in the distance were still blurry to Abubakari.

Abubakari walked their direction, slowly increasing his pace, until he was in a full sprint. Abubakari's feet pattered the sand crystals, and the air escaping his lungs grew heavier with every footstep.

18.

Mariama and Namandje sat on both sides of the ailing Abubakari, who rested upon his animal skins for warmth from the night air. The sweat pouring down his black face glowed from the candlelight along the walls of his private chamber.

Namandje rinsed a cloth in the water basin held by a young servant girl. "Return with fresh water. I want fresh water here for every moment. Do you understand?"

"Yes, my queen."

"And escort the royal physician directly here when he arrives." "Yes, my queen."

The servant lowered her head and scurried through the draped exit. As the silk cloth separated, Namandje could see Abubakari's two mysterious attendants standing outside. Abubakari's most trusted attendants turned slowly to espy the chamber before the silk curtain closed.

Namandje squinted at the pair with vexation. Her face then softened as she carefully placed the cloth on Abubakari's brow.

"They never leave his side," whispered Namandje. "How jealous I feel when they are near him. They strike me as very benevolent, yet as cold as a Saharan night."

"You have become somewhat callous since the first day you arrived in Niani," teased Mariama.

"N'na, why do you say such hurtful words to me?" whimpered Namandje.

Mariama smiled. "It is only appropriate that you change. You are growing older, and callousness is, at times, a queen's best weapon."

Mariama gently rubbed Abubakari's arm. There was great sadness and helplessness in her eyes as she stared at her only son. She kissed Abubakari's hand with watery eyes. Mariama had hoped that his symptoms were fleeting, but they appeared to worsen. Memories of her late husband pulsated through her mind. The heartache of having to watch her son suffer in the same manner sat on the edge of unbearable for the queen mother.

"My poor son, how you have suffered for so long," consoled Mariama. "You must remain strong and continue to be a good leader for Mali." She placed both her hands upon his. "You must forever remember these words, for they are true ones."

Soon Kongo entered, dressed in her elegant hijab. After greeting the two women who were already present, Kongo attempted her best sympathetic expression and softly placed her hand on Abubakari's pate.

"May Allah watch over him," declared Kongo. "It is such a dreadful day for the palace."

Namandje and Mariama shared a quick glance of disbelief. Namandje welcomed her, nonetheless. "Thank you for being here for Abubakari, Lady Kongo."

Kongo graciously bowed to Namandje. "He is a son of Mali. I also pray for his health."

Mariama glared at Kongo. "Kongo, I wish to share something with you." She quickly stood and moved to the corner of the chamber.

"Of course, Lady Mariama." Kongo followed her.

"Why are you here?" whispered Mariama to keep Namandje from hearing their conversation.

"Why am I here?" Kongo appeared to be taken aback.

"Yes, why are you here?" shouted Mariama. She looked over her shoulder to make sure she didn't startle the grieving Namandje.

"Can I not have concern for my stepson?"

"You have never been concerned for my son," responded Mariama. "Perhaps you should worry for Kankan Musa. His poor soul owes you for his distress."

"Kankan's heart weeps for his brother." Kongo arrogantly turned her back on Mariama. "That concerns me, I believe."

Mariama moved closer and spoke over her shoulder. "Do not feel at ease here."

Kongo smiled. "We should not let our distaste for each other hamper the love of our children."

"Hear me, Kongo, and hear me well. I remain civilized with your presence because Abu and Kankan Musa are siblings, and Kankan is pure of heart. But never believe that I am fooled by your pretenses."

"Your harsh words cannot prevent the inevitable," retorted Kongo. "Abubakari's days as mansa are dwindling, and soon Mali's rightful ruler shall take his place."

"If such a day arises, it will never change your status behind me." Mariama sauntered around Kongo and came face to face with her nemesis. "Remember, I was our husband's first bride, and you were just an object of a mansa's boredom."

Kongo's smile dissipated. "When that day does arise, I will make sure that you are shaved bald and paraded through the streets of Niani as a common harlot." Her smile returned.

"Only after I have taken a blade to your throat." Mariama's brows flared in anger. She showed her teeth, and they were long.

Their eyes shot sharp daggers at each other. They stared silently at one another, neither giving psychological ground.

"Only the future will tell." Kongo smirked. "Yes, it will," replied Mariama.

Kongo faced Namandje, who realized that the two older women were in conflict and looked on with concern. Kongo bowed to them both and departed, passing Mamadou on the way out. Neither acknowledged the other. Mamadou approached Mariama and politely bowed out of respect.

"Queen Mother."

"Mamadou, it is good to see you here. He whispered your name many times."

Mamadou nodded and glided over to the bedridden Abubakari. Namandje gazed upward with eyes unable to cry anymore. She held tightly to Abubakari's forearm. Mamadou could only offer a reassuring smile.

Without opening his eyes, Abubakari forced his lips to speak. "Mamadou."

"I am here, young lord," said Mamadou.

Abubakari swallowed and then took a deep breath. "Namandje, I wish to speak with my djeliba in private." "I cannot leave you—"

"Care for N'na. Can you do that for me?" hissed Abubakari. "Yes." She quickly wiped a sudden tear.

Abubakari coughed deeply as Mariama slowly pulled Namandje away from her husband. "Let us do as he wishes, Namandje."

With Namandje looking over her shoulder, the two women departed. Abubakari opened his eyes, lying stiff on the huge, furry skins. He slowly sat up, wincing from exhaustion and pain.

"The Twelve Doors of Mali are falling upon me, one by one. Tell me, Mamadou, have you ever had a dream that was so vivid, so pristine, so beautiful that you would do everything in your power to make it come to fruition?"

Mamadou thought for a moment. "No. I find beauty in what was and what is, not in what could be. It is a simple life, the life of a djeliba." Abubakari slammed his fist against the table holding the fresh water basin. He stood and, in a rage, began knocking over every item in the chamber—tables were overturned and urns were smashed.

Mamadou only watched as the two attendants hurried in the room followed by six sofa guards with spears in hand. They paused once they realized that it was Abubakari causing the disturbance. Mamadou put them at ease with a glance and waved them away. They left.

"I am going mad!" Abubakari curled in a corner as a soft cry came from the balled-up man. Mamadou could only look on with sadness.

"I have known for many days that I have very little time. I am dying, Mamadou," said Abubakari after wiping his tears and regaining his composure.

Abubakari lifted his head so that his eyes could meet his djeliba's gaze. Mamadou saw the eyes of the child from the hunt.

"Dying?" Mamadou's huge, spherical eyes widened even further. "What afflicted my father was passed on to me. Though, the curse has spread deeper and faster in my soul. Every day, I grow weaker. You are the only one I have shared this with, and it must never fall upon the ears of anyone as long as I am alive."

"The medicine men—"

"The royal physicians could not help Father then, and they cannot help me now," interjected Abubakari. "I had to maintain the attacks on Djenné, in hopes of uncovering the cure within their minds. My pride ruined that."

"We shall make an offering to the ancestors. Surely they will not abandon you if they receive a proper tribute."

Abubakari stood and walked over to his bedding. He reached under the furs and withdrew the two-foot-by-two-foot red box and let his hands glide across its lid.

"I shall build another fleet and see my dream come to pass, before I leave this existence...before my wraith lives on."

Mamadou's expression, as usual, had not changed. "Others will be up in arms, but..." He paused as one does when he experiences a revelation.

"What is wrong, accept for your normal concerns?"

"To build another fleet is one matter, but I feel the vexation in your soul. What are you not sharing with your djeliba?"

"You are my voice, Mamadou...greater than I will ever be. Yet there are important matters that must remain in secrecy, even from you."

"And what am I to say to those who follow? Those who ask of Abubakari the Second? What will I tell them of your legacy, young lord?"

Abubakari slowly replaced the box to its original location. "The truth, my friend. You will tell them the truth."

Sulayman squinted through the downpour to get a clearer view of Isa's home. His dark robe protected his tunic from the rain and helped him meld into the darkness of the street. Because the moon was hidden by the storm clouds, Sulayman could not discern the hour. He just knew it to be late, since passersby had emptied the streets and artisans closed their shop doors for the night.

Sulayman positioned himself on the opposite side of the narrow earthen path, just across from the wooden gate of the modest domicile. He was tempted to just announce himself and take her by the waist. Ah, to feel her bosom in my hand would be magnificent...to feel her soft touch and breathe her white flower scent, once more. Nevertheless, Sulayman respected her wishes and did not want to disturb her when she was in poor health. Besides, Isa's illness could have been extremely communicable, something that also gave Sulayman hesitation.

The wooden panels that covered the largest window glowed from the lamp inside. Sulayman's eyes widened as Isa's ebony silhouette passed the window. His wide smile tasted the salty raindrops as they trickled down the bridge of his nose. Sulayman made a commitment to gaze at the beauty the entire night, if necessary.

Suddenly, two shadowy figures came into view. Their lanky frames were covered in black, and dark scarves concealed their faces from the eyes down. The two unknowns dashed quickly along the gate and leaped into the grounds of the small home.

"Nothing good can come of this," said Sulayman as he unsheathed the shortsword from under his robe and approached the gate.

With the fluidity of a leopard, and with a single hand, Sulayman scaled the small gate and hurdled to the other side.

"N'ko!" shouted Sulayman.

The two masked men spun around with weapons drawn. One wielded a spear; the other held a shortsword. From the complexion around their eyes and their language, Sulayman determined that they were both Mandingo, but their dialect escaped his memory.

"Who are you?"

"What is your purpose here?"

"Odd. I was going to ask the both of you the same questions," replied Sulayman as he moved closer to the intruders. Before the melee began, Sulayman removed his robe and wrapped it around his free forearm. He then hunched in his fighting stance and secured his footing in the damp, grass-filled garden.

They attacked Sulayman simultaneously. Sulayman used his robe to shield the spear thrust and deflected the sword attack. As Musa taught him, Sulayman used the momentum of the attackers to move through the men and find the gate to put his back against, taking away the possibility of being attacked from the rear.

"Tell me who you are, and perhaps I may spare your life!" demanded the spirited Sulayman. The young Mandingo warrior boasted his talent by twirling his shortsword from the hilt.

The spearman charged Sulayman, nearly putting the spearhead through his abdomen. Fortunately for Sulayman, the tip embedded itself in the wooden gate. The frustrated spearman tried to pull the weapon out, without success. The swordsman quickly followed with a downward swing.

Sulayman fell to one knee and impaled the spearman in the thigh, knocking the spearman unconscious and to the ground. His sword immediately met the attack of the unknown swordsman. The clangor of blades increased as they exchanged blows. Though his enemy sought otherwise, Sulayman did not want to kill the men. He wanted to know from where they came and why were they preying on his Isa. "Do not interfere, you Keita goat!" roared the swordsman as the two locked swords and jostled for position.

"What am I interfering with?" screamed Sulayman.

The wooden door of the square-shaped residence unexpectedly creaked open. Locked at their hilts, both men heard Isa step from the light of the interior.

"Sulayman!" she cried.

The sight of Isa brought a sly smirk to Sulayman's face.

With confidence, Sulayman dropped and swept the feet from under his adversary. As the helpless swordsman tried to get off his back, Sulayman followed with a merciless thrust in the man's chest.

The melee was over.

Sulayman wiped his blade on the dead assassin's tunic and quickly searched the grounds for the missing spearman. Apparently, his wound did not prevent him from fleeing. Convinced that the other had escaped, Sulayman sheathed his sword and scanned the blood trail leading over the tall wooden fence.

Isa did not move. In fact, she appeared stunned by the entire situation, which seemed appropriate to Sulayman.

"Two men were here to harm you. But all is well now," reassured Sulayman as he removed the man's veil. He was definitely Mandingo, but Sulayman could not find any henna marks, thus he could not distinguish his tribe.

With her smooth, bare arms wrapped around herself, Isa moved towards Sulayman. She shivered along the way, whether from the chilly night air or the dead assassin who lay in a pool of blood. Her complexion was that of a sickly person, a pale gray with just a touch of burnt red.

"Do you know this man?" asked Sulayman as they hovered over the slain assailant.

Isa shook her head, staring deeply at the dead man.

"I will have this body removed and the other man tracked and found. You do not have to worry." Sulayman wrapped his robe around Isa and held her close. "I will also post guards to protect you." "That is not necessary. You have saved me." Isa glared upwards; her big russet eyes met Sulayman's. "How did you know to be here?" Sulayman looked to the stars above in search of a proper response. "Destiny?" he replied comically. "It is a good thing too, for your sake." His brow crinkled with wonder. "Still, who would send assassins after you?"

"My father is a powerful man in Krina. It would not surprise me if they hoped to kidnap me for his riches."

Sulayman gave an approving grunt. "Stay inside while I tend to the situation." He kissed Isa on the forehead. "Try to rest."

After Isa went inside, Sulayman pilfered the body for any clues to identify the attackers. Though he could not find any letters or items of interest, Sulayman did receive some insight as to where they came from. Emblazoned on the hilt of the assassin's sword was a snake with a sun behind it. Only a fellow warrior would quickly be able to decipher the crest of the Djenné standard.

19.

Musa was nearly finished preparing his wagon for departure. Unsure of his final destination, Musa had resolved himself to the fact that his presence in Niani caused unwanted turmoil. He would say farewell to no one, not even his mother and Sulayman. But before he would abandon all that he had ever known, Musa visited Niani's mosque one last time.

Musa rested upon his knees in meditative prayer. The late hour left the place of worship empty and silent. He was alone in a dark, secluded room of the mosque. Only the flicker of a single candlelight could be heard. With palms extended and tunic top at his waist, Musa's lean muscles glowed from the perspiration covering his body. In his thoughts, he was transported to the moment he and Abubakari stood on the Gambia after the hunt. The words did not escape his thoughts as with most childhood memories.

"Ever wonder what is out there?" "The sea."

"No, there…beyond the sea." "Nothing is there, Abu."

A slight breeze battled the candle, almost extinguishing it. He slowly opened his eyes, but remained in his stance.

"Who dares disturb me during my time of prayer?"

"Baraka, Kankan Musa. It is, I, Es-Saheli." Out of the shadows behind Musa, Es-Saheli slid into view.

Musa quickly turned on his knees and humbly bowed with his hands cupped. "Muezzin? Forgive me for my rudeness. I was unaware that it was you. As salaam malakum."

Es-Saheli eyes widened with his long smile. "Malakum salaam, Kankan Musa. You have my deepest apologies for interrupting your communion with Allah. Please rise, proud warrior. I wish to speak with you."

Musa stood. He noticed a hooded figure shrouded in darkness, standing a few feet behind Es-Saheli. The figure's presence sent an unnerving chill through Musa. He observed the stranger while speaking with Es-Saheli. Musa could only make out the man's forked goatee.

"You come not alone," asked Musa of Es-Saheli.

"He is of no concern. My interests lie with you, Kankan Musa. I am offering you a chance to serve Allah."

"As you are unaware, your eminence, I am leaving Niani." "Lady Kongo mentioned nothing of the sort," replied a surprised Es-Saheli. "Nonetheless, I must request that you remain in Niani. After you complete what I require from you, your departure will not be necessary."

"What do you wish for me to do?" Musa had already resigned himself to leaving, but he was curious as to what the cleric wanted.

Es-Saheli held Musa by the arm and pulled him to the corner of the room. "It is what you will not do that we ask of you," he whispered.

"Will not do?"

"You are next in the mansa bloodline and the deserving heir to the throne of Mali. We only ask that you remain silent as we make arrangements to see your destiny fulfilled."

"You speak of my brother?" Musa put comfortable space between him and Es-Saheli.

"Yes, I speak of Abubakari the Second. He is no longer welcomed as mansa in the eyes of Allah or the Mandingo. It is time you that you take your place, as your mother requests and as the people demand."

Musa had some inclination of the gossip that drifted through the halls of the palace. The people were unhappy with Abubakari as mansa and threatened to rise up if he did not concede to their struggles. Musa had given his brother ample opportunity to be a better man, to be a better leader for the people. His loyalty had reached its end. Musa had to consider his beloved Niani-ba.

Musa closed his eyes, forcing the words from his clenched teeth. "If it is to happen, Abubakari must surrender his title of his own free will."

"And if he does not?"

"Then he will remain as mansa," firmly stated Musa.

Es-Saheli sighed and placed his hand on Musa's shoulder. Musa eyes shifted from the hold to the face of the cleric. Es-Saheli could see that Musa would not budge.

"Your brother has gone mad, Kankan Musa," softly offered Es- Saheli. "The people of Mali have spoken. Allah has spoken. Abubakari the Second has a stranglehold on

208

Mali. He stands between your beloved kingdom and the lands beyond the Sahara. He stands between you and the Omniscient One."

"You would have me betray my brother?"

"Of course not," smirked Es-Saheli. "Although he has no respect for your existence, as he demonstrated to all many moons ago, I understand brotherly loyalty. Open your eyes, Kankan Musa. Your brother would rather jeopardize Niani and all of Mali than lose to a sibling who has always been the better warrior and leader."

By the expression on Musa's face, the cleric knew the intensity of his words had resonated. "There is more to ruling a land than maintaining the gold fields of Wangara and the copper mines of Takedda," is what Musa wanted to say to Abubakari.

"Indeed, much more," added Es-Saheli with a huge smile. "Imagine Niani having the largest mosque in all of Africa, where people from far away lands come to worship Allah. Truly, Allah's light would shine down on the man who let destiny take its course. Are you that man, Kankan Musa? Are you prepared to let the glory of Allah fall upon the Mandingo?"

"I must think deeply before I can answer you, muezzin," responded Musa while shaking his head. "He is still my brother. What ever is done, it would be an act of betrayal in the end. You must understand that."

"Destiny has not a beginning nor an ending," said Es-Saheli with an empathetic nod. "We ask only that you let the prophecy be fulfilled. Do nothing, Kankan Musa. Do nothing."

With that, Es-Saheli and the cloaked stranger faded into the darkness, leaving Musa alone to contemplate his inner feelings. His strength sank into his stomach, and only a terrible ache lingered in his chest.

Sulayman returned to Isa's dwelling a few hours after several royal attendants secretly orchestrated the removal of the assassin's body from the artisan district. He also had five sofa guards stationed on the home's perimeter for Isa's protection. Malian law dictated that all deaths that occurred within Niani must be reported to the appropriate court official. But having discovered the Djenné mark on the assassin's sword hilt, Sulayman had decided that he would report the incidence directly to Abubakari—after he was assured that Isa was in good health.

"Do not go!" cried Isa as she clung to Sulayman's robe.

"Isa, my love, there are guards posted with the orders to die before harm befalls you," laughed Sulayman. "I must return to the palace. It is my duty."

"I am afraid," Isa whispered in his ear. "Comfort me, so that I may sleep well tonight."

Sulayman felt her hands enter his tunic and seductively massage his muscular chest. Her moist lips touched his neck and the heavenly scent of white flower tantalized his imagination. It did not take long to convince him to shirk protocol. As they leaned into the bed, Sulayman removed Isa's top and blew out the last candle.

It was half past the Hour of the Owl before Sulayman and Isa finished making love. Since he had carried his new kora with him initially to Isa's, before he battled the assassins, Sulayman quietly strummed the string instrument, as they lay nude on the fur-covered bedding.

Only the wind knows,

What the rains washed away, Only the butterfly knows, From where it came, Only the clouds above know, Where our destinies lie

"That was the poem you told me when we first spoke to one another," said Sulayman while setting the instrument aside. "I do not have your gift for words, but I have the heart of a musician."

Isa curled into Sulayman holding a chalice filled with the sweet juice of Malian wine. As Sulayman placed his kora on the floor, Isa poured the violet libation down his mouth. The liquid carelessly trickled down the corners of his mouth, as he chortled from slight inebriation.

"I must return to the palace. It is late, and I must inform Abu...I mean my lord." Sulayman stumbled to his feet and donned his tunic. "It is late. Drink more and return at dawn," asked Isa. Her eyes followed the ring of keys that Sulayman moved from his satchel to his belt. She playfully came to her feet and jumped on his back. "Do you take me for a common village trollop? To come and go as you please?"

"It is nothing of the sort." Sulayman comically spun around with Isa on his back and slowly fell onto the bedding with her under him. "Stay," pleaded Isa as she stared into his eyes.

Sulayman caressed her cheek and smiled. He was relieved that she was more spirited than she had been in the past few days. Very soon, he planned to appeal to the mansa for her hand in marriage. For all direct retainers to the mansa had to gain the emperor's approval to wed, which depended greatly on the potential wife.

"I will soon return," responded Sulayman as he regained his feet and attached his scabbard to his belt. "Come and let my lips touch yours before I bid you farewell," came Isa's voice from over his shoulder. He grabbed his robe and kora and knelt beside her. She pulled him closer until he was also supine beside her. They kissed.

Isa maneuvered herself until she lay on top of him. The candlelight danced over Isa's auburn face. Her eyes of sadness and smile of deceit were his first and last warning to where her loyalties lay.

Thump. Thump. Slash.

Fright overcame Sulayman before the pain erupted. With his eyes wide open, his head slowly looked down the surface of his tunic. Isa no longer smiled as she slid off Sulayman with her double-bladed dagger in hand. The sadness in her stare remained. Sulayman shuddered before Isa, whispering to her, unable to determine what had transpired.

Isa, you betrayed me. Why? Why?

I loved you!

Sulayman slowly slipped into unconsciousness. As darkness flooded his vision, Sulayman felt Isa's hands tugging his belt and eventually freeing the keys for the palace's inner chambers from his person.

20.

Abubakari felt at ease while practicing his spear thrusts in the battle-practice chamber. Each downward strike that sliced through the air severed past regrets and resentful thoughts of the days ahead. His tunic was soaked in sweat, and the flames from the surrounding torches glittered off his face.

Ibn entered with sacks draped over his shoulder. He was dressed in the garments he wore when he arrived in Niani, dark tunic and trousers. Abubakari continued his strikes, aware that Ibn was allowed to enter the heavily secured chamber, but ignoring the Arab's presence.

"I shall have to depart Niani, Abu," said Ibn from across the room. "The life of a trader demands that one does not remain in comfort too long."

Abubakari continued practicing his swing. "Every man must follow his path. You must follow yours." The young mansa's feet left the floor as he twirled around, simulating defending himself from rear attackers. Thoughts of his brother and his stillborn drained the energy from his muscle and bones. He wondered if Musa considered the anguish that accompanied those who rule. If only we could have united as brothers. If only our paths were not so different.

Abubakari stopped his thrusts with a final strike on the porcelain floor.

"I came to say goodbye, but I am sure that my travels will bring me to Niani-ba once again," Ibn called out with a hardy smile. "Always know that I am never too far."

Abubakari smiled. "I believe our destinies will find each other, my friend."

Ibn turned to leave, and then he remembered that he had questions for his friend. "Ah, I understand that you are sending another fleet to the Green Sea of Darkness?"

"Yes," answered Abubakari.

"There are feelings of discontent within Mali. Take caution, Abu," said Ibn with a concerned countenance.

"I will."

Ibn nodded and turned to depart. He paused for a moment and faced Abubakari once more. "Oh, yes. You inquired once before whether one can be good and evil?"

"Yes, I remember," responded Abubakari with higher interest. "I do know this. Although it may seem comfortable to retreat into the darkness, it is so much better in the light. The Great Sahel awaits me." Ibn bowed. "Until our paths meet again, my friend."

"Until then, my friend."

Ibn winked and left the chamber. Abubakari sadly watched him leave, secretly wishing the Arab safe passage across the Sahara.

Outside the door, within the narrow passage leading to the battle-practice chamber, stood Abubakari's attendants. The way their white cloaks reflected the torches and the moonlight that slipped through the open portals above gave them a porcelain doll appearance. Eight more sofa guards lined the walls like statues.

Ibn exited the chamber and nodded to the women, who stoically lowered their heads as he passed. "Ladies." He continued down the well-guarded passage.

Isa dressed herself and opened the door for the cloaked man who waited outside. Peeking over the man's shoulders, Isa spotted the slain sofa guards piled atop each other in the middle of the small courtyard. More men lurked in the shadows near the gate.

"We are prepared," said the hooded man standing before Isa. His face was hidden, with the exception of the forked goatee that covered his pink lips. "You shall finally have your revenge."

"We will meet in Krina." Isa handed the man Sulayman's key ring. "Make sure you have his head in your possession."

"You and the cleric are making me far too wealthy to not fulfill my task. Leave quickly. Once we begin, escape may not be possible for a woman such as yourself."

"I must gather all traces of my presence. Then I can go."

Isa checked over her shoulder. "Have you gained access to the palace?" "Yes, our allies proved helpful. Gaining entry into the inner

chambers was our only hindrance."

"Very good," Isa replied. "I will make contact in Krina." After the mysterious man turned away, Isa closed the door and dashed into the bed area. She quickly began gathering her personal items from the rickety tables in the room. It never occurred to her that Sulayman was no longer on the bed, only the large bloodstain he left behind.

"You spit on the one who cherishes you," grunted Sulayman after appearing behind Isa and placing the blade of his shortsword under her neck.

Isa was startled but maintained her serene demeanor. "I had no choice. You were not supposed to come tonight." She slowly faced him. They were close enough to feel each other's breath. "I never wanted to harm you."

"Is that so?" groaned Sulayman. His other hand held tightly to his wounds, which should have been fatal. Bleeding to death was a possibility, but the vest given to him by Camara proved its worth. The dagger attack dug into his flesh but did not penetrate any major organs. Sulayman knew that Isa was not a professional assassin.

"I had planned to take the keys another day while you slept. But after witnessing what you did tonight, I could not allow you to inform the palace."

"You are planning to kill my brother." Sulayman kept the blade at her throat. His vision intermittently became blurred. Struggling to remain conscious, Sulayman gritted his teeth. "He has shown you and your brethren nothing but kindness! Why?"

Isa's watery eyes became slits filled with rage. "I am not

the daughter of a blacksmith from Krina. I am the daughter of Abayomi, King of Djenné!"

"Abayomi?" said an astonished Sulayman. He felt the wind leave his body, as he lowered his sword. The woman whom he had considered for marriage suddenly became a distant stranger before his eyes.

"My father sent me here to only gather information as to the sincerity of Abubakari's treaty," continued Isa. "But after your brother betrayed my beloved father, I could not leave Niani until I saw Abubakari dead."

"How can you be so certain that my brother was responsible?" "I am certain."

"So, this is about revenge! How far do you think your assassins will get before they are massacred by sofa guards?"

"Do not be so foolish, Sulayman," chuckled Isa. "I am not alone with this endeavor. I simply boarded a carriage that had already chosen its destination."

Never had Sulayman heard Isa laugh so hideously. As her laugh grew louder, the angrier he became. Yet a feeling of sympathy channeled through his weakened body. He sensed the madness in her voice and wanted to help her return to the woman he thought he knew. Nevertheless, Sulayman knew what had to be done.

Slash.

A single tear trickled down Sulayman's cheek, as he watched Isa's headless body fall before him. He could not look at her any longer. His eyes followed the bright red blood that streaked down his blade and poured from her neck.

Sulayman reached into his tunic and pulled out Isa's violet, translucent veil. He breathed in her white flower fragrance one last time as he considered his next steps. There were more people involved in this coup than he could trust.

Sulayman had to get word to the palace, but he did not want to alert those against him. Everyone was suspect, including some of his own men.

Once it finally occurred to him who to seek out, Sulayman wiped the blade of his sword with the veil and let the cloth fall to the floor. He had no time to spare. Leaving his kora behind, Sulayman stumbled out the dark abode.

Just outside the chamber where Abubakari practiced his halberd, twenty hooded figures slowly marched down the corridor to where the attendants stood. One man who was determined to see the mansa led them.

With their hands clasped on their forearms and covered by the large sleeves of their robes, the attendants lowered their heads before the man with the forked goatee. He removed his hood and revealed a pale face with sunken, cold eyes and a scar that ran from his eye to his chin. Known as Khalid in dark circles, he exuded a foreboding presence.

"I carry a message from the muezzin for the mansa," requested
Khalid with a slight bow.

Without lifting their heads, the two women spoke simultaneously. "The Great Mansa will no longer have an audience. Please accept our apology on his behalf."

"I must demand to see him. It is an urgent message."

"Please accept our apology and take your leave," monotonously replied the attendants.

Khalid took a few steps backward as a breeze suddenly caused the torches to flicker rapidly. The sofa guards uneasily closed in on the robed trespassers, and the attendants raised their heads in unison. Khalid let his robe fall to the floor to expose his black tunic, covered with black leather armor, swords, and an assortment of daggers. The other hooded figures, a mix of Africans and Arabs, also let their robes fall to the floor, exposing their arsenal of weapons. The sentries along the walls moved in, but to the surprise of the attendants, the dark sofa warriors joined the assailants with spears raised.

"I will have to insist," sneered Khalid.

Abubakari focused on every swing, every whirl. He combined strength and adroitness with each thrust of the halberd, unaware of what was taking place just outside the chamber.

Two of Khalid's men with broadswords hunched their way towards the two attendants. The women did not move to leave their station, but lifted their heads and glared at the approaching men.

"Step aside, woman!" demanded one.

"We do not have time to toil with servant girls!" teased the other. The women did not respond. Of course, when one lifts a stone from a serene creek, one never expects to see a poisonous viper lying underneath. The two men made the mistake of grabbing the women
by the sleeves of their tunics.

Simultaneously, both women unsheathed two double-edged shortswords from the sleeves of their robes. Before the men could react, their throats were dislodged from their necks by the fierce slashes of the ruthless females. The men fell instantly to the floor, gasping for air.

Khalid took a deep breath and angrily waved all the men forward. They charged ahead in full battle cry.

One attendant attacked while the other attendant remained in defense of the door.

The aggressive attendant met the charge with her two swords of death. With a snarl, she fearlessly danced through the rush, repelling sword blows and slicing the flesh of the men who screamed in agony as they fell. Blood splattered on her white robe. She repelled a sofa's spear thrust and proceeded to disembowel him with one stab after the other.

The attendant near the door crouched into a formidable stance as men rushed towards her. Their swords clashed with hers. She evaded their blows without moving from her position. As a blade whizzed over her head, she stooped and sliced through two of their legs as she twirled. Another sofa charged after, launching his spear. The attendant evaded the missile, and the spearhead embedded itself in the wooden door. She gutted him with her swords and kicked his lifeless corpse off her blades.

Khalid stood back and watched the melee unfold, waiting for his moment to strike.

Within his chambers, Musa prayed upon his knees. He closed his eyes and leaned forward to let his forehead touch his knees. Though he gave all praise to his god, Musa also prayed to the memory of his father. He begged for forgiveness and stated that he could do no more to help Abubakari.

"Forgive me, Abu. I must think of the good of the Keita and Niani- ba," muttered Musa in hopes that his thoughts reached his brother.

Musa then remembered the conversation with Es-Saheli at the mosque. Images of Es-Saheli's eyes, lips, and the man in the shadows behind the muezzin appeared. The words became clear as they resurfaced in his thoughts.

"Destiny has not a beginning nor an ending. We ask only

that you let the prophecy be fulfilled. Do nothing, Kankan Musa. Do nothing."

Musa's eyes widened with great realization just as Sulayman blasted into the room.

In crab-like fashion, Abubakari twirled the halberd around his waist and followed through with an upward swing. He practiced tirelessly, but he had yet to hear the deba play for him.

The battle paused for a moment in the corridor. Bodies were strewn along the bloody floor, and the attendants stood poised for more, breathing heavily from the melee. Their robes were torn and decorated with streaks of others' blood. Although there were only seven men left standing, the attendants were rapidly tiring.

Khalid waved the men forward. "Take the door before the mansa escapes. I will have a taste of this one."

The seven men rushed towards one attendant as Khalid approached the other near the door. Out came his large broadsword.

"What are your orders, my lord?" said Fela. He arrived at Musa's private chamber immediately after Musa's servant alerted the officer of the emergency.

"Gather our most trusted men and have them meet me at the battle-practice chamber as swiftly as possible," commanded Musa of the graying sofa warrior and his loyal retainer. "If I still know my brother, that is where he is located." Musa snapped the last buckle of his belt and secured his sword in the scabbard on his hip.

"I feel we must hurry." Sulayman winced as Musa's

male-servant cleansed and bandaged his deep wounds. The young Mandingo had used most of his energy hiding his wounds from onlookers when he returned to the palace. Sulayman could no longer stand, and he soon lost consciousness.

"Fela, you must move silently but quickly. They have access to the inner chambers. This is bigger than you and me, so tread carefully."

The veteran warrior nodded at Musa's words and departed. Musa knelt beside Sulayman and rested his hand on his younger brother's head. "Please tend to his health," he said to the servant, who obediently nodded. Musa worried for Sulayman but knew that he had to reach Abubakari before the men that Sulayman warned him of. Musa kissed Sulayman on the forehead and headed for the door. "Do not tell anyone that he is here," hissed Musa before leaving the candle-lit chamber, "not even our mother."

The two young women were trained to serve the mansa in every capacity, including sacrificing their lives if necessary. Abubakari the Second's attendants did not conceive their own thoughts. On the contrary, they became extensions of their lord, bred from birth with the mandate to shield the mansa from any unforeseen dangers. Thus, to die tragically was no different than serving their lord baobab leaf tea.

The attendant's limp body slid down the bloodstained blade of Khalid's broadsword. Blood trickled from the corner of her mouth as she glared into his evil eyes. She ultimately fell to the floor and died. Khalid wiped his sword on her white robe and waved his four remaining men to the battle-practice chamber door.

The men scurried over the body of the other slain attendant. After using Sulayman's keys to unlock the door, they entered the chamber with weapons readied, followed by Khalid.

21.

Abubakari stood sternly with his halberd extended. He was out of breath, and sweat poured down his brow. Shadows raced the perimeter of the chamber, alerting Abubakari that he was no longer alone.

One after another, the torches that lined the walls were all extinguished, as a whistling breeze swept through the spacious chamber. Only the blue rays of moonlight from the building's high portals provided Abubakari with illumination. The mansa discerned the shadows of the assassins darting across the blue rays and then dissolving out of sight.

"Who is there?" shouted Abubakari. "Show yourself!" Abubakari pivoted with each footstep and unsheathed sword that echoed in the darkness. What trickery is this? He readied his halberd, knowing that danger had entered the chamber.

"We have not had the pleasure to meet, mansa." From behind him appeared Khalid into the light, holding tightly to his two broadswords.

"Who are you?" Abubakari stared him down with curiosity as well as disdain. "How did you enter this chamber? It is forbidden to clerics!" Abubakari remained still, as his eyes followed the approaching path of the scarred Arab.

"Ah, but I am no cleric," laughed Khalid. "I am a merchant of life and death."

"Mercenary!" realized Abubakari. "Keep your distance

if you do not wish to perish at the tip of my blade!"

"Those who dwell in the darkness serve only one purpose, mansa. I am no different. If I am to die at your hands, it is my destiny. However, it is very unlikely that you can defeat me."

Abubakari suddenly became conscious of the situation. His guards and attendants were most likely slain at the hands of the man before him. With the exception of the royal guard who secured the inner chambers each hour, only Sulayman had access to every level required to reach the battle practice chamber. Had Sulayman died as well? Who conspired against me? Es-Saheli? Kongo? Kankan Musa?

"Who hired you, you dirty hyena?" snapped Abubakari. "I will have the lot of you strapped to the palace and castrated for such treason!"

"That I cannot provide. I can only tell you that Abubakari the Second will not live through the night. Is that satisfactory?"

The other four men stepped into view with their swords drawn, surrounding Abubakari on each corner. Abubakari's jaw tightened and he held firm to the long staff of his halberd. Using his peripheral vision, he shifted his glare to each assassin around him. Abubakari quickly twirled his halberd to put space between him and the assailants. His staff's blade hummed through the air.

"Stand back! I will have your heads, traitors!" threatened Abubakari.

"I am afraid that your reign has come to an end," sighed Khalid. Khalid slowly moved in as the other four men rushed Abubakari. Crouching low, Abubakari evaded the sword swing of one and repelled the strike with the tip of his halberd. He rolled and fended off the vicious swing of another. He regained his stance, but his illness unexpectedly returned. Bright red blood and mucous erupted from his mouth. As Abubakari coughed violently, he was sliced in the arm by another assassin's blade. Abubakari screamed in pain and moved out of the circle of men.

Khalid quickly pounced on him with repeated swings of both his broadswords. Abubakari stepped backwards, repelling each deathblow from both sides. Fatigue and the throbbing from his wound weakened Abubakari and allowed Khalid's last swing to gash his abdomen. Abubakari tumbled backwards, holding the wound that saturated his tunic with crimson.

Khalid exposed his maniacal grin as Abubakari struggled to regain his feet. Abubakari used his halberd to balance himself as pain permeated his face. Like wild animals stalking their prey, the five assassins closed in. Abubakari barely stood, with one hand to extend the halberd and the other to grasp the wound. He collapsed to a knee once more, and his head dropped. The sweat that commingled with his blood dripped to the floor.

"Perhaps, only in death can one find peace," whispered Abubakari to himself.

Suddenly, in his hazy state, Abubakari began hearing what he had never heard before—a sound that he believed would never occur. What he had hoped to achieve finally happened.

"I have done it!" Abubakari celebrated. It was the deba drum that played for the young mansa, deep within his thoughts. He heard the inner drum that guided the Mandingo warrior in battle, dictating his every move. Its melody reawakened Abubakari.

Abubakari's smile caused Khalid to pause momentarily.

He could not understand the joy in a man who was about to die. "Finish him," ordered Khalid.

An assassin swung for Abubakari's neck, but Abubakari effortlessly repelled the attack with his halberd and dug his spear's tip into the man's abdomen, through and through. Abubakari lifted his head to unveil eyes of steel. He forcefully lifted himself up and stood proudly with a defiant smirk. Abubakari ripped his halberd from the assassin's midsection, pulling flesh with it. The slain man fell.

Two more men rushed Abubakari with their swords drawn. Abubakari held the staff of his weapon on both ends and promptly used the pole to deflect their strikes. He then followed with a crouching slash across their bellies, concurrently disemboweling them. They wobbled, coughed, and buckled to their deaths.

Khalid held the remaining assassin from attacking and stared deeply into the eyes of Abubakari. In a single motion, Khalid folded his arms and then hurled two daggers into the upper chest of Abubakari.

Thump. Thump.

Abubakari swayed for a moment and dropped his halberd. He fell to his knees and rolled backwards. As blood trickled from the corners of his mouth, the deba no longer played for Abubakari. Abubakari gasped for air and blood filled his chest.

Khalid and the other assassin stood above him, grinning from ear to ear. "I commend you, mansa. You do not die very easily." Khalid placed the tip of his sword to Abubakari's throat.

Zip! Thump!

Khalid turned and found a javelin embedded in the chest of the man beside him. The man vomited blood and collapsed. On guard, Khalid turned and found Musa darting towards him while unsheathing his sword. Khalid launched throwing daggers at the oncoming Musa, but Musa easily deflected the projectiles with his blade and dexterity.

Just as Khalid unsheathed his second sword, his blades were met by the downward strike of Musa's sword. They pushed each other away and stood poised for battle. The blue moonlight bounced off the lean frames of the dark warrior and his Arabian adversary.

"Who sent you, snake-dweller?" shouted Musa. "Do not pretend you were unaware, Musa."

"N'ko. You are the one who hides in the darkness."

"So it seems." Khalid studied Musa for a moment. His eyes then expanded with wonder. "Wait! It is you! Do you remember? We battled in the Sahara many moons ago. It was you who gave me this scar!" Khalid raised his swords in preparation to pounce. "I have searched long and far for you, and I shall now have my revenge. This time, the wind will not save you, Mandingo."

"And I seek vengeance for my brother," Musa snarled. "So it is fate that one of us dies here."

Musa charged. His sword clashed with Khalid's blades several times before they came to another standstill. Both men were drenched in sweat and hunched for the next melee.

"You are much slower than I recall," taunted Khalid. "I am sorry to disappoint you, snake-dweller!"

Their swords clashed once again; back and forth they danced for an advantage. Their silhouettes before the moonlight backdrop was electrified with the spark created by the metallic weapons.

Khalid swung high, and the blades whistled inches from the crouching Musa, who quickly worked his way behind the

Arab. Khalid reversed his swing and brought his fierce weapons around for another attempt at Musa's head. Musa stooped and deflected the blows with his sword. Musa quickly rolled to a safe distance and stood with sword ready. Khalid waited with his glaring orbits absorbing the indigo of the moonlight.

Without warning, Khalid hurled two throwing knives at Musa. One struck Musa in the leg, and the other whistled past his ear. Musa grunted as he ripped the knife from his thigh. He noticed a green substance that coated the blade, which now entered his bloodstream. Poison. Musa knew that once the venom took effect, it was a matter of seconds before he would lose consciousness. Where is Fela? He had to end the fight as quickly as possible.

"Can you hear the drum?" said Musa with a confident smile, though he stumbled slightly from the immediate effects of the venom.

"What drum do you speak of, Mandingo?" Khalid was perplexed but entertained. "Foolish words cannot help a dying man."

Musa tensed up and brought the sword to his chest in a praying motion. The Keita prince closed his eyes in meditation, ignoring the merciless adversary near him.

Khalid twirled his blades in anticipation of another round of battle and charged ahead. He planned to sever Musa's arms and let the poison kill him slowly. After his death, Khalid expected to decapitate the Mandingo and keep his head as a trophy. The dark fire in his eyes could not be denied.

With both hands on the hilt, and with all of his strength, Musa slung his sword at the unsuspecting Khalid. It rapidly twirled through the air. Before Khalid could raise his guard, the projectile's sharp tip embedded itself into Khalid's throat and exited the back of the neck.

Blood spurted from Khalid's mouth, as he choked all the way to the mosaic floor. His swords fell from his hands and clanged on the floor, just before the Arab landed on his back. He looked up at Musa swaying above him.

"It seems that fate is on your side, but you are too late, Mandingo," gurgled Khalid as his chest became still.

Musa took a moment to watch the Arab take his last breath, before immediately making his way to Abubakari's side. Careful not to disturb the two daggers embedded in Abubakari's chest, Musa fell to his knees and gently lifted the limp Abubakari into his lap. Musa cared not for the blood that flowed from Abubakari and smeared his own tunic. The weak breath that came from Abubakari gave him hope.

"I am here, Brother, and will remain by your side, always." Tears poured down his face. "Allah, do not take his soul now. I beg of you." Musa's body quivered with each cry as he rested his head into the chest of Abubakari.

The mansa's stained hand suddenly clutched Musa's shoulder. Musa's eyes widened with astonishment to find his brother's eyes open and his face bearing a grin. Musa smiled in return. Elated, he chuckled.

Abubakari's mouth slowly crept open. "I heard the drum, Brother. I heard the drum." He then closed his eyes and drifted into unconsciousness.

Tears of joy pervaded Musa's cheeks. Perhaps the daggers in Abubakari's chest were not poisoned, though he had lost a great deal of blood. He held tightly to his brother as Fela and several sofa warriors flooded the chamber with weapons drawn.

22.

A golden-red radiance lined the Malian savannah as the sun peaked over its dry plains. A flock of blackbirds took umbrage under the huge silk-cotton Tree of Malabar just outside the palace, where African kings ruled for generations. Sofa warriors surrounded the palace and the walls of Niani, for the search had begun.

In her usual ivory hijab, Kongo exited the mosque with her entourage of six female-servants, just as several sofas, led by Musa, raced past her.

"Step aside, Mother." Musa did not waste any time to have the medicine man treat the poison and bandage his wound. Es-Saheli had betrayed Musa's emotions and played upon his Moslem faith to have his brother killed, and Musa wanted justice for the muezzin.

"Of course," Kongo acknowledged.

The sofas dispersed, revealing Mariama, Namandje, and their guard escorts. Kongo stopped and smirked at the two women as if she were regarding two untouchables.

Musa and his sofas shattered the door to the head cleric's chamber. The archaic room was filled with rare vases and golden- laid furniture. The men dispersed and searched the many clandestine enclosures within the chamber. They found several empty chests that were once filled with the gold donations of the Niani faithful.

"We are too late," resigned Fela.

"Do not worry, Fela." Musa sheathed his sword and sighed in utter disappointment. "There is no where he can hide that Allah will not find him."

Namandje stood inches from Kongo's face with a

scornful expression. Never had she held such a deep hatred for anyone until that day. As beautiful as she was to behold, Namandje's true beauty lay inside. She was queen, with the power to sentence almost anyone to death, justly or unjustly. Yet she believed that death had already caused great misery for all she loved deeply. Namandje made a promise to herself that she would undertake the reign of queen and use her power to create a more peaceful Mali.

"How fortunate that the mansa did not fall victim to this dreaded conspiracy. But he is alive, and that is what matters most," Kongo said. "Even now, you proclaim your ignorance," said Namandje as she shook her head in pity. "Everyone knows that you cater to Es-Saheli."

"I cannot be held responsible for the activities of a rogue muezzin."

"You are a liar!" Namandje spat angrily.

"Mariama, I see that you have not taught this little girl manners befitting a queen," Kongo smirked.

Mariama stepped between them, shielding Namandje from the evil woman. "I cannot prove your ties to my son's assassination attempt at this moment, Kongo, but I will."

"Mariama, you are amusing as usual," Kongo replied. "I could never understand why my husband took a fool such as yourself as his wife. Excuse me, I must return to the palace to care for my beloved Sulayman."

"That you cannot do, Kongo." The enjoyment in Mariama's voice was clear. "Indeed, your chamber has been confiscated until it is determined who was disloyal to the lord."

"How dare you? The council will not stand for it!" Kongo became uncharacteristically flustered, but she quickly gathered herself. "Nevertheless, I will have my servants gather my possessions, and I will reside at the mosque where I belong."

"We have already tended to that for you, Lady Kongo," offered

Namandje. "What?"

"Yes, servants removed your possessions and relocated them to where I thought you would like them to go," interjected Mariama. "I believe they were dumped in the forest to the north. I understand that you often travel there."

Kongo said nothing. She stared angrily at both women, and the unforeseen creases in her brow surfaced before their eyes. Kongo wondered how much more they knew about her escapades and decided not to retaliate verbally. She did not want to risk knowledge of her involvement with Abubakari's assassination attempt.

Musa and his guards exited the Niani mosque in disappointment. Musa immediately approached Kongo.

"Es-Saheli has escaped. Fortunately, we have taken several of his

marabouts into custody. Mother, do you know of his whereabouts?" "I do not know," she responded nonchalantly.

Musa returned his attention to the men exiting the mosque. "Disperse. Notify all surrounding villages that Es-Saheli is to be captured in the name of Niani-ba. All those who disobey and provide safe harbor shall be viewed as treasonous." The sofa warriors lowered their heads and dispersed as ordered. "Do not worry, Queen Namandje. We will find him." Musa gave Namandje a reassuring glance and quickly departed.

She did not hear her brother-in-law. Namandje never took her hateful eyes off Kongo until Mariama grabbed her by the shoulders. "Namandje, we must return to the palace," whispered Mariama as

she tugged at the young queen.

"A wise decision," said Kongo as her hateful glare followed their departure. "It can be very dangerous for a young woman outside its walls."

Namandje let Mariama pull her away. She realized there would come a day when she would have to deal with Kongo, and Mariama may not be there to guide her. If Namandje only knew how alone she was truly destined to be, she would have hurt much more than she did at that moment.

The moment Es-Saheli had learned that his attempt on Abubakari's life had failed, he had raped his mosque's treasury and headed northeast along the Niger. Under the guise of a traveling nobleman, he hired a carriage to take him as far as the large village. It took only eight days for Es-Saheli to reach Timbuktu.

"How soon can you depart for Khartoum?" Es-Saheli whispered to the bearded Arab who sat across from him in the dark inn. The pseudo-cleric glanced over his shoulder to ensure that the other three African patrons were out of earshot.

"Are you traveling alone?"

"Yes," Es-Saheli answered nervously.

"I expect half the payment before we depart and the other half once we arrive," said the man with conviction.

"Very well." Es-Saheli reached into his robe and withdrew a small purse filled with gold coins. He handed to the guide across the wooden table, careful not to singe his hand on the candle.

"Meet at the largest dune, just east of the city, at the Hour of the Owl. From there, we shall leave for the Sudan. I know that it is soon, but the best way to avoid Keita patrols is under the cover of darkness."

"I see. Excellent. That should give me nearly an hour to enjoy a goblet of wine." Es-Saheli was in good spirits. "Oh, wait! What of the items in my possession? They are somewhat cumbersome, but nearby."

The man sighed. "I will send one of my men here with a wagon to assist you to the dune. He will arrive here at half past the Hour of the Wolf. Is that reasonable?"

"Indeed," Es-Saheli responded with joy. His large eyes finally relaxed.

They nodded to each other, and the man departed.

Es-Saheli trusted the guide, since a mutual friend in Timbuktu recommended him, though the guide did not know Es-Saheli's identity. Actually, the cleric had little choice in the matter. Es-Saheli was deemed a rebel by Canco Palace, and every sofa warrior, villager, and bounty hunter searched for him. He could feel the snake coiling around his feet. Sooner or later, Es-Saheli knew that someone would see through his full beard and hood. But once he learned that his departure across the Sahara was secured, he felt at ease.

"Bring me a goblet of your finest wine," Es-Saheli instructed the young servant girl of the establishment.

"You are very fortunate," informed the petite server with a friendly brown face. "We just received a new delivery of the finest Fèsian wine available."

"Excellent. Well then, make it a carafe. I have little time to drink it, but I will try."

They have Fèsian wine. This is a clear sign that Allah is shining down upon me. How auspicious a moment this is. Es-Saheli also thought of the failed coup. He wondered how Lady Kongo was faring as the palace surely investigated other parties. Then he convinced himself that she deserved whatever punishment she received. Lady Kongo was the instigator; I was only the pawn in the entire scheme. I allowed myself to fall victim to a woman's charm. So, this is my reward for trying to bring some civility to this god-forsaken land!

The servant-girl returned with a flask of wine and a goblet. She carefully poured the wine for Es-Saheli and left him alone to sip the Moroccan inebriant.

"You did well," said the waiting stranger in the kitchen. He gave the servant girl a huge purse filled with gold coins. "Take this and leave quickly. It will give you a new life. Sofa patrols will find him soon enough. You do not want to be here."

The server smiled at the size of her reward. "Tell me stranger, why are you so kind to that traveler?" She reached into the sack and let the coins surround her fingers. "Why do you not give him the wine yourself?"

"I am just doing an old friend a favor. That is all. Now go." "Thank you for your generosity." She heeded the stranger's suggestion and exited the rear door of the inn.

Not long after, an old African man with a wagon arrived at the inn. He immediately recognized Es-Saheli seated with his head in his hands, especially since the cleric was the only remaining patron.

"Sir, I was sent to escort you to the dunes. Let us depart as soon as possible."

Es-Saheli did not respond.

"Ah, you should not enjoy life so much before traveling," amiably scolded the small venerable man. He moved closer to Es- Saheli. "Where are your possessions?"

Es-Saheli did not respond.

"Hey, we have no time to frolic." Slightly uneasy, the small man hunched down and nudged the unresponsive Es-Saheli.

Es-Saheli's arms fell limp and his face crashed onto the table, knocking over the carafe and scattering the wine across the table. He was dead. The old man panicked and immediately left the inn without notifying anyone.

As the wine dripped from the table's edge and splattered on the stone floor, Es-Saheli's large eyes had not closed, and his mouth gaped open. He bore the horrific gaze of one attempting to escape his evils, but to no avail.

The stranger mounted his camel, which he had tied in the rear of the inn. He reached behind him to ensure that the two satchels filled with gold were securely fastened to his saddle. Ibn then thought of his friend, Abubakari.

"We were right, Abu. Look inside the heart and you will find both good and evil."

Ibn didn't expect Abubakari to hear his words, though he said them with his normal sarcastic tone. He grabbed the reins of his camel and slowly trotted off into the night.

23.

1311 C.E.

Sulayman supervised the security for the collection of annual taxes, a duty that occurred every New Year's Day. As envoys for the various villages streamed through the palace's main gate, sofa guards guided them to the southeastern grounds, where court clerks assessed grain, gold, salt, and cattle.

"Ho, Master Sulayman! How are you?" came a man's

voice from over the young officer's shoulder.

"Ah, Camara!" Sulayman dismounted as soon as he saw the small man peeking through the palace gate. He had not seen his kora teacher since the assassination attempt and the night he lost Isa. "Come with me." Sulayman was thrilled but maintained his professional soldier persona until the two men were away from the guards.

"I have great news!" Sulayman nearly knocked Camara over with his friendly nudge. "I have negotiated a position for you as the official court musician!"

Camara was unmoved by the news.

"Surely, you are excited by such news?" Sulayman's enthusiasm slowly waned after seeing the musician's solemn expression. "I know that I have ignored my lessons in the last month or so, but now you are a direct retainer to the mansa. I can take my lessons within the palace." "I am most grateful by your generosity, my lord," finally answered

Camara. "But I came here to tell you that I will soon leave Niani." "Leave? Where will you go?"

"I must return to my native village of Tabon and care for my father. He is not well."

Sulayman had buried his feelings for his father, Abubakari the First, since the late mansa's death. They suddenly surfaced and his eyes watered in despair. Of all three of Abubakari's sons, his relationship with Sulayman had been the strongest. Perhaps it was due to the fact that the mansa's efforts to expand Mali had subsided shortly after Sulayman's birth.

"N'ko. I understand," said Sulayman as he patted his friend on the shoulder. "I will miss you."

"My lord, did you recover your kora?" "Yes."

The small man with soft features exhaled in relief. "Do

not let your skills diminish in my absence, Master Sulayman," Camara teased. "I will return when all is well and test your ability on the kora."

Sulayman laughed. "You are such a righteous fellow. The blood of the Soninke must run through your veins." The Soninke were known for their piousness and pompousness in equal proportions, attributes that made them excellent traders.

"A child whose hand is clean may eat with the elders," replied Camara with his normal dry humor. "What does that mean?"

Camara tilted his head in contemplation. "Unsure. But, it was something my father incessantly said to me as a child." Camara's chuckle grew to a hearty laugh.

Once their laughter dissipated, the two men clasped hands and came forearm to forearm in a brotherly grip. Camara appeared somewhat awkward, for this was the hold of the warrior. Their eyes met with the gaze of those who would never see each other again.

"You saved my life, Camara," said Sulayman, "and I will be forever in your debt. You are a Mandingo warrior in heart, and that is everything."

Sulayman's remark brought tears to Camara's eyes. He had never wanted to be warrior-class. He believed them to be barbaric and rash by nature. Yet meeting Sulayman transformed his perception of the sofa warrior. The musician had fallen in love with the warrior, though he swore he would never reveal that side of himself to Sulayman. Nonetheless, a timeless bond was made on that day—one that could revive itself, when needed, many years later.

"Farewell, Camara of Tabon." "Farewell, my lord."

Sulayman had not visited his father's grave since the late

mansa received his burial rites. He was just a child then, unable to comprehend that his father would never return to play with him. With his kora in hand, Sulayman found a comfortable spot to sit in the royal graveyard, where the remains of ancient kings and queens were laid to rest. Huge headstones dotted the grassy hill. To his left, there was his father's, decorated with gold and the crest of the Keita. To his right lay Kalabi Naman, the prince who died at birth.

He strummed a few notes on the stringed instrument, looking up to the clear blue skies. Sulayman could not remember the last time that the sky was absent of any clouds. Yet the sun did not scorch him, for a gentle breeze encircled the palace grounds.

"Such a propitious day, and so much has changed." Sulayman smiled with his eyes closed. He then looked to his left and then his right. "Shall I sing a song to my father and nephew?" He strummed a few more times as images of his father, Kalabi, and Isa streaked through his mind.

Only the wind knows,

What the rains washed away, Only the butterfly knows,
From where it came,

Only the clouds above know, Where our destinies lie

"One day I will learn another song. Until then, please bear with me." He closed his eyes with a gratifying smile and drifted asleep.

Abubakari sat peacefully upon the 3-tiered pavilion with silk- carpeted steps, just outside the palace's gate. The Tree of Malabar provided ample shade from the bright sun. Abubakari inhaled the sweet fragrance of the baobab fruit, which blossomed in the ninth month. Although his wounds were nearly healed, Abubakari's chest ached from his battles with heart consumption. His velvet tunic neatly covered the bandages.

Musa slowly strolled past the sofa guards at the base of the pavilion and took his seat next to Abubakari. The two brothers scanned the horizon, littered with village structures and people in the distance going through their day.

"I must believe that my dreams are not the thoughts of a madman," said Abubakari without looking at Musa.

"I do not agree with your plan to send another fleet to the Great Abyss, but I now understand your feelings," calmly replied Musa. "There is something else that I must tell you." Abubakari smiled.

"This time, I shall also take to the sea. I will go with them."

Musa faced his brother, bewildered. "You will go? But you are mansa. You are not permitted. You have a kingdom without an heir…"

"I am not well," interrupted Abubakari as he continued to gaze at the horizon. "The decision has been made. As for Mali, I shall leave you as regent and leader. My family will remain behind in your care. It is a heavy weight to bear, Brother. I am eternally grateful."

Musa became slightly agitated. "And what if you are not able to return? Have you considered that possibility?"

"I have considered many things in recent days," replied Abubakari with introspective overtones. "If I do not return in a year's time, then you will become mansa, Kankan."

"I refuse! It is a selfish and an unwise decision." Musa defiantly came to his feet. He did not want to lose the love that he felt for his older brother.

Abubakari also stood. He shared his beaming grin with Musa and emitted a sort of peace that reflected under the sun, creating a beautiful aura. "But it is my decision…one that I should have made many moons ago." Abubakari placed a hand on Musa's shoulder. "Perhaps, it may have saved the pain and suffering I have caused, especially to you, Brother."

"I have no pain. I have not suffered."

"I know I have caused you great heartache," whispered Abubakari. "When one finds peace, all that he has done, good and evil, is revealed."

"And he abandons his charge, his country, his blood?" Abubakari stepped into Musa's view. His smile faded, and regret followed.

"Kankan, I hated you. All my life, I hated you. I despised your beauty. Strong and pure at heart, you are everything I am not." A tear trickled down Abubakari's cheek. "And yet you remained by my side, always."

Musa's clenched his teeth to hold back the tears. "What else would a brother do?" said Musa through a fluttering lip.

"Forgive me, younger brother," pleaded Abubakari.

Musa could no longer hold back his tears, nor could Abubakari. He responded to Abubakari's apology with a simple nod. They then returned their gaze to the horizon.

"If you discover what you search for, Brother, come home." Abubakari nodded. "Father once said, we must stay united for a strong Mali. Somehow, we have." The sun was quickly descending into the horizon. Abubakari squinted from a sunray that penetrated the silk-cotton tree. He wiped the wetness from his cheek. "I will always be part of Niani-ba, even when I depart what is known."

The landscape swallowed the red sun as the two silhouettes watched from the pavilion.

24.

Six Months Later

In her private chambers, Namandje prayed before a small memorial for Kalabi Naman. Between the two candles on the pedestal were a colorful blanket that she had woven during her pregnancy and the small gown she expected to dress him in. Above those articles sat a statue of Lebe Serou, the primordial ancestor of Dogon.

After prayer, Namandje caressed the part of her robe that covered her slightly protruding belly, which brought a smile to her face. She was once again with child, though no one had known of her condition until four months after Abubakari departed. The young queen knew, but did not want to burden her husband with the knowledge that he was leaving behind a child as well. Namandje wanted Abubakari to have his dream, but his absence saddened her deeply. She prayed for his return.

The serenity of the dimly lit chamber was interrupted by a voice behind the door.

"My queen, Djeliba Mamadou Kouyaté requests an audience with Your Greatness."

"Yes, he may come in," she replied, remaining in her kneeling position.

Mamadou entered. The spiritual figure bowed his head and withdrew a scroll from his heavy robe. He handed it to Namandje, who accepted it with care.

"The mansa asked that I give this to you once his journey had long begun. Only then could you read this."

Namandje unrolled it and somberly scanned the writing on the scroll. Mamadou bowed and began to exit.

"Mamadou?"

He paused at the entrance. "Yes, my queen?"

"As I watched my husband leave, I looked into his eyes and felt as though he struggled with something sacred… something he wanted to share with me, but could not." She did not look up at the storyteller.

"Is that so, my queen?" said Mamadou with a single eyebrow raised.

"I believe so," stated Namandje.

"I believe that is the Mandingo way, my queen." Mamadou bowed again and exited.

Namandje's gaze fell to the scroll in her hands. As she read, she could hear the serene voice of Abubakari, her beloved husband and mansa.

My Namandje, I can imagine your beautiful eyes peacefully reading my pitiful words. How you must wonder what would impel me to leave so much behind, for but a foolish boy's dream. How can one tear away from love and power so easily? There are matters that we cannot decide for ourselves. This decision was made many years ago.

Namandje could envision the fifty-foot-long, curved, banana- shaped, dua la mtepe command ship that Abubakari embarked on, cutting through the ocean with the sail flapping in the wind, escorted by thirty similar ships. The boat's deck sat about six feet above water level, and its many oars were in the up position. The deck of this ship was wide and fitted with a poop deck that sat a pempi, shaded from the unforgiving sun with a bird-emblazoned parasol. Upon that pempi sat a bearded Abubakari, dressed in a white robe. She read on…

I am not confident what I will find in the abyss. I do know that it is not an abyss. The Arabs say that only a small, sandy, barren island exists in the turbulent waters to the west. Yet I do not expect the waters to be of any concern. The Somono, who will sail with me, have assured me that our ships' small design will skip across the vast waters as a pebble spun across a small pond.

She could see the dark clouds invading the blue sky as Abubakari sat by candlelight in his tiny cabin. Namandje felt the rocking of the ship that caused unattached items in his personal quarters to clatter to the floor. She heard the rain splatter the roof of the below-deck cabin as Abubakari sat uncomfortably on makeshift bedding and opened the same two-foot-by-two-foot red box he unveiled earlier in Niani.

I shall tell you of the dream I had as you slept in my arms. The waters are not blue at all. They are blacker than the night sky. I watch the moon dance, becoming my guiding light in the darkness.

Abubakari reached in the box and revealed the necklace made with the cowries he gathered as a child. He studied them with kind eyes.

N'ko, the sun is brighter than the Sahel. I believe it is Father keeping my heart filled with warmth to battle the coldness of fear, for there are times in my dream that I am afraid.

Abubakari slowly placed the necklace around his neck. His eyes gazed upward when he heard the thunder and crackle of lightning.

It is a long journey, not without its tribulations.

Lightning struck in the dark skies above the ship as Abubakari's fleet suffered through a terrible storm. Screaming Mandingoes were washed overboard, trying to control the wild mast and the oars. Part of the mast splintered and plummeted to the deck below, catching an unsuspecting African seaman by surprise. He screamed just before it crushed him.

Abubakari was drenched, and he struggled his way across the wet deck. He tried to help one man up, just as a wave slammed him into the railing, almost knocking him overboard. Abubakari held tightly to the starboard-side railing. Prone on the deck, blood dripped down his forehead and the downpour washed it away. Water emptied into Abubakari's ears, leaving only the muffled screams of the dying. Tears covered his eyes, and he soon lost consciousness.

Abubakari awoke the morning after the storm to the sound of the ocean waves crashing against the ship's hull. Blood was smeared along his cheek. He slowly lifted himself up to the surrounding coughs and moans of his men licking their wounds. Staggering, he scanned his damaged ship. He then espied the ships remaining in the fleet. A seaman approached Abubakari to help steady the mansa, but Abubakari refused the man's assistance and pushed him away. Abubakari reached the bow of the ship and only saw water touching the horizon.

Will I ever get there? Does "there" even exist?

As night fell, Abubakari walked along the deck beside a graying, older man, who was hampered with several scrolls cramped under his arm. Abubakari donned his ceremonial white tunic and white trousers. His beard was a little scruffier. The man directed Abubakari's attention to the stars by swinging his finger back and forth. Abubakari was captured by the starry night. He gazed upward with his hands folded behind his back.

The Keita ancestors are watching.

He saw the North Star brighten.

As months passed, Abubakari remained in his

compartment. He sat stoically near a small open portal. The ocean tide thumped the hull from outside. He held the cowry necklace tightly and sipped broth from a bowl to replenish his strength.

Suddenly, the disheveled Abubakari was interrupted by the whistle of a blackbird that landed on the edge of the portal. For a moment, Abubakari stared at the bird, watching it from several head- tilt angles, until he heard a shout from above.

"An bara kissi! An bara kissi!" screeched the seaman. Abubakari's eyes illuminated with excitement. He dashed out the cabin. Once on the deck, Abubakari could see that all the men had gathered on the decks of each ship. Their ivory grins under the bright sun brought a smile to Abubakari.

"What is it?" demanded Abubakari.

"An bara kissi! We are saved, Great Mansa!"

Abubakari maneuvered through the crowd and reached the bow of the ship. He was frozen in awe. Far in the distance sat a majestic coastline, with palm trees, sand, blue waters, and seagulls circling above.

"Na' kamma," said Abubakari with confidence.

The Malian ships beached at Tula. Abubakari was the first to waddle through the clear water and step onto the white sands of Central America. His Mandingoes, armed with spears and swords, followed. Abubakari cared not that his white robe and velvet tunic was getting wet.

I see white sands that appear as though they have never been walked upon.

Abubakari fell to his knees and cupped the sand in both hands. He let it sift through his fingers. He brought his hands together and closed his eyes in deep thought. He then roared in extreme joy.

Abubakari and a small party trekked along the coast as the Mandingoes moved supplies toward the jungle's edge. They were saved from the intense heat with a pleasant coastal breeze.

I see a civilization, unlike Niani-ba.

Abubakari held the caravan with a hand raise. He squinted for a moment and then his eyes widen.

I see beautiful people made of gold.

From out of the flora, nearly a hundred brown Toltecs emerged. They appeared as small people, decorated with many feathers and little clothing. They approached cautiously with spears and other pole arms extended. The Mandingoes reacted defensively and readied their weapons. Abubakari quickly calmed his men with a steady hand.

Abubakari separated from the warriors and unsheathed his sword, slowly moving towards the Toltecs. The Mandingo warriors watched their leader in amazement.

Abubakari stopped and placed his sword upon the hot earth. He removed his sandals and let his toes sift through the white sands.

This is my dream. It is as clear as the open savannahs.

Abubakari's white robe glowed from the sunlight, drawing the Toltec warriors to him. There were both men and women. The natives lowered their weapons and cautiously surrounded the smiling Abubakari. They touched him out of out of amazement, sporadically whispering to one another. "Quetzacoatl...Quetzacoatl...Quetzacoatl..." Soon, Mandingo and Toltec warriors greeted each other with commonality.

If I do not wake from this dream, know that part of me is there beside you and Kalabi Naman...beside Kankan... beside N'na.

Remember me, Abu, your husband and mansa.

Namandje placed the scroll down. She stared at the flickering candles. At that moment, Namandje realized the possibility that Abubakari would never return to Mali.

"I believe you will be a prince," said Namandje to the unborn child in her belly. "I shall name you Maghan. When you come of age, I will tell you of your father, Abubakari the Second. You will learn about the man he was and the man he wanted to be."

25.

1359 C.E.

"Nothing good can come from this," Sulayman said to himself as he led his defeated army out of the throes of Mossi territory. Sulayman reached into his bloodstained hunter's tunic and withdrew a tobacco root. He chewed it vigorously.

A sofa officer trotted beside his horse. "Mansa, I beseech you. Let us make camp here and counterattack in the morning."

"No, Basel," sternly replied Sulayman. "We will return to Niani and recuperate." The vivacity in Sulayman had abandoned him. It resonated in his dull eyes, gray beard, and his drooping cheeks. The young warrior had grown old. He no longer had the tenacious battle readiness he once possessed.

A column of battered sofa warriors trailed behind them. Their chain mail armor reeked of blood and the shredded Keita banners flapped in the wind. The Malian army entered Burkina Faso with a force of eighty thousand men. They left with only a little over forty thousand.

"Their Moro Naba is quite a leader. Perhaps I will meet him one day," said Sulayman to his officer of the Mossi ruler. The Mossi had subdued the Dogon people, and Sulayman knew they would advance in time. He needed to regroup and discuss tactics with his war council. How quickly events change course. When his army first departed to engage the Mossi, spirits were high. The warriors cheered as their mansa led them into battle. Sulayman was a warrior- king. Unlike his predecessors, he wanted to see the battle unfold from the advantage of his saddle. He witnessed his warriors get routed by the ruthless Mossi. The times were changing.

Sulayman looked forward to seeing his family. For years, his love of women had escaped him. It was only fifteen years before the Mossi attacked that he had taken a wife. This was after constant pressure from his retainers complaining that the kingdom needed an heir. She was much younger than he and ably gave birth to twin boys.

As the Malian cavalcade made its way along the Bali River and wove through the shea and gum trees, Sulayman reminisced of days long gone. Never before had he felt so alone.

Musa had eventually reigned as mansa. His rule had made Mali the largest empire in the known world, and Sulayman took pride in Musa's achievements.

"Ah, Kankan, you were amazing," whispered Sulayman to himself.

In 1324, Mansa Musa made the pilgrimage to Mecca, with 60,000 people in his caravan. With gold, cattle, and determination, Mansa Musa crossed the Sahara, establishing new alliances with Arabia and fulfilling his dream to make the Hajj. He was only the second mansa to ever do so. Mansa Musa also had glorious mosques built across Mali, including the Grand Mosque in Djenné. He had finally achieved permanent peace with the defiant city-state. Musa died in 1332, leaving Maghan, Abubakari's son, as mansa.

"Such heartache. Such heartache." Tears flowed from Sulayman's eyes.

Maghan would only rule for four years. He died in 1336. What caused the young mansa's death was never determined. Rumors of assassination due to poison filtered through Canco Palace. It tore at Sulayman's heart that Abubakari never saw his son sit proudly upon his pempi and die tragically under the silk-cotton tree.

Maghan's death proved too much for the queen mother to endure. Days after her son's death, Namandje severed her wrists and bled to death in prayer. As she requested in a poem to Djeliba Mamadou Kouyaté, Namandje was buried beside Maghan, Kalabi Naman, and Lady Mariama, who had died peacefully in her sleep.

Sulayman thought of his own beloved mother as he swayed in his saddle, fatigued from the long ride. Lady Kongo had remained a bitter soul until her death in 1338. Fearing reprisals from court officials for her accused hand in Maghan's death, Sulayman, who had subsequently assumed the throne, banished Kongo to a mosque north of Walata. He had heard that she fled to the Moroccan Court, only to be turned away at the palace's gate. Sulayman never saw her again.

"Ah, it is good to see Niani," shouted an officer from behind

Sulayman, bringing the mansa's attention front and center.

They had been retreating for fifteen days, and finally, they reached the outskirts of Niani. As the war-torn sofa warriors clamored into the walled city, natives prostrated themselves along the side of the road, celebrating the return of their king.

"We are most grateful to see you in good health, my lord!" "Thank you for working so hard for us, my lord!"

The people of Niani loved Sulayman as leader and as a Mandingo. During his reign, more of the palace's wealth reached the villagers. Education for children was widespread while Sulayman ruled. And the arts were even more celebrated than Mansa Musa's time. Sulayman normally addressed the populace when in public view. But from the main gate of Niani to the walls of Canco Palace, his gaze stayed straight ahead, ignoring the cheers.

"Even in defeat, they cheer me," muttered Sulayman to a nearby officer. "They deserve better than I."

Sulayman kicked his horse into a faster gallop and stormed through the palace's gate, with his officer corps trailing. Once he reached the main entrance leading to the bollon, or the main anteroom, Sulayman dismounted. His djeliba and several retainers greeted him.

"Welcome back, my lord," said the djeliba as he bowed.

"It is good to be back, my friend," replied Sulayman as he patted his djeliba's shoulder. "I only wish I could speak of victory."

"One who lives is always victorious, my lord," said Camara with sincerity. Sulayman's old friend and former kora instructor remained small, but his wisdom had grown as long as the gray mane that covered his head and face. He needed the support of his crooked staff to follow Sulayman into the palace. "Shall I convene the war council?"

"No, I am tired," snapped Sulayman. "Inform the queen that I have returned." Sulayman scanned the elaborate corridors leading in many directions, unsure of his destination. "Where are my sons?"

A sofa guard escorted Sulayman to the battle-practice chamber. As the mansa removed his chain mail breastplate and unfastened his torn hunter's tunic, he abruptly entered a training session. The instructor immediately prostrated himself before his lord, and the two boys shouldered their wooden staves and bowed to their father. "Your return is most pleasing, my lord," shouted the instructor with his face to the floor.

"Do not let my presence interrupt their training. Please continue." Sulayman waited until his sons lifted their heads, as servants hurriedly entered with pillows and clean water for the mansa. His sons were twelve years of age. Their faces were identical, both resembling Abubakari the Second in the most striking way. Even the soothsayers could not explain it.

"Welcome home, Father," said one of the lads.

"Ah, it is good to see you, Abu," replied Sulayman, "as it is to see you, Kankan," smiled Sulayman to the other boy.

"Did you bring us something from the battle, Father," asked Kankan of Sulayman, "perhaps, a gift?"

"Perhaps," grunted Sulayman as he slowly lowered himself to pillow provided. "But after your studies, you may have it." He waved his hand at them. "Now, go on with your lesson." Sulayman raised his hand, and a female servant immediately started fanning the mansa.

"I am too old for the fathering sort." Sulayman chuckled to himself as he watched his sons engage one another. The teachings had not changed since the days of Sundiata, The Lion King. Sulayman grinned as the instructor constantly hammered the boys with the "sound of the deba" and their failure to hear it.

Sulayman leaned on another pillow and rested his head

in his hand. His eyes blinked repeatedly from fatigue. For a moment, his brothers appeared to him. They sat on both sides of Sulayman and eagerly watched their nephews' practice. The old mansa assumed that he was more tired than previously conceived. The two ghosts appeared as the youthful warriors Sulayman remembered as a young man. Nonetheless, Sulayman pretended that all was normal and that the brothers of Keita were once again side-by-side.

"They are as stubborn as the both of you were," said Sulayman to his translucent brothers. "But they also have your hearts, and only good can come from that."

Having said his piece, to the clangor of staves, to the drumming of the deba, and to the war cries of two young Mandingo warriors, Sulayman took a well-deserved nap.

EPILOGUE

And thus, the two brothers followed their paths, as the ancient ones watched from the heavens. So were the ways of the Mandingo.

Mansa Sulayman died in 1359. His sons, Abubakari and Kankan Musa ruled once again. But the kun-tigi would not follow the boy- kings to battle the Mossi. Civil war erupted between the tribes, and suffering spat its forked tongue, giving way for the Songhai to take power. Oh, Lord Maghan, who generously spared the lives of the two princes, bow to Mansa Abubakari's wisdom. Would you have walked the path once traveled upon?

My lord Abubakari the Second would never return to Mali, the land of the Bright Country. Be well, my lord, for your wraith harbors no ill will to the Mandingo people.

And what of me? Did I live or die? Of course, I am alive.

My stories are alive; therefore I live.
  For the world is old, but the future springs from the past.
  Djeliba Mamadou Kouyaté